CLUB TRIPOLI

Terry Wright

DEDICATION

I dedicate this book to all the struggling writers I've known and labored with over the years. Without their help and encouragement this work would not have been finished. In particular, the members of The Panama City Writers Association and the Clarksville Writing Society have been of invaluable service. And good friends all.

ACKNOWLEDGMENTS

I particularly wish to recognize my wife and son, Mary Anne and Trevor Wright, for the encouragement and patience they provided to keep me writing and working.

I must also acknowledge the Wikipedia Commons for the use of their photograph of the Uadaan Hotel and Casino in downtown Tripoli on the cover of Club Tripoli.

ABOUT THE AUTHOR

Terry Wright lives and writes in the beautiful hills of Northeast Georgia and has published numerous articles and non-fiction books, as well as poems and short stories in literary magazines.

- 1 -

Trapped. I felt like I couldn't breathe—my face itched and my pits dripped, and if I didn't get off of this lousy plane pretty soon I'd come out of my skin. I inched my way along in the big Air Force Super Constellation, angry and impatient. The rest of the passengers showed at least as much irritation as I did. Tempers were short and we were barely moving. Up and down the long aisle people groped in the overhead bins, backing up traffic while we tried to shuffle on toward the door. We began to move a little faster as I lugged my guitar down the aisle. I turned it to slip through the doorway onto the platform of the tall, metal stairway.

Oh God! Air. Fresh air and sunshine. I took a couple of deep breaths and searched for Dave Walker, my buddy from Laredo, the only person in Libya who knew me. A sparse crowd of people waited near the terminal but I couldn't see him among them. Where was he? He'd made a big point of saying he'd meet my flight. I spotted him at last. So he had come, after all. There he stood, beside a chain-link fence in the long late-afternoon shadow of the MATS passenger terminal. Over all the flightline noise—the high-pitched whistle of the jets and the gruff, throaty roar of the props of the transport aircraft—I could barely hear his shouts.

"Ted! Over here, man. Over here!"

With relief I cleared the bottom step at last and jogged over to the open gate. Dave's face split in a wide grin. He shook my hand and pounded my shoulder. "Ted, you useless son of a bitch! Did you get lost or something? Miss your damn plane? I've been checking the arrivals board for two days and no Ted Miller."

I ignored his pounding blows. "Come on, man. You know it's a long haul from Charleston to Tripoli. But it's sure good to see you,

Dave." I punched his belly. "Gained a little weight over here, haven't you? Man, you look even chubbier than the last time I saw you."

"Who me? Screw you, Miller. What took you so damn long?" Dave frowned and dug a pack of Lucky Strikes out of his shirt pocket. "You're two days late."

I laughed. "Yeah, tell me about it. It seems more like a week. We had to change out an engine halfway here and it took forever. 'All Enlisted Personnel are restricted to the transient quarters until further notice.' You know the drill."

"Yeah. I remember, all right. Hurry up and wait."

As we left the flightline, Dave lit his Lucky, blew the smoke out of the corner of his mouth and his big grin was back. "Anyway, you're here now, Ted. Wheelus Air Base, the garden spot of North Africa, like it or not. Man, what a place this is. There's so many things I want to tell you about Tripoli I don't even know where to start."

It was only April, but sweat poured down my face and back. "Please—start by telling me it's not always this hot and gritty here."

He chuckled. "No, man, today is hot. The wind's off the desert and that raises the temperature about twenty degrees. You'll get used to the grit, more or less. But it'll cool off some when we get away from the runway. The temperature climbs to a hundred and thirty out here on a bad day. And that's killing hot."

We watched the Libyan ground crew move in slow motion. Dave scowled and shook his head. "Look at those guys. I see you kept your guitar out of the checked baggage," Dave said. "That's good. These Arabs are really slow, even when it's not this hot. Dim-witted A-rabs. We'll come back by here on our way to the barracks and find your luggage. What do you have, just your duffle?"

"Yeah, just the duffle bag. I sent some civvies and my winter uniforms over on the cargo ship, but it'll be a while before that arrives."

"Like hurry up and wait, right? Screw it. Right now I want to take you to a great place offbase—Club Tripoli. It's the coolest nightclub in Libya, and maybe the best in North Africa. I've got to work there for a couple of hours this evening, a small combo gig. You could sit in, man. What do you say?"

"Yeah, sure. I haven't played since that layover for the engine change. An offbase gig, huh? Does it pay good? I mean, I figure the only good thing about an eighteen month hardship tour in Libya is to use the time to work and put away some money. I need to go home with enough bread to start college."

"Yeah, I hear you man. Anyway, the money's pretty good at the club but I'll bring you up to speed on all that later, okay?"

We walked over to a rough-looking old Jeep parked by the fence. The bodywork showed a collection of rust, dents and peeling patches of paint, but when Dave got in and pushed the starter button it cranked right up and rumbled like a brand new '57 T-Bird. I could tell from the deep burble he hadn't kicked his horsepower habit.

We left the flightline and drove straight out the main gate. "Whoa, man," I said. "I don't have a class-A pass or anything."

"Man. You haven't changed a bit, have you, Miller? You worry too much. Take it easy. The Air Police all know my Jeep, and security isn't very tight here. You'll be all right."

I hoped the APs agreed with him. I gawked at everything like a tourist, but Dave drove too fast for me to see much, just glimpses and flashes of passing scenes. He looked over at me and said, "Relax man. I'll give you the big Tripoli tour tomorrow or the next day. Right now we need to get to the club."

* * *

We parked in the back lot and came through the employee entrance. Dave's group had hit the bandstand fast, already setting up their equipment to play in the back bar of the place. I unpacked my guitar and tuned up. My hands felt a little stiff from lack of practice, but I knew everything would loosen up in a few minutes.

We played to a crowd of noisy Air Force lieutenants and Dave filled me in. "These guys are all pilots from the European Tactical Air Command bases. They're down here in Tripoli to do their gunnery and bombing training, flying their F-100s out in the desert, in the gunnery range, El Watia. What a bunch of maniacs—but they're big spenders, and that's good for the club. Big tippers for the band, too." He grinned. "And that's good for me."

We kicked off a set and Dave took a long ride on "Tutti-Fruiti," as he honked away on his alto sax. I had my mic pulled in close and turned way up, and I banged out triplets in a steady, monotonous chain, rock-and-roll style. The crowd loved it and they tried to sing along. "I got a gal named Sue. She knows just what to do. Got a gal…" They went all out on "Womp bomma loo mop—b-lamp, bam, boom!" Everybody had a great time except me, banging out the triplets till my hands got sore.

At last we finished the set and Dave called a ten-minute break. I walked over to the bar and asked for a beer. The bartender gave me a tall frosty mug of draft and wouldn't take my money. I leaned on the bar and checked out the big room. Fancy, with lots of mirrors on the walls and a flock of little tables scattered around a big polished dance floor. The girls in the room worked the pilots—they hustled a lot of drinks and talked them into trips down the hall. It looked like a busy place, all right. Reminded me of Nuevo Laredo.

I felt relieved not to have to make any conversation. The noise level, the clamor of chatter and shouts, sounded so loud in the bar I couldn't hear myself think. Sometimes I hated nightclubs and bars. Dave and I had played in all kinds of places back in Laredo on both sides of the border for a couple of years and the routine of constant gigs in noisy clubs full of loud drunks had turned into a tired scene.

"Now—where in the world has Dave gotten off to, anyway?" I asked myself.

He'd disappeared somewhere between the bandstand and the bar. I looked around, and thought I spotted him in a booth in the corner of the room. Yeah, I'd found him all right—sitting with a guy with long deep creases in his face. Permanent frown lines, like a sad old man.

I started over to his corner with my beer. As I walked up to the booth it looked like Dave handed the guy something from his coat pocket. "Hey, man. Mind if I join you?" I asked.

He jerked around and stared at me, frowning. "Miller, you dumb bastard! Don't come sneaking up on me like that."

What! Where did that come from? The other guy in the booth slid out and left, but I'd had a good look at him. Dave still glared at me with narrowed eyes.

"Sorry, man. I didn't mean to startle you," I said.

"Just mind your own business, damn it. That was a private conversation."

Conversation? Hell, it looked more like a transaction, like somebody dealing. That shocked me. We'd seen a lot of people using drugs back in Texas and Mexico, but I never thought Dave dealt in the stuff. So had he? How would I know?

Enough. To change the subject, I asked, "How about some folk music in the next set, Dave? There's some songs I'm working on I'd like to try. Good stuff."

He looked blank. "Huh?"

"On the bandstand. When we get back, I'd like to play and sing a tune called 'Goin' Down the Road,' a Woody Guthrie thing. You know, a singing, talking blues. What do you say?"

"Oh. Yeah, sure. We can start with that on the next set. Just make sure the piano man knows what you're doing." He scowled again. "Look, man. Be careful around here. Don't be walking up on people when they're busy. You about got more than you could handle, understand?"

Damn. There he went again, acting like a stranger, like some street tough instead of the friend I remembered. "Dave—save the bad-ass routine for somebody you can scare, okay? Don't waste that crap on me."

His tough expression faded away. "Take it easy, Ted. Be cool. I didn't mean to come on that strong. Listen, why don't we go try your blues number?"

I briefed the piano player, gave him the key and the chords and kicked off the tune in a moderate tempo. I played the first chorus with some good, strong bass runs and sang the first verse. I'm not sure whether it was the "Lord, Lord" stuff or maybe the "I ain't a-gonna" business but a few of the pilots standing at the bar had turned around to stare with pained looks replacing the big grins they'd been wearing. Dave's eyes were bugging out, like he'd remembered the whole song, all the other verses. He stood up and grabbed the next chorus on his sax and honked his way through the simple melody. After playing the one chorus he signaled an ending for the drummer, cut off the band, and the song.

"What in the hell are you doing?" I asked.

"Man, if we played about one more chorus of that I'd be out looking for a new gig. This club doesn't have any tolerance for country music, you dig? And neither does our audience."

I sat there with my guitar in my hands and my mouth hanging open. Dave went up front and started singing "One, two, three o'clock, four o'clock rock!" and the drummer jumped right on it. When did Dave decide to censor my music? Oh, well. I guess he didn't favor folk music a whole lot.

At the end of the song he muttered, "Dusty road, my aching ass."

I'd had enough and decided to put away my guitar. I turned off the mic, moved it back and began wiping down my strings.

Dave asked, "You packing up, man?"

"Yeah, that's it for me. Must be that long flight over here. I'm beat."

He stared at me for a moment and tossed me a ring of keys. "Here. Take the Jeep back to the barracks for me. I've got some late errands downtown for these guys and one of them can drop me off at the base."

"Well, thanks, man. I appreciate that." I wondered what kind of errands he'd run in downtown Tripoli in the middle of the night, but then remembering his tense conversation in the shadowy corner booth, I decided not to ask. I didn't want to know.

* * *

Dave had given me good directions. I breezed through the main gate of the base and headed for the flightline. His Jeep reminded me of the new Chevy my dad had just bought. He let me drive it some when I was on leave before I caught the plane to Tripoli. What a sweet ride that was, with the hot fuelie V-8 setup. Dad had always been picky about what he drove so I guess I'd come by my passion for cars honestly. Dave and I had been the biggest car enthusiasts in the squadron back in Laredo.

I pulled into the terminal lot, parked the Jeep by the chain-link fence and found the luggage desk. After making me sign two triplicate forms, the night man dumped my overloaded duffle bag on the counter and I dragged it back to the Jeep. Another few minutes and I pulled into the rear parking lot of one of the flat-topped, mud-colored three-story buildings along barracks row.

"Okay," I muttered. "First find the CQ's desk, third floor. Get my room assignment, then find my bunk." My miserable duffle bag felt heavier each time I lifted it.

The CQ rolled off his made-up bunk in full uniform. He looked me over like I'd gone out of my way to ruin his good night's sleep. He took a copy of my orders, entered my name in his roster and showed me where to sign in. "You're on this floor, in 315. Here's your key. First formation's at 0700 in the dayroom. Class-B uniform. Be there."

"Yes, Sergeant," I said. I wanted to thank him for his gracious welcome to my new squadron, but decided against it. Maybe I'd better learn the lay of the land before I started laying on the sarcasm. With a heel-pop and about-face, I grabbed my bag and headed down the hall.

- 2 -

The next morning I walked across the street with Dave for coffee and pastries at a small place, a snack bar called the Oasis. His sturdy Boston-Irish good looks suffered from a patchy reddish sunburn in strong contrast with his clear blue eyes and blond hair. Dave was taller than me and he carried more weight. My Irish heritage was from the Black Irish side and the dark coloring of my brown eyes and hair, complemented by the heavy tan I'd picked up during my furlough spent on the beach, created a strong contrast between the two of us.

The heat and intensity of the brassy North African sunshine had struck me the moment I'd cleared the front stairs and stepped out onto the sidewalk. We'd just begun the day yet the sunlight felt fierce. Dave looked cool and comfortable in his lightweight tan tropicals with the short sleeves and short pants. He wore the new Air Force summer uniform, but my old-style, long-sleeved GI khakis were way too heavy for this heat.

The Oasis had a low counter with a row of stools which outlined the rear of the snack bar and several tables sat nearer the front windows. The place wasn't crowded and we dropped our hats on a table, went through the short cafeteria-style line by the counter and gathered up coffee and cheese tarts. Dave paid and we walked back to our table. As we sat down I loosened my dark blue tie. "Thanks Dave. I owe you one."

He waved that aside as he abandoned his customary morning silence. "Remind me when we get back to the barracks. The houseboy brought me two sets of clean tropicals yesterday and I can loan you a set. Since we're both still airmen second class, the shirt will work."

"That sounds good to me. These khakis are killing me." I stirred my coffee and took a bite of one of my tarts. They were tasty and not too sticky. "But you know I heard promotions were easier to get overseas, yet you've still got the same crummy two stripes you wore back in Texas. What's the story?"

"What do you think? It's the same tired crap it's always been. If you decide you want a third stripe you have to re-enlist for it." He laughed. "No way, man. They can stuff their lousy stripe, you know?"

"I'm with you, Dave. I won't sell my ass to the Air Force to make airman first class. No buck sergeant for me. It's just not worth it. Anyway, I appreciate the offer of the tropicals. That'll be a big help."

He patted his stomach. "Like you said, I've gained a few pounds since I got here, so the pants might be a little loose on you. At least they're shorts so the length won't matter. But you'd better get yourself down to the Base Exchange and invest in a couple of sets. You'll see. They're the best thing to wear here at Wheelus."

As we drank our coffee, Dave began to fill me in on the local music scene, where the gigs were and how the pay scale stacked up. I sat up straight. "Now you've got my total attention, man. I need to save me some money—as much as I can get together before I ship back to the States. I've tried to build up a decent college fund, but it's still way too small. You and I both know you just can't save much money on our lousy pay."

"Ain't that the truth? You're lucky if you have enough for cigarettes."

"Yeah. But I mean to finish this crummy four-year enlistment and get out—stay out and go to school," I told him. "I've paid my dues as a crappy little peon. Enough to last me a long, long time. But I know getting out and staying out is going to take some money. Maybe a lot of money."

Dave sat up straight and squared his shoulders. "I know, I know. You're preaching to the choir, Teddy boy. And I'll clear that hurdle, too, if it kills me. If you let this crummy mandatory service turn into a re-enlistment, you'll be an old man when you get out. And that's not going to happen to me. No sir!"

He shuddered and bit into his pastry like he wanted to kill it. "Now listen. The NCO Club is in a contract with a German band from Wiesbaden. We should squeeze those Krauts out of there and take their job, but they're good, and the bastards work cheaper than we do. A lot cheaper."

I took a swallow of coffee. "Man. How bad is it? I need to make some bread. I have to!"

Dave laughed. "It's not all bad, Ted. The Officers' Club books the squadron's big band most weekends and they use my rock group some on weeknights. The Airman's Club is always good for a night now and then, but they don't pay as well as the Officers' Club. Anyhow, there's money to be made here."

My coffee cup was empty and the pastry I'd eaten tasted good enough to make me want another one. I went back to the counter for seconds. Back at the table Dave flipped through his pocket calendar. "We've got the usual crap for today, rehearsals and the Retreat Ceremony, but there's a group playing in the Airman's Club tonight you'll want to hear. They're from Club Tripoli—where we went last night—and there's a couple of guys in the group you've just got to meet."

* * *

That evening, we walked down to the Airman's Club and Dave led the way through the noisy chaos of the main bar. We'd missed first call but it looked like every other enlisted man on base was lined up at the bar as they clamored and yelled for beer. We walked past and entered a small lounge with soft lighting near the back of the club. It was a quiet haven compared to the main room, with enlisted men at the bar and a few couples who sat at the tables scattered around the small dance floor.

We joined an airman who wore band brass on his class-A, leather-billed hat. Dave didn't introduce me to him and that seemed strange. He was tall and well-built, a black airman first class, thin and ascetic looking in the face, like someone who'd been through a recent illness. The sunglasses he wore, dark enough that I could barely see his eyes, made him seem distant and aloof.

The guy reinforced his austere air with quiet humming. He seemed to stare at a point just above my head, but I couldn't be sure. My mind wandered. Maybe I still hadn't adjusted to the time change and the long trip from Charleston to Tripoli. The airman with the sunglasses cocked his head, got up from our table and walked up to the bandstand, nodded to the piano man and pulled a trumpet case out from under the big grand piano.

"There he goes," Dave whispered. "He's ready now, but when he hums like that you can't talk to him. A waste of time to try. But listen to this guy. Listen!"

He transformed himself the moment he put the horn to his lips. His vagueness vanished as he started to play very softly behind the piano, drums and bass for the remainder of the current chorus of the song. He asserted himself on the next chorus and improvised carefully around the melody without actually playing it. He wove a mournful, muffled, complex counterpoint with the piano and string bass. While the guy seemed weird, his skill and talent with his horn impressed me. He sat in for a few more numbers. Then without a word to anyone, he popped his horn back in its case and shoved it under the piano.

He returned to our table and this time Dave introduced us. "Meet Bob Rodrigo, our lead airman in the trumpet section." Dave gestured to me. "Bob, this is my friend Ted Miller."

Rodrigo pulled off his dark shades and squinted at me. "I answer to Bob, man, but mostly they call me 'the Pres.' Like Dave here will tell you, I play the coolest horn in North Africa."

Oh great. Another modest musician. "What's the 'Pres' thing?" I asked. "Is that like 'The Chairman of the Board' or something?"

Bob tilted his head to one side. "Yeah," he said. "You get the idea. The guys at Goose Bay gave me the name, out of respect, you dig?"

I extended my hand. "Yeah, I dig." What a jerk. "Well, you can call me Ted. Or Miller."

"Oh, yeah. The new guy from Laredo, right?" he asked. "Dave's been telling me about your guitar playing. Says you're pretty good—but then he's your friend, isn't he?"

He sounded pretty snide with the 'friend' comment. The smirk didn't help. "Pres, I'll let you decide for yourself if I'm any good when you hear me play. I do all right."

"Now where have I heard that before?"

We continued our light sparring for another minute or so. Then he pointed out the members of the trio. He talked with enthusiasm about the piano player and leader, Joe Scarlatti.

When the set ended, Scarlatti announced a ten-minute break and walked over to our table. We exchanged introductions. Pulling up a chair, he sat down with us and moved the ashtray over to his side of the table. He was older than the rest of us and wore a neatly trimmed mustache and an expensive looking European-style suit. He lit up and spoke in a deep bass. His faint accent sounded a little British. "It is good to meet you, Mr. Miller—Ted. We are trading off with one of your squadron groups. They play tonight at Club Tripoli, my place downtown. Dave says you are a solid guitarist—and we need another rhythm man for this group. Are you interested?"

I'd just gotten to Tripoli, but it seemed to be a constant stream of surprises and complications. What was an Italian with a British accent doing in a city of an Arab kingdom owning and running a club? I delayed my response to his offer of a job by asking him about his situation. "Joe, you sure don't look Arabic and Scarlatti sounds Italian. So what are you doing running a nightclub in North Africa?"

Scarlatti smiled politely. "And you don't sound like a solid student of history, if I may say so," he said. "You see, Mr. Miller, Libya has been an Italian colony here in Africa since the early part of the century. We took this land from the Ottoman Empire in our Italo-Turkish war back in 1912. But our brilliant Italian leadership of the 40s led us into a disastrous situation. *Il Duce*... Following the war we were ruled by the British until 1951 and then the United Nations turned the country over to the Arabs. So, for the last six years we have been an Arabic kingdom."

He shook his head with an air of weariness. "Yet, as a third generation colonist, I cannot abandon the fruits of forty years of Italian industry and hard work. My brothers and I continue to prosper as owners and operators of Club Tripoli."

Italo-Turkish war? I hated looking like an idiot in front of everybody and I could see a trip to the base library in my near future. I didn't doubt what he said, and he'd hit it right-on about my ignorance. But it wouldn't happen again. A little quiet reading would take care of that.

I thought about his unexpected offer to work with his group. He hadn't even heard me play and I didn't want to get pinned down before I understood the situation a little better. I smiled and said, "Well, I want to think about the spot in your band. That does sound interesting, but let me get settled in first."

I turned to Dave. "What about your group, man? Was that it downtown last night?"

"Yeah, and as you heard, it's the usual crap. Raucous and rough with me honking on alto and a lot of drums."

Yeah. That's what it had sounded like all right. "Do you need a steady guitar man in the group?"

"Sure. I could use a good guitar man, one who's good at triplets and wow-wow." He paused. "One who doesn't screw around with any twangy country crap."

Dave didn't mince his words a lot. "You know, man, playing rock and roll isn't my favorite gig, but if the money's there you can call me Bill Haley."

Scarlatti crushed out his cigarette and cleared his throat. An expectant silence fell over our group. "The real money to be made here is downtown at my club," he said. "My Club Tripoli is a first class resort where many of the oilfield exploration people come to spend their money and blow off the steam."

Bob had his dark glasses back on. He shook with soft, steady laughter. "Resort? Oh, yeah, nice little place. The best casino and whorehouse in—"

"I'll explain my club if you don't mind, Mr. Rodrigo," Scarlatti said in a hard flat voice.

They exchanged a look and Rodrigo's eyebrows climbed. He ducked his head slightly. *What?* He seemed cool and tough—or did he? He acted kind of like a suck-up instead of a fellow musician. Like maybe he was afraid of Scarlatti.

It had gotten harder and harder for me to concentrate on the conversation. My body was at four a.m. instead of ten p.m. I could feel myself fading fast and decided my time lag problems weren't over yet.

I turned to Dave, but he'd anticipated my complaint. "Ted, you're looking kind of droopy. I guess you haven't quite adjusted yet. Let's get you out of here. Ready to go?"

"Yeah." I took a deep breath. "I'm ready."

* * *

We said goodbye to the group at the table and started for the door. Dave dropped back and said something to Scarlatti. He opened the door of the little lounge and we passed through the noisy main bar and into the quiet parking lot. The heat had moderated, a breeze stirred the palms and the fresh air perked me up a little. As we walked toward the barracks, tonight's conversation ran through my mind again. "What were Bob and Joe talking about tonight? They came on strong. And they sure were aggressive about trying to hire me. You know, they've never even heard me play."

Dave chuckled. "Yeah, they do that. Plus I've really talked you up to them, you know? Anyway, they always try to recruit new help. Club Tripoli is growing and it seems like they never have enough people to keep up with the business, mostly entertainment and finance."

If I remembered Bob's outburst right, that meant whorehouse entertainment and casino finance. And who knows what else, I thought, as I recalled Dave's transaction in the back bar last night. Why the veneer? What was he up to with all the pretty words? I mean, it couldn't be much worse than the places we'd worked at back in Nuevo Laredo.

He continued. "Scarlatti's organization is growing here in North Africa. They need people, but they hate to use the Arabs, causing friction with the locals, the King and his people, but they're pretty stubborn about it."

That sounded dumb to me. "Friction? Maybe snubbing the Arabs is not too smart, since they're the ones in charge."

"Well, Scarlatti thinks they can fill the gap by recruiting Americans from here on base. Lots of Italians have left the country over the last six years, ever since the Arabs took over from the British back in '51. There aren't that many Italian people left to choose from, but their scarcity leaves a nice gap for guys like you and me to fill. We can pick up some good money in the process of giving them a hand, you know?"

Traffic was light, but we waited for a truck to pass and crossed the street. "So where do you and Joe and Bob fit in with this club?"

Dave turned toward me slightly, and lowered his voice a notch. "Scarlatti, he owns the place and Bob works there nights and weekends as a kind of connection with the GIs who go there."

Connection? Or pimp? More pretty words. "And you, Dave, What do you do?"

He shrugged. "I'm a musician, only I have a lot of other duties. Part-time bouncer, some-time courier, keeping the girls in line. Lots of different jobs to do, but it sure pays well. I mean good money. There's big opportunity at the club for all of us. Bob is sort of like Scarlatti's main man, his right hand." He chuckled. "At least that's the way Bob tells it."

"I don't know," I said. "It looked to me like Bob may be scared of Scarlatti. He sounded like he was sucking up—or backing down.

What's that all about, anyhow?"

We reached the barracks and sat down on the rear steps. Dave studied his garrison cap and twisted it in his hands. "Well. Sometimes Bob tries a little too hard. But he worries about things. How he rates with Scarlatti means a lot to him. I'm betting he'll apply for discharge here at Wheelus and stay with Club Tripoli. Like he sees that as a whole lot more attractive than going back to the States, or back to the South."

I paused to think about what he'd said so far. There was an undertone to a lot of what he said. I got this strong feeling he wasn't telling me everything, like he skirted issues or slid past the rough spots.

One thing bothered me the most. It seemed like the big opportunities might require my involvement in a whole lot more than just playing guitar. And this business about conflict with the Arabs didn't make sense. "Tell me, do Scarlatti's people have a lot of problems with the Arabs and the King? Do the Italians get along with them? Are they in some kind of bind now that the power has shifted?"

He dropped his eyes and squirmed on the concrete step. "Yeah, maybe so, man, but that's not my problem. Not yours either, and there's not a lot else going on in Tripoli. It's the only place around here that pays good money. Hey, I'll take you down there tomorrow night and give you the whole tour. Dinner, the show, everything. You'll see. It's a great place."

- 3 -

Dave drove through the main gate and onto the road to town. We'd just cleared the air base when he slammed on his brakes to stop for a creaky-looking old man, wearing a fez and long white robes, trying to herd a bunch of sheep across the busy road. The old Arab maneuvered his long crook with dexterity, clucking like a mother hen to its brood, herding his flock of fat-looking sheep toward safety. They blocked both lanes of traffic, and nothing moved in either direction.

I glanced over at Dave. His behavior struck me as out of proportion—overwhelmed with disgust and frustration. I started laughing, but Dave didn't look amused. "Miller, you won't think this is so damn funny when you've seen it about a hundred times. I don't get it. How do these dim-witted Arabs expect to build a modern nation when three-quarters of their people are still living in the eighteenth century? These damned A-rabs don't know enough to come in out of a sandstorm. Just look at this guy."

His comments seemed as extreme as his expression. I might be the new guy here, but I couldn't understand Dave's vehemence and irritation. I thought about the funeral processions we'd wait to pass back in the States, down south. We sat for two minutes, ten minutes whatever it took. But nobody I knew got upset about it. It was just something that happened. And here this old man tried to get his herd to market, or back home, or whatever. He didn't look to me like he could rush right out and buy a big truck to do it with. "Come on, Dave. He's just trying to make a living."

He glared at me, like I'd become part of the problem.

At last the sheep completed their crossing and he slipped the Jeep back into gear. "Idiots," he muttered. "It's about seven miles from the base gate to the club but it can take over a half hour to drive it. Sometimes it's quicker, but you never know what to expect."

We drove west into the late afternoon sun, and Dave's old Jeep purred like a kitten. "Man, where did you get this sorry looking heap?" I asked. "I mean, it runs good but it looks like it's ready for the junkyard. Did you bring it over from the States?"

"No way, man. The Wheelus motor pool put it on surplus and sold it. I bought it cheap, but I had to turn right around and rebuild most of the mechanical gear—the engine, transmission, four-wheel drive and a lot of other stuff. It's reliable, you know, but sometimes it needs some help. There's still too many tired, old parts on it, but I'm getting ahead of it."

"Do you do your own mechanical work?" I asked.

He raised his eyebrows. "You got to be kidding, right? I found this Arab mechanic who can do anything."

What was this? Praise for an A-rab? From Dave? I wondered.

He never missed a beat. "I mean, for an A-rab he's pretty smart. He even swapped the engine for a Ford V-8 and changed out the gear set in the rear end. It's a sweet setup." He stepped on the gas pedal and screeched the back tires to make his point. Then he looked over and grinned. "I guess you're right, Ted. I ought to get it cleaned up a little, but first it has to be dependable. It has to run, see? That's the main thing."

Dave filled me in a little on the local history as we rode. He'd been reassigned to the Air Force Band here in Tripoli a couple of months ahead of me and he knew way more about the place than I did. "Wheelus had been around since the thirties when the Italians built it. They called it Mellaha Air Base, I think." he said. "The Italian Air Force used it for a while and the German Luftwaffe took it over in the big war. Then the British 8th Army liberated it from the Germans in'43 and the Army Air Corps took it over in '45. Now the U.S. Air Force has it leased from the United Kingdom of Libya for use mostly by Military Air Transport Service, along with the Air Training Command and the Tactical Air Command. The 'Welcome to Wheelus' booklet they gave me when I boarded the plane in Charleston has all that in it. You got one, right?"

"Yeah. But I haven't read it yet. I suppose I should."

* * *

As we approached the heart of town, the traffic grew heavier. The horse carts and the camels gave way to modern cars and busses. We cruised along with the traffic when, without warning, the people on the sidewalks started to run and spill out into the street in a stampede. With loud screeching of tires and honking of horns, the traffic ground to a stop. The Arabs yelled and screeched in high-pitched voices as they pushed and shoved each other. They screamed and bounced off hoods and fenders in the street swarming with people.

"What is this, man? What's wrong with these guys?" I asked.

Dave shrugged. "Who knows? I wish we had the top up, but it's too late now. We'll just sit this one out and hope the king's finest show up quick."

He reached under his seat and came up with a pair of hefty looking clubs. He handed me one and said, "Here. Keep this handy, but don't use it unless we have to. Follow my lead, okay? The police shouldn't take long to get here and they'll make short work of these guys."

I held my billy club, feeling like an idiot. Then a dozen big Arabs in white uniforms charged up the street. They swung their night sticks and knocked everybody out of their way, whacking heads as fast as they could swing. They hit anybody that moved. One of the policemen yanked his big revolver out of its ornate white holster and fired a couple of shots in the air. The whole street got quiet.

As things settled down, Dave grinned. "Not bad. They must have been nearby. The king picks the biggest, meanest toughs he can find from out in the desert for the police force. Bedouins. They're trained to kick ass and get the job done." Dave's grin faded. "If we'd been on foot when this broke out we might have had a problem. They go nuts like this for no apparent reason. Scarlatti says it's about religion, but who can say. I don't think he knows much more about it than I do."

He lit a cigarette. "But if you're walking around you learn to keep your eyes open and be alert. And you look around for cover, a safe place, like a doorway, a foyer, some place where you can get clear of the brainless mob until things blow over. You hear me? It'll become a habit pretty soon, but you can't afford to get too confident or careless, and you don't drop your guard. Just remember, these guys are all crazy. Unpredictable and dangerous."

"That'll take some getting used to, but now that I've seen it for myself I don't think I'll forget. Thanks for the warning."

Dave grimaced. "Well, at least the police have all the guns. And they're fearless. Nothing scares those guys."

With the mob dispersed, we continued toward the center of the city. My heart had stopped pounding and I'd resumed my sightseeing. Dave pointed out Club Tripoli from a block away. The building was beautiful, stunning with its white walls brilliant in the sunshine, its high tower in sharp contrast with the clear blue sky and dark blue water of the harbor.

Dave must have noticed me acting like a tourist. "This is the prettiest part of the city, and the nicest time of the day," he said. "The Arabs have a phrase they use for Tripoli that means 'The White Bride of the Mediterranean.' I guess they mean the big buildings here along the harbor and the snow-white seawall along the Lungo Mare. You'll have to see it from the water to understand and appreciate what they mean."

I looked over at him, trying to guess whether he was putting me on or not. He glanced at me and furrowed his brow. "Well. That's what it says in the Air Force welcome book they gave us."

* * *

We parked in the back again but entered through the main front doors this time. "I thought we'd have dinner, then check out Scarlatti's house band and see the show," Dave said. "But first let me give you a quick tour."

He led me through the main hall, past the reception desk and into the game rooms. They weren't busy this early in the evening, except for a few dour, determined card players. Some of the games I couldn't identify and I stopped to take a closer look.

"Come on, Ted. You'll be way ahead if you stay out of here."

I laughed at the gloomy expression on his face. "Just looking, man. Just looking. Don't worry about it."

We went on to the main bar for a drink. The room had an old-fashioned feel, with lots of mirrors and brass fittings and soft lighting. I glanced at the pretty waitresses and the hotel guests. The guests looked elegant and were of all ages. There were young business types, some middle aged couples and a few older guests who appeared a little too well fed.

Dave looked around the room. "We get a lot of visitors on holiday from southern Italy and Sicily, and some from France and Germany. Scarlatti siphons off some trade from the big casinos on the Riviera, offering lower prices for accommodations and food. He makes the real money on the gambling, and there's no discount there."

The people did look kind of prosperous. Almost like you could smell the money. Or the management could. The staff treated everybody with great courtesy and respect.

We continued our tour. The dark marble flooring and paneled walls of the large, formal dining room struck a sharp contrast to all the white linen and glassware. We got a table by the windows looking out over the old castle and the harbor.

Dave sat there as if he owned the place—and the view. "Take your time with the menu," he said. "Everything's good, but the veal scaloppini is a specialty of the house."

We both chose the veal. Throughout the meal it seemed like the entire staff paid special attention to us and they all seemed to know Dave. Most of the waiters were Italian while the cleaning people and the busboys were Arabs who worked under a steady stream of harsh, demanding orders from the Italians.

When they brought us the check, Dave scrawled his initials on the back and tossed it onto the tray. I raised my eyebrows and said, "Don't you need some help with that?"

He glanced over at me with one of his a big smug grins. "Hey. It's on Scarlatti, man. Compliments of the house."

After dinner, they gave us an up-front table for the floorshow. A big ensemble band did the backups for the show, and I recognized a couple of guys from our squadron in the group. There were six girls performing, all wearing skimpy belly dancers' costumes. They worked in a complex weaving, whirling swirl, moving their hips and bellies in ways that I'd never seen or even imagined possible. As the tempo of the music increased, the dancers grew more aggressive and bold until they seemed to be approaching an erotic frenzy. By the time they stopped I was breathing hard. Dave laughed at me, but hey, they were all right.

Following their performance, three of the dancers came over to our table and showered Dave with breathless, affectionate greetings. I gaped at them. They looked middle-eastern, Arabic or Turkish, with big dark eyes and dark hair, a little plump for my taste, but hey. Dave leaned toward me and whispered, "Be cool, man. Sit back, relax and have some fun."

Well, they turned out to be a whole lot of fun and we ended up in one of the luxurious, two-bedroom suites. Before the evening ended, the girls taught me some things that I had never even considered. My world dissolved into a steamy maze of hot wet flesh and titties, of gasping mouths, groping hands, tangled legs and squirming bodies.

Dave brought me back to reality as he banged on the door of my bedroom. We had regular duty in the morning and he said he couldn't be late, like he couldn't afford another gig from the first sergeant this week. *Christ.* I groaned aloud, but untangled myself from my dancers and tried to hurry. Clutching my clothes, I stumbled out into the big living room of the suite and dressed.

Dave and I walked down the hall toward the back exit of the hotel talking about the girls. He chuckled. "Man, that Tina is something else, isn't she?" The door to one of the nearby rooms popped open and two young Arab boys came out. I caught the briefest glimpse of a tall, black, naked man in the room as he closed the door. *Was that Rodrigo?*

* * *

By the time we got back to the base, it was almost three o'clock. We rolled up to the gate, but there was no automatic wave through from the AP on duty. Dave pulled up, reached into his shirt pocket and handed the sentry two gaudy colored cards with the Club Tripoli logo printed on them. The AP took them. "Get the hell out of here." he said over his shoulder. He reentered his guard shack.

As we drove on toward the barracks, Dave chuckled. "They're always happy to get those passes. They're good for just about anything the club has to offer. And they won't give us any trouble about the curfew for a while."

We pulled into the barracks parking lot, and sat there for a moment. I asked him, "What's going on with Rodrigo? Two boys in his room?"

Dave hesitated and looked over at me. "Well, old Bob likes to play with the Arab boys."

"Does he?" I'd thought the Arabs had some pretty strong religious strictures about that kind of behavior, but it wasn't my fight. Whatever. "Everyone to his own tastes, I guess."

"Huh. Bob's tastes include the flavor of the little girls on the cleaning crews *and* the younger busboys, at least the pretty ones."

Where was he going with this? He didn't make me wait long.

"Bob's not the only one who uses the kids, and he's open about it," he said. "Want me to fix you up?"

Was he serious? Sometimes it was hard to tell if he was pulling my leg or not. "I don't need that kind of stuff, Dave. I'll save my strength for the dancing girls. I tell you, those girls were something. But I don't need any kinky stuff. Just not into that, you know?"

I leaned back in my seat and asked him straight up. "Tell me. What is it you do for these people at Club Tripoli? Free drinks, free dinners, free girls, and free passes to hand out?"

He stared through the dark windshield in silence for a moment. "That's just fringe benefits. I do a lot of stuff. It's hard work, but it pays well."

It sounded to me as if he deliberately tried to be vague. Like he worked hard to avoid letting me have much information, and painted a big rosy comfortable picture without much detail. That bothered me—made me uneasy. The place really didn't look much like a small-town country club but I had a feeling it might be rougher than Dave described. "So. What's with all the gambling and the other stuff?"

He grinned. "And other stuff? Listen, man, don't be so fussy. They want you. You can start with a spot in the band with Scarlatti and see what develops. If they like you they'll offer you a position, something that pays better than playing the guitar."

I wondered what he meant by that. Somehow, this whole setup was giving me the willies. It looked too easy, too pat. "You know, Dave, I need to look around a little, see if I can land some decent gigs here on base. That'll let me send home a few bucks to build my college fund."

Dave narrowed his eyes. I tried to make myself clear. "I don't need to get rich. Just save enough to go to school back in the States. You know how I feel about the Air Force. I've got to make it as a civilian and that means I have to get out and earn a degree. Get a good job and stay out!"

He leaned back again. "I hear you, man, I know. But how much money is enough? You're smarter than me, Ted, but sometimes you're too conservative. Opportunities like this don't come along every day, you know. Besides, they play the best music in town, right there in Club Tripoli, and quite a few of our guys work in their bands. Think about it."

He did make sense. This might be a chance for me to make enough money to get a big leg up on going to school. It sounded like fun, too. Still, I didn't want to get in over my head.

There seemed to be too many angles for this job to be on the up-and-up, like totally legitimate. But hey. Dave was an old friend. He wouldn't get me involved in anything dangerous, would he? And yet, he seemed different. Not quite the good ol' Dave I knew back in Texas. Smoother, maybe. Or tougher.

He cocked his head and eyed me with an air of expectation. "Okay, man," I said. "I'll think about it."

- 4 -

The next day I reported to the squadron first sergeant, Master Sergeant Andrews. He'd just gotten back from a temporary assignment in Europe and during his absence the squadron had saved my official check-in process for him. He was a small man with a full head of gray hair. He looked like he'd seen a lot of years of service, and he was all business. With a hangover and not enough sleep, I struggled to stay alert.

"Hmmm. Miller. Theodore L. Miller, A/2C, AF13558137. Let's see your orders, Airman, and get you posted on the official roster."

I dug out my orders and handed him the package that contained my medical and personnel records. He thumbed through the stack, checking off the items against a master list as he grunted and tapped the desk with his pencil.

He pushed the stack aside. "Okay. Now, I assume you brought some currency with you from the States."

"You mean money, Sergeant?"

"I mean U.S. currency. Greenbacks. You have to turn it all over to me. Now."

"What? Give you my money? I don't understand that at all."

"It's all explained in the 'Welcome to Wheelus' brochure they gave you on the plane, Miller. But of course you haven't read that, have you? So read it. It's got a lot of useful information in it, good stuff to keep you straight—and out of the stockade. First things first. You have to turn in all your greenbacks to me. I'll give you a receipt, and swap them out for you. We use scrip here at Wheelus. It's only good on base, but you can exchange it for Libyan piastres at the American Express office next to Finance."

He had me confused by all this and I said, "But, Sergeant—"

He waved my objections away. "The whole thing is about currency smuggling and the stability of the Libyan money. We don't allow use of U.S. currency here because it can end up on the black market and cause a lot of problems. Understand?"

"No, Sergeant, I don't."

"Well, you don't have to understand. Not required. Just give me any currency you have on you, and we'll swap."

I knew when to quit in an argument I couldn't win, so we swapped, and I broke out laughing. "Sarge, this scrip stuff looks like play money, like the stuff you use in Monopoly."

"Yeah, only cheaper. But hang onto to it. It spends the same. At least here on base. Downtown you need Libyan currency."

In about five minutes more he had me squared away. He leaned back in his chair and smiled. "Welcome to the 7272nd Air Force Band Squadron, Miller."

"Thanks, Sergeant. Can't say I'm glad to be here, but at least the assignment is officially started. And now I've got only five hundred and thirty-eight days to go."

The first sergeant snorted. "I hear you. This is a place where almost everybody counts their days. But seriously, I don't recommend day-counting because it's too discouraging, especially right at the start of your assignment. The thing to do is stay busy and look for ways to make use of your spare time. Then it won't drag so much. You'll see."

"Yes sir. Dave Walker said something about doing regional PR. How do we fit in there?" I asked him.

"We cover the Mediterranean area for NATO and the U.S. We do concert tours and visit military bases all over the region—public relations gigs. I just got back from Italy where I set up the itinerary for a concert tour of American military installations and several Italian towns and cities."

"Italy. That sounds a little better than Tripoli," I said.

He smiled. "You bet it is. We'll take the big concert band this time, and that includes everybody in the squadron. Sometimes we send just a few men up to France or Germany to augment the Air Force Band units up there if they're shorthanded. Then it's a TDY— a temporary duty assignment. You'll probably do one or two of those while you're here."

He turned back to my records. "Let's see. This shows your primary instrument as trombone and your secondary as guitar. We've got a full trombone section for the concert band, so you'll be on guitar there. We'll use you on trombone for the marching band to give us a full front row. The trip to Italy is our next big tour and it's another road trip. Concerts and dances in big theatres, village squares and mess halls—and long hours on the bus."

Long hours or not, the whole idea of the tour appealed to me. A new country, new people. That sounded good. "I'm looking forward to this trip, Sergeant."

Sergeant Andrews reshuffled the papers on his desk. "I think you'll have fun, but remember—we've got a job to do. You'll get to mix with the local people and see the country, but try not to cause a problem with the local girls. It's supposed to be a good-will tour."

I made a wry face. "Yes, Sergeant. I understand. No rough stuff with the women and try to stay out of jail, right?"

Sergeant Andrews gave me a hard look. "You get out of line in some of the countries we're going to visit and you'll wish you never heard of trouble. These guys can play pretty rough when they want to. I guess they're tired of smart-mouthed GIs and they won't put up with any crap. Got it? We have a couple of men on the roster who're still in prison in Turkey. Don't know when we'll get them back—if they're still alive. So keep a lid on it, Miller. I don't need those kinds of problems."

I sat up straight. "I don't need those kinds of problems either, First Sergeant. I'll be cool."

He gave me another look and began to putter around with an old, disreputable pipe while he talked, patting all of his pockets looking for a light. He gave up, "Have you got a light on you, Miller?"

I smirked. "No, First Sergeant."

He looked at me for a moment. "Oh. A non-smoker. Well, I smoke too much anyway and I ought to cut down. Filthy habit." He patted all his pockets again. At last he found a tattered book of matches in the lap-drawer of his desk. After he got his pipe going he took me in to meet the Old Man, the squadron commander, Chief Warrant Officer Mackey. I saluted and the Old Man welcomed me to the squadron. He encouraged me to concentrate on getting the most out of my eighteen-month tour of duty at Wheelus.

He flipped through my records on his desktop and stopped to study a page.

"Hmm. It says here you're qualified on the Colt .45 caliber semi-automatic in addition to the carbine. That's unusual for an airman."

"They made me an auxiliary Air Policeman at Laredo, sir. I had to qualify on the forty-five there."

"Do you like to shoot?"

"Yes, sir, shooting's okay. It's been a while, though."

He smiled broadly. "You need to try out for the base team."

That sounded like something way over my head. "I don't know, Mr. Mackey. My experience in competition shooting is a big fat zero."

He looked stern. "I run the pistol team here and we need more people involved. The team can't be competitive unless we can scare up a few more shooters. Besides, you don't want to sell yourself short on this. You can't find out your real capabilities unless you work at it a while."

"Yes, sir, I guess you're right."

He smiled. "Of course I am."

He turned a few more pages of my records. "You know, Airman Miller, this could be an opportunity, a real chance to improve your skill level with the forty-five. You can't always tell. Someday you'll appreciate having this ability. We'll get together at the base firing range and do some shooting, maybe competition or just plain old practice."

It sounded like we were done, so I stood. "Yes, sir, Mr. Mackey. Just say when."

He dismissed me and I wandered out to look for a cup of coffee, glad to escape the pressure I'd sensed from the Old Man.

* * *

That evening Dave and I and a few others from the squadron sat drinking beer at a table in the main bar of the Airmen's Club. Just as I tried to order another round, a flightline mechanic stumbled over from the bar and bumped into the corner of our table. The idiot knocked bottles over and spilled our beer. He laughed like a braying donkey. "I always said you bunch of piss-poor band fags couldn't hold your beer. Look at this mess," he slurred.

Dave grabbed him by the shirt front and slapped him across the face, making a harsh, resounding splat. He heaved him in the direction of the other mechanics sitting at the bar. They all jumped to their feet and the bartender, a big senior NCO, came over swinging a heavy sawed-off bat. He glared at both groups. "Any tough guys here?" he asked. "Come on. Step right up."

It got real quiet and he didn't find any takers. He stared at us. "If any of you punks show up in here in the next week, I'm going to personally find out who's tough and who ain't. Now. Out of my club! Move it!"

We filed out of the Airmen's Club and headed back to the barracks. There were footsteps behind us. We turned as the guy who'd been slapped ran up to us. He started cursing and made a grab at Dave. Laughing, Dave spun him around and kicked him square in the ass and knocked him down. The guy got slowly to his feet and began to circle as he cursed softly, making short jabs and feints. Dave waited. The mechanic stumbled and Dave stepped forward and delivered a strong kick to his right knee. The guy went down in screams with his lower leg bent at an unnatural angle to his thigh.

Dave muttered something I couldn't understand and kicked him in the crotch. He quit screaming and started puking and gagging. Another quick kick and he got quiet.

We heard a siren in the distance and rushed up the barracks stairs before the APs got there.

As we stared down from the third floor balcony, I said, "Good Lord, Dave. Where'd all that come from? You looked like a mean barroom brawler."

He threw his head back and roared with laughter. "Come on, man. You don't grow up in South Boston being polite to assholes."

I'd known Dave for a long time, but I'd never seen him do anything like that. He'd crippled this kid, mostly for being dull or for drinking too much beer. Yet I'd never seen him pick a fight or even get involved in one. The Dave I knew wasn't anybody's gentleman, but I'd never seen him act like this. Had he changed that much in the months since he'd left Texas? Or maybe I just didn't know him as well as I thought.

We stood leaning on the rail while I tried to decide whether to hang it up for the evening. Dave lit up a Lucky. "By the way, Ted, I've meant to ask you. Do you have any greenbacks left?"

"Well, no. Not since I met the first sergeant. He said I had to turn them in to him, exchange them for scrip. Crappy looking stuff, but he said it's the only legal money I can carry."

"Did he? And you gave them to him. You got hustled, man. I could have gotten you piastres for that money, and a lot more than the crummy exchange rate they'll give you at Finance or American Express. Hell, he saw you coming, Ted. Another green kid just off the plane." He swore under his breath.

"What else could I do? Lie to the first sergeant and go out and look for some black-market trader? Right—and get busted on my first week in Tripoli or something. I'm not that greedy. Or that dumb."

"Oh, right. You don't call giving all your money to the first sergeant dumb?"

"Dave, just drop it, okay? It's over and done with, and there's nothing I can do about it. And it was my money and no skin off your ass. Forget it."

Dave gave me a hard look, then heaved a sigh. "You're right, man. Live and learn. But there's a lot of sleazy people around here. Most of them on the make, one way or another. If anything else comes up where you have any doubts, talk to me. I can't have people screwing around with my friends."

He'd put me on instant alert. His sudden swing to a sympathetic self-righteous posture didn't ring true. Did he feel disappointed because I hadn't given him first shot at being sleazy? Like maybe he'd missed out on the easy mark.

I said, "All right, Dave. But don't be playing games. I'm a big boy now."

- 5 -

I got up early the next morning and struggled to make up my mind about working at the downtown club. Sleep had been hard to come by. As I stood in the hot shower it finally dawned on me. The club didn't want to marry me. They'd offered me a good paying job in a band. That had substance, something I could feel in my guts. From the age of about twelve I'd worked hard to be ready for such a chance, and put in long hours to learn music and improve my playing. Maybe that earned me a good paying job. Anyway, if it didn't work out I could always quit, right? And still be a few dollars ahead.

The main thing was the music, the opportunity to work with good musicians, Scarlatti in particular. He stood out among the musicians I'd known—he knew what he wanted and his music always worked. A big sense of relief swept over me as soon as my decision was made. Why did I always have to worry so much?

I got into uniform and waited in the dayroom for Dave to come by. We walked over to the Oasis. "I've decided to take the job with Scarlatti," I said. "It sounds like fun and the bread is damned good."

Dave's face lit up. "Hey, Ted. That's good news. He'll be real pleased. Me, too. You're not going to regret this. We'll have a great time at the club and you'll make the money you need for college."

* * *

A few days later, I started the job at Club Tripoli, three nights a week, playing guitar with Scarlatti's jazz quartet. It brought in a hundred a week to send home and the nights were flexible so I could avoid conflict with my Air Force duties. He paid me in scrip and I'd asked him about that. He told me they took in a lot of it from their Air Force customers, so it would be more convenient for both of us than paying me in piastres. It worked for me. I could walk into the American Express office on base, make a deposit to my account and they were greenbacks, just like that. A hundred a week meant more money than my monthly pay as an airman second class. And it came with some nice fringe benefits, like free drinks, food and a chance to fool around with the waitresses and dancers working there. Was it a little too good to be true? I hoped not.

I had fun there, and I enjoyed playing in Scarlatti's quartet. I'd based part of my gamble in taking the job on my certainty about his skills. I'd figured he had more competence, more expertise than the Air Force musicians, after listening to his deft, complex improvisations on the piano. That meant a lot of good with a little bit of bad. He pushed me hard, harder than the others did. Yet, my attitude changed and my playing improved.

Most of the worst irritations about Club Tripoli grew out of the constant oppression and arrogance of Scarlatti's junior managers. They seemed more interested in intimidating the workers and roughing up the women who worked there than in running a smooth operation. Stupid.

One evening as I left the bandstand for my break, a noisy row developed in the kitchen, loud enough to be heard in the dining room. The disturbance surprised me. One thing I'd thought you could count on at Club Tripoli—the place ran like a well-regulated machine, in spite of the heavy-handed actions of some of the managers. Scarlatti demanded order and he got it. There must have been something seriously wrong back in the kitchen, but still, it didn't much concern me. He paid me to play in the quartet, period. I walked up to the bar to get a drink and Rodrigo and one of the security guards cut me off. Bob grabbed me by the arm and said, "You come with me, Miller. We need some help in the kitchen to straighten out a couple of workers."

"Bob, what are you trying—?"

"Don't argue with me, Miller. Move it."

"Get lost, Rodrigo. I'm not one of your mindless goons and I don't take orders. Got it?"

He grabbed me again and pulled me close to his face. I could see the veins bulging in his forehead. "I can't stand here and argue with you," he said. "We've got a job to do, but I'm warning you. Don't get in my way. And don't try to make me look bad around here, or you're going to wish you'd never met me. I'll kick your scrawny ass from here to Sunday, you sweet little Southern boy." He muttered to himself and hurried toward the kitchen with the security guard in tow.

What? Did I have to take that kind of crap from this jerk? I did not work for Rodrigo and I wouldn't.

Dave sat at the bar staring at me with a sardonic grin. He must have been there through my whole run-in with Rodrigo. He chuckled. "Well, now you know what a prick Bob can be, don't you?"

"Yeah. I guess I do. Dave, where is he coming from, ordering me to help him whip up on a bunch of under-nourished Arab kids?"

He slid off his stool shaking his head. "Listen, take my advice. Stay out of his way. Scarlatti's in charge, but, like I told you, Bob has a lot of ambition. He wants to be Scarlatti's right hand man and move up, so he tackles all the mean, dirty jobs."

"Well, I've had enough of that guy," I said. "I won't put up with—"

"Look, man. Just stay out of his way. It's that easy. Don't pick a fight with him. He's not worth the trouble. He's a jerk, you know?"

We agreed on that score. "Enough of this, Dave. I can't tiptoe around Rodrigo or anybody else at this club." I walked out to the back bar to escape the argument and cool off. I felt too riled up to think straight about the job, Bob or anything else.

- 6 -

The job with Scarlatti's quartet gave me a chance to improve my skills and expand to a wider range of music. His steady careful discipline forced me to give up some of my bad habits and weak performance. He'd wag his finger in my face. "You must understand, my boy, that a lazy musician will never make excellent music. Music takes discipline and hard work and accuracy. Sloppy substitutions when the music calls for more complexity or subtlety are inexcusable."

To his credit and my gratification, Scarlatti seemed as quick to praise improvement in my playing as to criticize poor execution. "You continue to improve, Ted, but you must move away from the simplicities of country music and the imitative jazz you like to play in the squadron."

Like I didn't know my own shortcomings. He was right, but there was a limit to how hard I wanted to work for him. Or anybody else in Tripoli, Libya.

One evening after our last set, we had a glass of wine, a Marsala, something special from his private stock shipped in from Sicily. He sniffed, sipped his wine and sighed. "Do you play other instruments besides the guitar?"

"Yes, sir, I do. Trombone and tuba with the marching band."

He chuckled quietly. "No, no. Real instruments. Like the violin or the cello, or perhaps the mandolin?"

"Uh, no. I don't." I did play the cornet a little but wasn't sure that was a real instrument either.

He looked down as he paused, then continued in a quieter voice. "Too bad. My son played, as he put it, anything with strings. He was a natural talent, a prodigy."

He remained silent, holding a fixed stare across the room for a long moment and I asked, "Does he still play?"

"Ah, no," he said. "I—I lost him in the war. He fought with

Graziani and Rommel against the British, trying to help us save our colony here in Libya. He died in a tank at Tobruk."

I didn't know what to say. Dave had told me that Scarlatti had lost family in the war and almost never mentioned any of them. "The people back home say the war lasted a long painful time," I said. "Seems like nearly every family in America lost a man in battle."

Scarlatti looked up, his skin stretched tight across the gaunt structure of his face. With a tremble in his voice, he asked, "How many of your American fathers lost *all* their sons in battle?"

The little I knew about his family hadn't prepared me to handle his response. There didn't seem to be anything else to say and I sat there, tense and silent, waiting for his next move. Then he rose. All expression had vanished from his face and voice. "I left a great deal of work in my office. I must attend to business now."

I sat there for a while, awash in feelings of inadequacy, like I'd fallen short or failed a test of some kind. I finished my wine and walked over to the back bar to check out the scene. Dave sat at a table with a drink, talking to a couple of waitresses. Business had slowed down for the evening, another quiet Tuesday.

I sat down with him and he grumbled at me. "Scarlatti is running me ragged. There's no way to satisfy the man. Every time I finish one of his little jobs, he just gives me two or three more things to do. He is absolutely driving me crazy."

I'd heard enough about Scarlatti for one evening, yet I understood Dave's irritation. "But, Dave, that's why he pays you so well. You're always there for him. Always."

"Huh. Maybe I need to start hiding out or taking days off."

I ordered a beer and took a long pull on the bottle. "So, what is it now? Anything I can help you with?"

Dave looked up with a startled expression. "Yeah. Maybe you can. Scarlatti's got me going in three directions at once tonight. I have to make a drop-off for this major on base at ten. But I can't do that and keep my eye on the new bartender here at the same time."

I put down my bottle. "I'm leaving for the base now. What are you dropping off?"

He frowned and looked away from me. "Just listen to you, Ted. When are you going to learn not to ask for more than you need to know? I want your help, but you sure don't need to know what's in the package for the major."

Here we go again. What I needed to learn was how to keep my stupid mouth shut in the first place. "Listen man, I don't need your lecture, okay? Make up your mind. Do you want some help or not?"

We were sitting there staring at each other, in a standoff, when Scarlatti walked into the bar and spotted us. He walked straight up to Dave, stopped and gave him a long hard look. "Good evening, Mr. Walker. You seem to be at loose ends, as they say." He stared at Dave with a cold smile. Dave began to squirm on his bar stool.

"S-s-sir," he stammered. "I'm just leaving to check on your supply delivery. I-I asked Ted if he could handle a drop-off for me. It's a conflict for me, time-wise, and I've asked him to pitch in, sort of, and help me out."

Scarlatti focused his cold gaze on me and I tried not to squirm, not to react at all. He tilted his head. "Good. Good, Ted. We all need to pitch in at times. It seems I sometimes ask Mr. Walker for a little more than he's able to handle. I appreciate your sense of cooperation and your offer to help."

I tried to think of something to say—anything. He snapped a short nod at us and stalked off, heading for the main salon. I looked over at Dave. He'd broken into a light sweat and mopped his brow with a handkerchief. "Thanks," he muttered. "I do appreciate it, Ted." He reached in his coat pocket and came out with a thick brown envelope. It looked like the one he'd given to the man my first night at the club, at the booth in the back bar. He handed it to me. "Here's the packet of 'don't ask' for the major. You need to meet him at the beach pavilion at ten. That's ten exactly. He'll be driving a little black Fiat two-door sedan, a Topolino."

I took the package, regretting my offer to help him. I was pissed off at Dave, Scarlatti and myself. What a dumb situation. He needed to transact another deal with this major, only this time he'd gotten me involved—I'd offered to help. Dumb. "Okay, man. Okay."

"It's a piece of cake, Ted. No money exchange, just give him the package. I'll remind Scarlatti what a great team player you are." He handed me the keys to his Jeep. "Take these, man. You don't have much time to meet the major and I can get a ride back to the base with Rodrigo."

With reluctance and a few second thoughts I drove back to the base and swung by the deserted beach pavilion. I'd arrived a little early so I drove on past and came back a couple minutes later. The place still stood empty except for a tiny dark sedan parked in one of the slots. I felt ridiculous sneaking around in the middle of the night, but I pulled in beside the sedan. I recognized the sad-looking major from the incident with Dave in the back bar of the club on my first visit there. I got out and handed him the package through his open window. Without comment and no change in facial expression, he slipped his Fiat in gear and left the parking lot.

* * *

At Club Tripoli a week later, we left the bandstand for a break. Scarlatti led me over to a rich leather sofa on a raised dais in a corner of the main bar, where he surveyed the crowd from a commanding view. As I settled down in the luxury of the soft Italian leather, a waiter hurried over and Scarlatti ordered us a glass of wine. He lit one of his English cigarettes and said in his deep rumble, "You make good progress, Ted. You are a quick learner and have worked out well with the quartet."

It felt good to be commended and I'd struggled to deserve it. "Thanks, Mr. Scarlatti. I appreciate your saying so."

"And the help you gave Dave the other night, I appreciate that as well." He smiled. "You are doing a good job for me, but you can do better than playing guitar. Our organization needs runners and pick-up men and people to travel to our clubs in Morocco and Sicily."

I squirmed on the sofa. He must know I couldn't take off for a trip out of the country just any time he needed me. "Uh, sir. Don't forget. The Air Force still owns me seven days a week and I can't just simply—"

"Relax, Ted. I have worked with Air Force people for a few years now. There are ways to get things done."

That sounded oversimplified to me, but he continued along the same line of thought.

"What I'm talking about now is important work, responsible work," he said, "but it is not difficult. And my couriers make more money than my musicians. What I need is a man to make the run out to Homs every week, about seventy five miles up the coast. Do you know Homs?"

"Yes sir. Out by the old Roman ruins, isn't it?"

"Exactly. I need a man to carry the payroll out there and bring back the weekly proceeds from our operations. I need someone who is reliable and smart, who knows how to follow directions.

Explicitly."

I thought about it. That seemed simple enough, like a routine kind of working arrangement, easy to manage and fit into my schedule. "Now, that's something I could do here in Libya, and without any conflict with the Air Force. But, you know, sir, I'm not so sure I want to—"

"Of course you do," he said. He smiled. "All you have to do is ride out there, meet my men at the inn, deliver their briefcase and pick up mine. Takes perhaps two to three hours. As easy as that. Get back here and pick up two hundred dollars. Sound good?"

Well yeah, it sounded good. A couple hundred bucks a week for a few hours work meant really good money, more than I made on the bandstand for a lot less effort. Dave had said this kind of offer would come. The job promised a lot of money, but an uneasy feeling gripped me. "Why do you need a new courier? Did your regular driver quit?"

"Ah, well. He had an accident on the road back to Tripoli. It was late and the idiot crashed on his motorcycle. Perhaps he fell asleep? We do not know. The body had deteriorated somewhat by the time we found it."

I shuddered. A courier could make an easy target out there on the empty coastal road from Homs. All at once the big, safe organization Dave bragged about didn't sound quite so rock-solid anymore. Like the easy money might not be all that easy. It hadn't helped that courier much. I hedged. "Sir, what if I have to be out of the country? We do these TDYs to Europe, Morocco and Turkey and all and I can't just tell the First Sergeant I'm busy, you know."

He frowned. "As I said earlier, there are ways to work things out. One of my security men can cover your occasional absence. You forget I manage a big organization, perhaps. That's not a problem to worry about."

That was a nice quick answer, but maybe it was a little too smooth. Sometimes Scarlatti seemed to kind of shave the truth a little close. "Sir, I'm not very experienced on a motorcycle. You know, I'd probably crash on the way to Homs on my first run." With a sincere-sounding laugh, I said, "But I am interested. Let me think about it over the weekend."

He sat up straight. "No! It's a yes or no offer. I need a man now for this job. So make up your mind."

Scarlatti could get tough when he wanted something. Tough and mean. I'd seen him in action with Dave and the Pres, but I'd seldom been his target. I felt the pressure strongly. My decision depended on whether fear of the job outweighed the good money. Getting wasted out in the desert seemed like a definite risk, but I didn't want to pass up the chance to fatten up my college fund. Besides. It didn't have to be a permanent arrangement. If it seemed too dangerous, I'd quit. Simple as that.

Here goes, I thought. "Well, then, Mr. Scarlatti, I'll give it a try. Make the runs in the early afternoon using a borrowed car. That sound all right to you."

He patted my shoulder and smiled. "Good. Be at my office at noon next Saturday. You'll make your initial run with one of our club security guards to show you the ropes and give the people on the other end a chance to meet you."

"Thanks, Mr. Scarlatti. It's generous of you to make the offer. I appreciate it." We shook on it.

I still felt uncomfortable with Scarlatti and his organization. It seemed hard to come to terms with all the things Dave had to do, and hard to follow his lead. But the money would kick my college fund up a big notch—and assure my planned escape from the Air Force. I stopped at the bar on the way back to the bandstand, got a straight whiskey and sat there staring in the mirror for a long moment. I noticed my hand shook just a little as I picked up the drink. *What am I getting myself into, now?*

- 7 -

The next day, Dave and I took the rock and roll combo out to the Royal Tank Corps base near Homs. They were a holdover from the days of the big war and had leased their base and the rights to carry out war games in the desert from the United Kingdom of Libya like we had leased Wheelus. I knew I'd get a chance to take a look around and check out the dusty little inn where they carried out Scarlatti's local trade. And I wanted to get a look at the old semi-restored Roman ruins of the ancient seaport of Leptis Magna.

On the drive out to Homs, Dave filled me in on his relationship with the tankers. "The British Army has this sailing club on Tripoli Harbor. It's a recreational facility for their men and for the British embassy staff, too. They keep about a dozen little sailboats there with full gear at their dock in the shadow of the seawall. It's kind of tucked under the Lungo Mare along the southwestern edge of the harbor. The harbor's big and it stays pretty calm most of the time, with pretty good winds off the Mediterranean."

"Do you sail there? I've seen sailboats but I've never been in one. They sure are pretty. It looks like a lot of fun, but I've never had a chance to try it."

Dave grinned. "Truth be known, it's why I do this nearly free gig at the tank base. I don't charge them much for the band, the tankers blow off a lot of steam and the British let's me have sailing privileges at their club on the harbor. If they knew how much I love sailing, they'd probably charge me to play at the base."

I chuckled. "And here I thought you were entertaining these guys out of the goodness of your heart. You, Dave? Working an angle? What a shock."

"Yeah, right. Good old Dave," he said, shifting his hands on the wheel.

We drove on in silence for a while. As we neared the town of Homs he explained a little about Scarlatti's operations there. "He keeps gambling and whores available for the troops, and the Tank

Corps command structure turns a blind eye most of the time. I think the deal depends on keeping the operation smooth and trouble-free for the British command. Right now, things are going good. Scarlatti had to shut down the drug trade for a while, at least in the official sense, and concentrate on booze, gambling and prostitution."

"So is Scarlatti in bed with the British Command? Or is all of this just a hands-off kind of unspoken deal?" I asked.

Dave gave me an unreadable look. "I think that's another one of your 'don't ask' kind of questions, Ted. You don't need to know and the information could be dangerous to you. Got it?"

I got it. We were back to the tough guy routine, but I didn't expect it to last, and it didn't. The tankers' isolation at the edge of the desert meant they had few distractions from their dreary surroundings and the boring routine of their combat training. Scarlatti's operation gave the men a limited outlet for entertainment.

* * *

We arrived at Homs and the intense heat and dryness, with the wind blowing off the desert, made the tank base a barren miserable place, plain and inhospitable. The morale of the men just had to be a real problem. I tried to imagine a daily existence at the base, but I couldn't get the feel of it. And I didn't really want to spend enough time there to get that feel. No way. We met with the officers in charge when we arrived, then went to the mess hall to set up the combo and get our concert underway.

We kicked off with "Long Tall Sally." Dave honked away on his alto sax for the first chorus, and I banged away with the triplets, just about peeling the covers off of the amplifier speakers. I had plenty of competition from the drummer, and the Brits loved it. Then we sang the first verse in unison, trying to keep together on the lyrics. "Gonna tell Aunt Mary about Uncle John, Claims he has the music but he has a lot of fun . . ." It wasn't Little Richard but we rocked along.

Good lyrics, but the chorus grabbed everybody. "Oh baby, yes baby! Oh baby, yes baby . . ." The tankers all joined in, competing for loudest voice, and I didn't have to sing along anymore after the first verse.

All those guys were dancing with a bottle of whiskey in one hand and the other balled up in a fist waving around over their heads, stomping their heavy boots on the mess hall floor. They sure hadn't forgotten how to raise hell. But these guys were more like happy drunks than the mean drunks I remembered from some rough clubs I'd played.

I kept turning up the volume on the amps, and playing a heavy rhythm guitar while the drummer beat the hell out of every gadget he had in his setup. We played some of the latest American rock and roll tunes, took requests and turned out a wild, uninhibited sound.

At the first break, Dave warned me, "They're always glad to see us, but watch out. They're more than generous with the liquor, and they always try to get us drunk. I'm telling you, I've never seen anybody who could hold as much Scotch as these guys can." And they were a little tiresome, trying to get us to drink more than we were used to.

We did one set of nothing but Chuck Berry tunes, staying late and playing hard. I guess I did drink a little whiskey. I remember singing "Maybellene," and I couldn't remember all the words. But hey, I don't think anybody cared or even noticed.

When we finished our last set, three NCOs staggered up to the bandstand. The drunkest one didn't quite make it. He walked into a wall behind us and keeled over in a heap. The ranking NCO insisted on shaking all our hands. "Bloody good music, men. Bloody good. Loved it. The men loved it. We all did."

I thought he'd go on forever, but he looked around and saw there were about as many Brits lying down as there were standing up. "All right you men. Let's clear this up, and drag the bodies back to the barracks. We'll all have a good run at dawn!"

A long, loud chorus of agonized complaint rose from those still on their feet. "Enough grumbling, lads. Don't forget when it's time to pay the piper!" The sergeant snapped, "Up and out, men!" I thought maybe he was teasing them, but he wasn't.

The next morning the men showed up for breakfast at the mess hall. They looked tired but definitely sober.

The Tankers were generous in their thanks and appreciation for our visit. "We enjoyed your playing tremendously," they said again and again. I couldn't be sure who remembered what from last night. But Dave and I remembered the generous breakfast spread they laid out for us. The tankers ate good, better than the Air Force, and I always enjoyed going out to Homs.

* * *

On a Saturday, a week after our visit to Homs, we arrived at the sailing club about mid-day. I'd been out on the boat with Dave a couple of times and I felt like I was getting the hang of it. An easy breeze blew across the seawall. The sailing club manager, a crusty old retired tanker, offered us one of the Snipes, a small sloop-rigged open boat designed for a crew of two. He asked if we could take someone out with us. "You'll be safe enough," he said. "It's a fair calm day, not much chop on the harbor. Your passenger is just a wee lass, you see, and won't take up a lot of room. She wants to learn a bit about sailing."

I glanced at Dave. "We can take her along, right?"

Dave shrugged his shoulders. I looked at the girl, small and dark, with brown hair pulled back in a ponytail. She had dark brown eyes, nearly black, and a petite, trim body. Definitely feminine, but small. I had the eerie sensation, just for an instant, that the wind and the noisy birds had all grown silent. I felt lucky I didn't have to say anything right then. I don't think I could have. Her white tennis shoes, a white jersey, old faded jeans and a self-assured, confident smile all made her look normal and casual, yet I hadn't seen any girl as pretty in Tripoli. I tried not to stare.

She'd been hanging back and the manager introduced us. "Penny Crawford, I want you to meet Dave Walker and Ted Miller."

I smiled and said hi. Dave said, "Hey. It's a pleasure. Where you from?"

"Oh, all over. I'm an Air Force brat and it seems like I've lived in about half the States, Europe, the Far East. And now Africa."

The manager broke in. "Penny's recently graduated from the Wheelus High School and her dad is with the Air Police unit on your base."

I finally found my tongue again. "Oh, no. You weren't one of those kids in the brat pack were you? The ones that claimed they owned the beach?"

"Yeah," she said with a lopsided smirk. "The Uaddans."

"The wah-what?" I asked.

"Uaddans! That's the Wheelus High School mascot. It's a Libyan sheep, big and fat with curvy horns. But I'm not a Uaddan anymore. I've graduated and I'm ready for college."

The manager interrupted. "Penny, you'll find that Dave, here, is quite the sailor, experienced back in the States. I've sailed with him as crew in a race or two and found him quite capable. So. I'm putting you in good hands. Right, lads!"

He left us standing on the dock. I looked Penny over. "Ever sailed before?"

"Yes, once, but I want to learn how to run the boat myself."

Dave stepped forward "All right, then, but you've got to pay attention and listen. This is a small boat and we can't be stumbling around, you know."

Penny's brows knitted. "Just tell me what I have to do."

"Okay. If I say 'coming about' or 'jibe ho' that means get your head down immediately." Her eyes widened. "It means the boom, this part, is going to be swinging across the cockpit of the boat, here, quickly. If you don't duck you'll get hit hard on the head. Maybe hard enough to knock you out cold." Dave pointed out the other parts of the boat as he talked.

The boys at the dock had rigged our Snipe and we were ready to go. I settled into the crew position, forward near the mast and the centerboard. As crew, I'd manage the jib, and have Penny sit next to me on the wide gunwale to learn by example. Dave sat in the back to handle the tiller and the sheet for the mainsail.

"All right, Penny, watch everything Ted does and listen to the chatter," he said. "Stay close to him and move with him as we maneuver the boat. Now, let's see how it goes."

I pushed us off and Dave paid the mainsheet out to catch the wind. We sailed away from the dock until we reached the middle of the long, wide harbor. Then we eased into the wind and tacked to head toward the east end of the harbor.

After a couple of gentle changes in heading requiring minor adjustments in sail and jib, Dave snapped, "Enough loafing. Coming about!"

Penny and I ducked as Dave eased the bow across the wind, coming onto the other tack with a gentle tiller. I slipped under the sail and moved to the other side. Penny peered at me under the sail and I reached out and pulled her over to my side, nearly landing her in my lap. She glared at me and I felt like a clumsy fool. I laughed, trying to cover my embarrassment. "You'll catch on," I said. "Remember. Crew has to move to the side away from the sail when we're on a tack."

She gave me a strained smile. "Sorry about that. I'll do better next time." She moved close to me again and I felt the warmth of her leg pressed against mine. Either she wanted to be aggressive with me, or my imagination ran wild. Whatever . . .

As we approached the pass from the harbor out to the open Mediterranean, the sea birds rose in waves from the rocky jetty. Gulls and terns screamed their plaintive, lonely cries as they circled us, diving in close, looking for handouts. Penny made throwing motions and the birds went wild. They turned and jostled for position with all the others crowding the air around us.

The tenseness that had grown between us vanished. We chuckled together at their greedy antics. Dave interrupted our amusement by shouting, "Damned birds!" We turned to see him scooping up water with one hand, wiping bird droppings off his face, and trying to handle the tiller and mainsail with the other.

The boat wobbled and wandered off course until Dave burst out laughing at himself. He quit his attempts to recover his dignity and righted the boat back to its proper course. When he had us on a good heading away from the rocky jetty, he leaned back against the transom. "All right. I need a volunteer to act as the target. Here they come again!"

It seemed like we'd been on the water just a short time, but our daylight had started to fade. Time to head back toward the dock. We set up for a steady run downwind, sails full out. A stunning sunset bathed the harbor. In the rosy light and quiet of the moment, I studied Penny's face and her dark, dark eyes, and watched the way her ponytail moved along her slender, sun-tanned neck, with wayward strands wafting in the gentle breeze. A sudden surge of warmth and unexpected feelings of tenderness engulfed me. She leaned against me and smiled.

* * *

Dave maneuvered the Snipe into the slip and I stepped onto the dock to secure the bow and stern lines. Our return to the solid feel of the dock and the real world of responsibilities and obligations jarred my carefree mood. The familiar hot, tarry smell of the street swept over us with the strong mixture of odors that emanated from the old city, from the dung of the camels and sheep, to the sharp stench of human urine.

Penny thanked us for her first real sailing lesson. "I hope it won't be my last. I had a lot of fun, really."

Dave stood there smiling in the glow of her generous words. "Yeah, we've had a nice day for a sail," he said.

Penny looked up at him. "And you make it look so easy."

"Maybe today," Dave said, "but it's not always so easy. Next time we'll let you have the tiller and the mainsheet for a while. That's a bigger challenge."

As we started toward the seawall, he turned to me. "Ted, I need to stop by the club for a minute. Scarlatti said he had to see me this afternoon. It shouldn't take me too long. Do you mind?"

Penny must have noticed my grimace because she broke in. "I'm going straight back to the base," she said. "I can give you a lift if you need to get back right away."

I felt a little jolt in my guts, but I tried to stay cool. "Hey, that'd be a big help. There's a few things for me to catch up on at the barracks." We all climbed from the dock back up to the street and Dave rumbled off in his battered Jeep, treating us to the incongruous burble of his V-8 engine. Penny unlocked her car, an old pre-war Ford coupe, and we climbed in. I sat back in the fading light and watched her drive. Apparently she sensed me observing her and turned to look at me. "What?"

She caught me off guard. I felt the earlier tenseness grow between us again and couldn't think of a quick, smooth rejoinder. "I must have been daydreaming," I ad libbed. "It's been a nice day and I'm about to fall asleep. Good thing you're driving. I was watching you drive, thinking about home and everything I miss about it."

She looked back at the road for a moment. Her face softened and she turned to me. "Yeah. You know the idea of getting homesick worries me. I'm going off to school this fall and I've never been away from home. What's it going to be like without my family?"

My thoughts went back to my early days in the Air Force. "Listen, everybody gets homesick, but it doesn't have to be too painful. It lasts longer for some people than it does for others. The main thing is, you need to stay busy and look ahead, not back."

She eyed me closely with a bemused look furrowing her brow, as if she doubted my sincerity. "If you're going to be sympathetic with me and give me such sound advice, I won't know how to handle it. What? No teasing? No tough guy stance or something?"

"Oh sure, that's me, the big tough guy. But, seriously. You're talking to one of the survivors. A bona fide homesickness survivor.

No scars, just the memory."

As we drove through the main gate of the base, she smiled and waved at the APs.

She looked over at me. "So. Where do you need to go?"

"I'm dying of hunger. Why don't we stop at the Mirage and get something to eat. What do you say?"

Penny smiled. "Food! Yes. Does sailing always make you this hungry? I could eat a horse."

* * *

She pulled into the empty parking lot. We went inside and she grabbed one of the battered booths. We ordered cheeseburgers with fries and milk shakes. As the waiter left, Penny got up to check out the selections on the jukebox. Going down the list she stopped. It seemed to me as if she were holding her breath. Penny relaxed with a long sigh. "This song was one of Cynthia's favorites," she said. " 'Dream.' She loved to sing it."

"Who? Cynthia?"

"Oh. Just somebody I used to know. A girl. Look, there's a new record from the Duke Ellington band."

"Are you kidding me? Yeah, there it is. Duke Ellington. Do you want to play it?"

She chuckled. "Sure. It's about the only new thing they've had this month."

I checked my pockets for jukebox tokens. What a nuisance. The scrip I had on me came in all sizes from five cents to ten dollar denominations, but a "paper nickel" wasn't going to play the music. I walked over to the cashier, handed him a paper "dollar" and got a handful of tokens, quarter sized coins. Penny put a token in the selector and picked out several songs she liked. We danced to the gentle melody and slow tempo of "Dream," nice and easy and moody. I figured I'd better quit dancing while I was ahead and walked her back to our booth.

We sat and I listened to the Ellington number, "Satin Doll." His subtle meter and complex chord structure kept me off balance. I wanted to work it up on the guitar, but unless I got the sheet music, I'd have to fake a few of the chords, complex top-heavy chords that were about half-dissonant and hard to figure, just listening to the record.

When the number ended, I noticed her watching me. "So," she

asked, "what do you do in the Air Force? Are you a pilot?"

Damn, I thought. If she thinks I'm a pilot then she probably thinks I'm an officer. Oh, well, let's get this over with. "No, I'm not a pilot. I'm a musician in the band squadron, an airman second class." From her expression, I must have spoken in an aggressive tone of voice, like I had a chip on my shoulder.

Penny looked down at the table. "Take it easy. Don't get offended. Just making conversation." She glanced up at me with an abrupt toss of her head. Her eyes were narrowed and she didn't look apologetic at all. The conversation lagged while I tried to come up with something else to talk about.

She helped me off the hook of my embarrassment, saying, "I've never known any musicians, and I've never seen anyone concentrate so hard listening to a record. Music must be important to you."

I tried to be cool and gave her my biggest smile. "Sorry. I was trying to figure out the tune, or Ellington's arrangement of it. You know, the harmonics, the structure of the thing." She looked a little blank, so I shifted gears. "Anyway, that must be a kind of a giveaway. But, you probably have known other musicians without being aware of it. Often the topic doesn't come up. Like Dave. He's a musician too, and in our case, we're doing our required military service in the Air Force Band System."

Her eyes lit up. "That sounds like fun. Do you enjoy it?"

"Yeah, really. And it's easy duty. Only thing though. It's hard to get into the system. There's a lot of competition for not very many slots. The only way to qualify is by examination."

She stared. "You mean like an audition?"

"Yeah. Scary experience. Or it was for me."

"I'd be terrified," she said. "But you must have done okay."

I laughed. "Well, yeah. They accepted me, but I can't remember the whole audition. One of the senior bandsmen at Lackland Air Force Base put me through some hoops to see if I could read music and do sight-reading. He even made me do some ad lib work to see if I could follow his piano accompaniment. I made it, but whether it was barely or positively, I'll never know. The guy just filled out some papers and said I'd get the results from my basic training squadron commander. They wrote a letter that said I had a new AFSC description as a trombone/guitar player."

"A what? AFSC?"

"Oops. That's Air Force Specialty Code. Sorry. I guess I dropped into airman-speak there."

"Ugh. I hear that stuff around the house all the time, but I try to ignore it if I can."

I laughed. "Yeah, I'll bet. The career guys in my squadron sound like they're speaking a foreign language sometimes. It gets irritating, down-right tiresome after a while. Makes me want to get away, and I do if I can. You know, just go somewhere else. The library, the beach, anywhere they aren't. Anyway, being in the band is fun most of the time. I guess the worst part of it is there's not much rank handed out. It's hard to get promoted in a band squadron."

"Isn't the band what my Dad calls 'soft core'?"

"More airman-speak? But yeah, we're definitely soft core. Headquarters allocates stripes to us like Old Mother Hubbard handing out bones. Not many and not very often. But I sure don't plan to make a career in the band, or in the Air Force. When I finish my enlistment and get out of the military, I'm going to get a degree in engineering. So I can make a decent living."

"An engineer? That's a long way from being a bandsman."

"Well. My dad is an engineer and I think I can—"

"I didn't mean you're not smart enough to do it."

More silence. I remembered Penny's dad served with the Air Police. "So, your dad's an AP, then?"

She hesitated for a moment. "Not exactly. He's the Provost Marshal. But he used to be an AP."

Whoa! The Provost was in the top brass on any airbase. I scrambled mentally to regain my balance and decided to view that as a challenge rather than an obstacle. And see if she could take a little teasing. "Oh. *That* Crawford. Now, don't get defensive about it. He's not an airman, then, is he?"

She rolled her eyes upward and sighed. "No, he's not an airman. He's a bird colonel, but he's my dad and he's a nice man. I've never seen him throw his rank around."

I snorted. "That's kind of unusual for a bird colonel, wouldn't you say?"

She held her ground. "Not this colonel. *And* he's had enlisted men as friends, as long as they weren't in his command."

I could feel my smile fading away, a frown settling across my face. "Would he mind if you dated an enlisted man?"

She hesitated. "Hmm. That question's never come up, so I don't know, really. My guess is that neither he nor my mom would be thrilled about the idea." She tilted her head and studied my face for a moment. "Why? Are you asking me for a date?"

I laughed. No shy or timid act for this girl. "Well, I might ask, so maybe you should check with them, see what they say."

Our food finally came. We were ravenous and tore into our cheeseburgers without another word. She finished her food quickly and I asked, "Do you want another burger or more fries?"

She swallowed hard. "Oh, no. I'm a light eater."

I almost choked on my shake. "A what? A light eater? I haven't seen food disappear that fast since the last time we had cold-cuts night at the mess hall."

We walked out to her car and I watched her walking ahead of me. Nice. And she caught me watching. With just a hint of impatience, she asked, "Where can I drop you off, Ted?"

"Can you take me over to the squadron? It's on barracks row."

"Just show me which one." We climbed back into her car and she drove us across the base to the long block of three-story buildings where I lived. She pulled up to the curb by the band squadron sign and said, "I'd better go, Ted."

I got her phone number and went on up the stairs of the barracks two steps at a time, humming "Satin Doll." My mood had faded by the second flight. Tomorrow night I worked at Club Tripoli, and on Saturday I had to make that run out to Homs. The bread would help me go to school, but I still couldn't feel comfortable with the job and the club.

- 8 -

Getting more involved downtown cramped my spare time. I put in a big piece of my Saturday making the run to Homs now, in addition to my playing three nights a week in Scarlatti's quartet. Spare time was becoming a faint memory of the past and I wished I had more time to spend with Penny Crawford. Then, on the Wednesday after my first solo run as a courier, Mr. Mackey cancelled our scheduled rehearsal for the big band. He had to attend a staff meeting for unit commanders in the 7272nd Air Base Wing. With no notice at all, I had an afternoon off with no commitments. The clock said ten and I decided to call Penny and see if she could go to lunch with me. Asking her for a date with such short notice made me a little uneasy, but I decided to gamble. We had dated twice since we'd met at the sailing club, but had kept things low-key. I didn't think her family knew she was going out with an airman, and I didn't want to raise that issue with her. Being with her was fun and that was enough for now. Any future with her was a big open question in my mind.

I phoned Penny at home. She finally answered after about six rings. "Hey, this is Ted Miller. The Old Man just gave me an afternoon off and I thought about you. How do you feel about going to lunch? Downtown at La Loggia. Do you know the place?"

"Yeah, I know about La Loggia. I've been there with friends for coffee and snacks. Lunch? Sounds good to me."

"Great. I'll borrow Dave's Jeep and be at your place in, say, ten minutes."

"Don't bother Dave. I've got my little Ford coupe. I'll pick you up and you can watch me drive—again."

"That's a great idea. He's generous with his Jeep, but I need to be careful. I could wear out my welcome on a thing like that."

"All right, then," she said. "See you in ten minutes."

I prepared for more like twenty minutes or so. She had to do her makeup, fuss around and decide what to wear. Growing up with two older sisters had taught me a little something about women. I changed to civvies and waited in the shade on the top floor landing.

Sure enough, about twenty-five minutes later she pulled up to the curb out front. I trotted down the stairs and got in the car. She looked good in khaki slacks and sandals with a white button-down oxford blouse. It looked kind of preppy, but it made her dark coloring and her tan look great. Every time I saw her, it took me a minute or two to get my tongue untied, to relax enough to carry on a normal conversation.

She drove and I watched. We found a rare parking spot by the fountain on the Castle Square at the harbor and walked the couple of blocks to the café. La Loggia was a cool place, a nice little sidewalk café near Independence Street, downtown on 24 December Street. It wasn't far from the harbor, and it had small tables out on the sidewalk, arranged around the columns of the building. Some of them sat out in the full sunlight, with awnings and umbrellas set up for shade. Other tables were tucked back in the arcade beneath the second floor overhang.

We chose one of the sheltered tables in the shade. The early June weather felt a little too warm for a table out on the sidewalk in the bright sunshine. The waiter brought the drinks and pizza I'd ordered and we sat in the breeze from the overhead fans. We felt comfortable enough in the shade and the iced drinks helped.

Penny grinned. "You know, these Arabs are weird. Now, why would they name their main street after Christmas Eve? That doesn't make a bit of sense."

"Oh. 24 December Street. That is confusing, and I had to check it out at the base library. Turns out, that's the day the United Nations turned Tripolitania over to the Arabs, to King Idris."

"Really?"

"Yeah. It just happened to be on Christmas Eve when they made it official. It's their fourth of July."

"Gee. I feel so dumb."

"No, no, not dumb. Every American I've ever talked to, the GIs at least, make the same mistake. I remember that I did. 'Gee. Why do Muslims have a Christmas Eve street?' Everybody does it."

Conversation slowed down a little and Penny talked about shopping. "There's so much stuff I'll need when I go off to school.

And then there's the presents for relatives and friends back in the States—but I just don't seem to be able to get organized and get started on it."

Her talk of going off to school dampened my mood. It always did. She'd babble on and on about leaving, getting away from home, and I'd start getting depressed about losing her. I mean, she wasn't mine to lose, exactly, but that's how it felt.

I signaled to the waiter. "Why don't we go over to the old market now? I know you can find some things for gift-giving there. Hey, if you can't find it in the souk it's something you don't really need or want."

She hesitated. "I've never been there. But if you want to take me I'm sure it'll be all right."

I chuckled. "It sounds like somebody's been telling you those old tales, the ones about girls wandering into the old city and getting dragged off to the desert to spend their life in slavery in some sheik's harem. An ugly, old, smelly sheik."

"Mom says—"

"Yeah, Yeah. I've heard those stories, too, but you can't track down a single word in the papers or at the base library where anyone's disappeared or gone missing. Nothing. Not a word."

Her eyes narrowed. "Yeah? Well, maybe it's a kind of cover-up. Something nobody talks about. How do you really know, anyway?"

"I don't know. That sounds pretty far out to me, but there's no way to really know, I guess. Anyway—here in the city, the only real risk is when the Arabs go spooky and start screaming and running around. Then you've got to take cover and not get trampled."

A troubled look creased her brow. "That's what they say, but I've never seen them go crazy. And I don't really want to."

My mind flashed back to my first trip to downtown Tripoli with Dave. "Yeah. I saw them go nuts once, when I was first here. And once was enough for me." I looked at the check, put thirty piastres with it and got up. "Come on, let's walk over there. It's only a couple of blocks and we won't stay long, but you've got to see this place. Got to."

"Okay. But stay close to me."

"How close do you want me?"

"Not that close."

I took my hands off her. "Come on." I handed an extra coin to the busboy and we walked over to the tall arched gateway in the wall surrounding the old city of Al Tarablus that served as the main entry to the souk. Beyond the wall a busy, crowded maze of narrow lanes lined both sides of the street with small shops.

During the hottest summer months, the cloth merchants rigged long strips of bright-colored, newly-dyed cloth from wall to wall across the passages. This arrangement blocked the direct sunlight, yet allowed free circulation of the air. It wasn't air conditioning, but their ingenuity impressed me. It beat baking in the sunshine. As we cleared the gate, the overhead cloth panels burst into a brilliant tapestry of reds, greens, yellows, blues and whites.

Penny craned her neck, looking up at the radiant display. "Oh, look. It's like the awnings Dad put up over our patio. It's so pretty."

I glanced around the street. "Yeah. I love this place. I think I've bought brassware or tapestries for everyone I know back in the States. But I still love to come here to look around, and haggle with the Arabs."

I looked through a rack of leather belts in front of a tiny shop. Penny had gotten very quiet and she grabbed me by the arm. "Ted. Isn't that Dave Walker over there? What's he doing?"

I looked up and across the narrow street. Dave and Bob Rodrigo were entering a vegetable stall. Bob disappeared from view and Dave remained visible, blocking the entry into the stall. I could hear Bob talking to someone, sounding harsh and insistent. I couldn't understand what he said but it sounded like money talk. Then he started out of the little shop, moving with a determined stride. A boy who couldn't have been more than eight or nine years old followed him out of the stall. The boy jumped on him like an angry lion, screaming and pounding on his back and shoulders, all outrage and courage, but he was small and light.

Bob shook him off and slammed him against a wall. He wrecked a display of baskets filled with fruits and stunned the boy to silence. The customers scattered from the shop like chickens running from a yelping dog. Dave and Bob went back inside, then re-emerged, dragging a small man out by his hair. They threw him down in the street. Bob put his foot on the little Arab's neck and shifted his weight onto him until the man began to croak and gurgle.

Penny grabbed my arm. "Ted! What are they doing? They're hurting him. And the little boy—"

"I don't know. I can't tell what's going on." I looked down the street and cupped my hands like a megaphone. "Rodrigo! What do think you're doing, man? You're acting like a thug. Let him go before you kill him, you dumb bastard!"

He turned in my direction, face distorted with rage. Dave looked like he had in the back bar of Club Tripoli a month ago. Bob started toward us, but Dave grabbed him by the arm and said a few words I couldn't make out. Bob grabbed the Arab, shook him and cursed him for a moment. Dave kept talking and pulled Bob away from the shop owner. After a few more words, Dave and Bob walked away, heading deeper into the maze of the market. I soon lost sight of them as they ducked into a side street.

I looked at Penny. She was still holding onto my arm. I couldn't just leave her there and go chase Dave and Bob. Anyway, I wasn't sure what I'd do if I caught them. Penny was crying. "Oh, that little boy. Let's see if he's all right."

We walked over to the shop and the man had the boy cradled in his lap. He wiped the boy's face with a grubby rag and made soothing sounds. They both looked okay to me, but the crowd was closing around us and you didn't have to understand Arabic to feel their hostility. Penny tried to talk to the little man. "Are you all right? Can we help?" But he ignored her and she sputtered into silence.

I looked around at the solid wall of angry Arabs. "Come on Penny. Let's get out of here." I stared over the heads of the people in the street, avoiding eye-contact, and took Penny by the arm. As we moved away from the stall, the crowd got out of the way and let us move back to the archway of the main gate with only an occasional rough jostle. Having cleared the gate, we walked over to the fountain on Castle Square where we'd parked and got in the car. I leaned back and took a deep breath.

Penny looked at me with a pinched face and wide eyes. "What's going on?" she asked. "I thought Dave was your friend, but he acted like a gangster."

"I don't know what's happening. I've got some vague ideas about Bob in particular. There's rumors around the club about a few of the guys running a protection racket, a shakedown in some of the smaller shops in the old city. But I didn't know Dave was involved."

"You be careful, Ted. I wouldn't trust either one of those guys."

I sighed. "Yeah, I hear you. Anyway, we're okay. No harm done, I guess, but things felt a little close in there, didn't they?"

Penny stared at me. "Close? I was scared to death, and I've never felt scared of a crowd of people in my life. Not in Tripoli or anywhere else."

I put my arm around her shoulders and pulled her toward me. "Take it easy. We're okay now. I'll talk to Dave and try to sort this out."

I meant to hold her and try to reassure her. And I kissed her, but the kiss became something much greater than reassurance. She responded with a hungry embrace and kissed me hard. She put her arms around my neck, nearly choking me. We broke apart and stared at each other, catching our breaths. She took my hand. "Just be careful," she said with a slight tremble in her voice.

"Okay, okay." I held her close and sensed her regaining her equilibrium, calming down. I thought back over the scene in the market. "You know, Dave's kind of an odd duck. You think you've got him figured out, then he does something bizarre and throws your whole view out of kilter." I held her for another minute. She heaved a big sigh, started the car and we headed back to Wheelus.

* * *

The next weekend Penny and I had come to La Loggia again for lunch. She liked the place because you could order a light snack and sit there listening to the buzzing of the traffic and the chatter of the people speaking Arabic or any of a half dozen European languages. Lingering over cups of coffee, we watched the people on the sidewalks passing by, hurrying to get back to their jobs or to finish their shopping. The European women were dressed in the latest styles, cool and elegant. Watching them reminded me of a fashion show. Penny would try to explain this style or that match of colors to me and I gradually soaked up more about fashion and design than I ever wanted to know.

That afternoon we were talking about our families and I was telling a long story about me and two of my brothers and a .22-caliber rifle. The story had a dark background to it, and the events of that afternoon had left my brothers and me feeling stunned and frightened. But I tried to relate it to her in a light-hearted manner by putting emphasis on the learning experiences that we boys went through rather than the idiocy of our adventure. It ended with me getting hit in the head with a ricochet bullet, just above the eyebrow.

My older brother Ray sent Fred back to the house, and he snuck a pair of tweezers and some Merthiolate, gauze and tape out to us. Then Ray used the tweezers to grope in and pull out the bullet.

I showed her the small white scar in my left eyebrow. "It didn't hurt all that much because my eyebrow and the area around it were still numb. They held a gauze pad on my eyebrow until the bleeding stopped then bandaged me up. What would we tell Mom, and how could we explain the bandage? What were we going to do?"

Penny was trying not to laugh. She shook her head. "Oh, Ted, your poor mother. With five boys her life must have been one nightmare after another." She sat there with a disbelieving look that said she had her doubts about the story. "My mom used to say she was glad I had only sisters, and I didn't understand why. But she'd had two brothers so I guess she knew from experience what a mother had to go through."

Penny got quiet then, looking out over the traffic.

Sisters? I watched her for a moment. "Just now you said something about sisters, but I thought you just had the one younger sister. Are there others?"

She looked at me and hesitated for a moment. "There's one more. My older sister, Cynthia. She's four years older than me. She's been gone for a few years."

"I've never heard you mention her before. Or is that the girl you mentioned at the Mirage, the one who liked *Dream*? You meant your sister."

She sipped her café latte, playing with the spoon. Then she looked up and said, "Well, yes. But we don't talk about her much. She used to call me some times and ask about the folks. I think she worried more about Sandra than me. Every now and then, she'd mail me a card. You see, she—she ran away from home."

Her eyes narrowed and her features took on a taut, stiff look.

I waited for her to go on.

She sighed. "I guess Cynthia didn't like living by the rules at home. Who does? She left home when she turned sixteen. Ran away with a boy who'd dropped out of school and did some kind of drugs. She said they wandered around, working a little and panhandling. But I don't know what all they did." Her eyes seemed to be fixed on a faraway point across the square, blank and vacant. "She was an arrogant, reckless, self-indulgent, spoiled brat and she always asked for money. And yet, I still miss her sometimes."

She looked at me with a pale tight face. "I don't know why I'm telling you about her. You'll think we're all white trash or something."

I thought about her sister. "A drop-out, doing drugs. I've never known anybody who did that. They're just people I read about in the paper. I guess I don't understand them." I tried to catch the waiter's eye to get him back to our table.

Penny looked up from studying her coffee cup. "Judging by Cynthia, I'd say they want to play and have a good time and never grow up. Then there's the drugs."

"Yeah. I guess I'm pretty square." If you don't count the booze and the pot.

"Well, I've given up trying to make sense out of what she did and I'm past caring— or I try to be. I've watched my folks cry and suffer over it, but nothing changes. Cynthia had all the answers and my folks don't have any."

I reached over and held her hand. "You only talk about what she did and what she was." I hesitated, afraid to go on. "Where is she now?"

Penny looked away from me. The silence grew between us and I knew I'd gotten onto very shaky ground, afraid to continue, yet compelled to resolve the mystery, the dilemma her sister seemed to represent.

She looked up at me, shaking her head. "I'd like to just forget. But no. I can't just walk away from the memory of Cynthia. She's gone. She's dead. Her happy-go-lucky alternate lifestyle killed her. Or her boyfriend did."

She sat there for a long silent moment. "There's no way to know what happened or why. The police said he'd put her out on the street to make enough money for drugs and his miserable lifestyle. They found her—" Penny's voice tightened and cracked. She shuddered and tried again. "They found her in a dumpster. Dead. Tied up with a rope and naked. Cuts all over her. Smeared in garbage and shit."

She stared at a point on the table with her face locked wide-eyed in a grimace of pain. I could feel, just for that moment, the emotion that so vividly gripped her and seemed to reflect all the horror of her sister's death.

I wanted to run, to escape her agony. But I reached over and put my shaking hand on her cold and unresponsive one. "Penny, I'm sorry. I didn't know. And I didn't mean to open old wounds and cause you a lot of pain. I'll—I'll try to put away the past if you will." I kissed her hand, feeling inadequate and helpless. What could I do or say that could make any difference? I decided that silence beat idle chatter, and signaled the waiter to fill our cups.

The waiter wandered away and I tried again. "You know, sometimes you need to move on, to get on with your life. Living in the past—I've done that. But life goes on whether you're involved or not. In the end, it's your choice. You have to decide for yourself."

I'd run out of words and got quiet again as we toyed with our coffees and watched the people. It seemed to me she'd seen a lot more, lived a lot more life than most of the people I knew. Somehow, the thought of her sister's body lying naked in the filth of that dumpster formed a vision in my mind that I couldn't shake. Maybe Penny could begin to take me seriously, make a commitment, but who could be sure? I knew I'd been looking for someone like her, someone pretty and bright and sensitive, who had a mind of her own and knew how to use it. Yet I felt like I didn't quite understand the complexity of her experience. Feelings of inadequacy washed over me, in a way I'd never experienced before. I thought, *Come on, enough caution. Maybe I need to take a gamble, and quit being so scared and nervous, so defensive. She needs something or someone. Is it me?*

- 9 -

I pounded my way down the beat-up coastal highway after another Saturday afternoon run out to Homs. Scarlatti's men had met me at their small, dusty café. Making the exchange of the briefcases had made me nervous in the beginning, but you get used to anything after a while. We made our swaps and I headed west, back toward Tripoli, pulling out of Homs not long before sunset. Evening approached but the light hadn't started to fade much yet. I pushed the Jeep harder than usual, trying to make up some of the time.

The decrease in tension and concern about making the run made the drive itself seem boring, a tiresome trip on a tired old road, passing low barren dunes. I moved along, trying more or less to put together a country song about driving on an old empty rural road.

"Driving down a blacktop two-lane highway . . ."

I could almost see the old southern back-roads as I sped along. A second line, which held the meter, sounded okay, but it just didn't fit what I wanted to say.

"Through the used up land, past signs without a town..."

It seemed vague and unfocused, and my attention shifted to thinking and worrying about how Dave and I seemed to be getting in deeper with the organization. We fought the same kinds of demons, but his problems weren't under my control. The last time we had talked, he sounded upset about his latest trip over to the Morocco club.

"Making those runs gets more hairy with each trip," he'd said. "The security police at the airport in Rabat took us all into custody on the last trip and started an inspection of the aircraft. Most of us didn't have any papers, but we got lucky. The bust turned out to be a small-scale shakedown. Rodrigo managed to fix the problem. He used the cash he had on him, a few hundred dollars in greenbacks and a few Libyan notes in pounds and piastres."

I recalled his harried expression as he relived the experience. "Everybody stayed cool," he'd said, "and things settled down okay, but I don't feel any big urge to make another run to Morocco real soon. Except—the money's so good, you know? The only good thing about the trip was seeing Rodrigo get completely reamed out by Scarlatti. Heh, heh. The money he used to get us off the hook in Morocco was supposed to come back to Scarlatti after turning a profit in the money exchange in Rabat. Man, Scarlatti got pissed. And Rodrigo had to stand there and take it."

My mind wandered and the Jeep's speed had picked up some, making me slow down for one of the tighter curves, then settle back into a better cruising speed. This stretch required some attention to the road. In the most barren parts, a crosswind could drift the fine desert sand and quickly cover the whole highway. I didn't want to hit one of those drifts at high speed. Still, since I drove mostly on asphalt, I'd stayed in two-wheel drive. If I needed the added traction of four-wheel-drive, I'd have to stop to make the change.

I slowed down from inattention in spite of myself. My thoughts drifted away from my unfinished song and turned to Penny. She held a special place in my mind, but it made sense not to build any fairytale ideas about my chances for a future with her. Maybe she thought I didn't fit into her class, or maybe I really didn't. Yet, I couldn't keep my mind off of her either. Listening to my inner voice, I thought about falling in love. Who, me? No way.

Rounding another curve, I squinted at the road. It looked like a drift had formed up ahead. Should be shallow, though. I'd come through here only a couple of hours ago.

Braking steadily, I planned to hit the sand at about ten to fifteen miles an hour. As I got closer I saw it didn't look like a real drift at all. A barricade had been set up across both lanes. When I'd nearly reached it, four or five men in burnooses jumped up from beside the road. One of them shook a big, mean-looking weapon at me. The others held handguns, waving them overhead, all yelling at once, screaming at me. My legs trembled and turned to rubber.

What in the world's going on? The briefcase! That damned briefcase I carried around like some kind of idiot messenger boy. Oh no! These guys wanted Scarlatti's money.

I went through the motions of stopping, wishing I'd set up my four-wheel drive. I shifted down through the gears while my mind raced ahead. What did I have to fight back with? Nothing. The only thing even resembling a weapon in the Jeep was a flare gun, a signal pistol. Where was it? In the back, behind my seat. I pawed around behind me. There! I scooped it up and checked the charge, and, yeah it had a load. Live or dead? Find out soon enough.

As the Jeep slowed, they lowered their guns and chattered rapidly to each other. Almost to their barricade, I leaned below the dashboard and floored the throttle in second-gear. They jumped back as I yanked the Jeep sharply to the right, plowed past the end of the barricade, picked up speed, hunkered down and headed straight up the low, gravely dune close to the road. Now they were pissed off, and started shooting. I reached back over the seat and pulled the trigger on the flare pistol. The bright red flare hissed toward the men at the barricade. They screamed and yelled, and tried to get out of the way. The flare gained me a few seconds but some cracks and a rattling sound started up behind me. It sounded like the .45-caliber automatic "grease guns" we'd seen in our perimeter defense training back at Wheelus. While the automatic ripped, I shook and shouted and prayed to God.

"Sweet Lord, help me!"

Nearing the crest of the dune, rounds pinged off the Jeep's heavy metal while others cracked over my head. Then I crested the dune with a huge sense of victory, a surge of joy.

I made it down to the level stretch at the bottom of the dune and the traction got better. I steered back to the left and ran parallel to the road, using too much throttle, but my hands shook and my fear drove the Jeep. Too frightened to force myself to slow down, I desperately hoped to beat them back to the road and make a run for it.

As I turned back toward the road and started up the dune I heard the sound of renewed screaming. Were they getting closer? The Jeep crested the dune again and slewed around some. I couldn't afford to get bogged down. Not now!

I forced myself to drop the speed and eased the Jeep on down until it got back onto tighter, firmer footing. My traction improved—not much, but enough. The Jeep crawled but gradually picked up speed.

Nearing the road, my miscalculation leaped out at me. They were coming straight for me, with the trigger held down on the grease gun! Rounds snapped past my ears and cracked overhead as the muzzle climbed irresistibly higher from the heavy recoil. Time seemed to stop for an instant. I recalled Penny's description of her sister's body in that filthy dumpster. Like a flash, she'd shown me a horrible vision of my own certain death. They were so close now my next act came from survival instinct in the hard grip of my fear. I ducked, shifted down a gear, stomped the gas and headed straight toward them as the Ford V-8 began to snarl.

Angry voices changed to screams as I charged them. One—two solid, heavy thumps and I'd cleared the path. Back on the road, my speed rose steadily. Remembering to change to a higher gear to avoid blowing the engine, my hands were shaking so badly I nearly missed the shift.

My speed kept climbing. "Forget about drifts across the road," I muttered. "I need some distance from these maniacs." Being clear of danger for the moment didn't make me want to slow down. Those guys didn't walk from town to put up that roadblock and I felt certain they'd be after me. I drove hard and fast and hoped the old Jeep would hold together. My hands trembled and my breath rattled in my throat, but I kept the Jeep at nearly full throttle until another series of curves forced me to slow down.

I kept nervously checking the rearview mirror, afraid of seeing headlights. There hadn't been any yet, and I didn't want to see any. Finally, after about ten minutes, my hope began to rise. But five minutes later there were headlights behind me, closing the gap between us. There remained enough light to make out the outline, the low, dark shape of a Citroen sedan going all out, sweeping smoothly through the curves. I had to lose these guys, even at the risk of blowing this V-8 engine or stripping the old Jeep's transmission.

I put the pedal down all the way and prayed. Now Dave's V-8 took on a new note. The snarl got harder and began to sound more like a wail as it accelerated. The engine still had reserves of power and my speed picked up steadily. The old Jeep's speedometer pegged out. And my speed still rose. With my foot down hard and squeezing the wheel, the Citroen began to fall behind. I tried not to worry about all the old parts Dave talked about. Those headlights began to disappear part of the time in the curves. Finally they weren't back there anymore. And the awful vision of Cynthia's body had begun to fade. I silently thanked Dave's "A-rab" mechanic. I owed my life to him and his skills under the hood.

As I passed Wheelus, the traffic became more congested. I

slowed down and approached downtown Tripoli. Still no Citroen—and I began to breathe again. Maybe they had quit chasing me, finally, or maybe I'd just flat outrun them. Or maybe I was the luckiest son of a bitch on the face of the earth.

* * *

Back at his office, I gave the briefcase to Mr. Scarlatti, feeling exhausted, sick of the whole operation. "Mr. Scarlatti, I just had a bad scare. A group of thugs set up a roadblock on the coastal road. They tried to rob me. Tried to kill me. I didn't expect to make it back here. It had to be a setup. Somebody who knows when I make the run, somebody—"

"Don't try to make something grand from a small incident, Mr. Miller. Here you are, standing and talking to me about it. How bad could it have been? The light out there is strange at that time of the evening. Sometimes we see more than there actually is to see. Perhaps the Libyan police were holding a training session with firearms."

I stood there, speechless. It sounded like he wanted to pass the incident off as a case of nerves on my part. He didn't make any sense. "Mr. Scarlatti, I know what I saw out there."

He folded his arms and stared at me. "I don't pay you to worry. I don't pay you to be afraid. Is that clear to you, Mr. Miller?"

The vision I'd had of my death out there in the desert held no interest for this man. I swallowed hard. "Yes, sir."

He counted out my money for the run and for my week's work with the quartet. I pocketed the money and went out to Dave's old Jeep and sat there for a while, trying to calm down. So that's how it felt to have somebody shooting at me, somebody trying to kill me. I didn't need that kind of terror. No sir.

Checking the Jeep over, I looked for impact marks or bullet holes, but it had such a collection of old dents and scars that I couldn't be sure. I couldn't see anything that looked like real damage. The radiator wheezed slightly and gurgled. I saw a broken taillight, but I'd have to ask Dave about that.

As Scarlatti saw it, I was either hallucinating or the Libyan police were using grease guns. Right. He had implied that this kind of problem belonged to the job. It went with the good pay. In his book, you were on your own out there. On your own wits, cunning and firepower. Yet, it seemed hard to feel that tough. Or be ready to start shooting at people over a briefcase full of money. Maybe a gun made sense, though. Being completely defenseless out there in the desert had been an awful feeling, not the kind of thing I wanted to repeat. I didn't want to count on being that lucky again.

My fundamental dilemma didn't change. In my pocket I felt the big wad of bills that Scarlatti had handed me, nearly five hundred dollars. Enough to fund me for another quarter of college when I got back. If I got back. The vision of how easily, how quickly I could have died out there in the desert had receded with the vision of Cynthia's body. And in spite of my fears and worries, my feelings about Club Tripoli went back and forth. I sat there with my pocket stuffed with money. Now that felt good. It was money I had to have to make my dream of escape from the military life, from life as a peon, become a reality. And the dream would succeed if I held firm. And it felt good, very good, to know I'd outsmarted the Arabs. I had beaten those thugs at their own game, out there on the road to Homs.

I took a deep breath and sat up straight. Enough. What I needed right now was a tall cold drink and a little company, the company of a few people who led simpler lives, people who weren't trying to serve so many masters at once. I turned the key and pushed the starter button on the old Jeep. The V-8 rumbled to life as I backed out of my parking slot and turned toward the base. I wanted to flush the whole complicated set of demands and pressures of Club Tripoli out of my mind. And feel a little less like a tired old man.

- 10 -

I'd planned to have a long talk with Dave, but didn't see a lot of him over the next week or so. Maybe he'd tried to avoid me again and had fallen into one of his weird, dark moods. Sometimes he'd go a week or more without talking to me—or anybody else, as far as I knew. But I stayed busy anyway, finding more work on base.

One morning on the way out of the day room, I met one of the older NCOs, a tech-sergeant. The old tech had a little gray hair over his ears but not much more hair than that. He and Sergeant Andrews were in deep conversation in the orderly room, and I needed to check something with the first sergeant.

Sergeant Andrews looked up from his paper work. "Ted, this is Sergeant Henry Carter. He's been on an extended TDY assignment in Frankfort for a couple of months and just got back. Carter's our lead man in the percussion section and a great drummer."

I stood there for a moment, and finally remembered. Back in Texas a couple of bandsmen had talked about a Sergeant Carter, a man they'd been stationed with in Anchorage. And here he stood, right in front of me, an unassuming NCO, with an athletic appearance in bold contrast to his graying hair and apparent age. "Sergeant Carter," I said, "There were two guys in Texas who knew you up at Elmendorf. They said you were the best, at swing, jazz, concert and show."

He put his hand to his chin and wrinkled his brow. "There's a lot of good drummers out there. And a lot in the Air Force. They must have been talking about somebody else."

I didn't try to push him on it. He had a reputation for being modest and hard-working, unusual characteristics among most bandsmen. "Where do you play, Sergeant?"

"Mostly at the Officer's Club. I have a trio we use a couple of times a week and that's about enough to suit me. Don't like working every night or all night anymore. Old bones and a stiff back are slowing me down these days."

He didn't look like an old man and he didn't move like one. "I'll try to catch you at the Officers' Club," I said.

"Do that," he said. "And bring your axe, man—sit in a little."

"I will, Sarge. Tonight."

Sergeant Carter listened to me play that evening and hired me to work with his group. His bass man had returned to the States, so the group consisted of him on drums, a guy named Williams on piano and me on guitar. We played at the Officers' Club on Sundays, smooth music, old ballads and show tunes, in an understated light jazz style.

As he explained it to me, we had the job of providing an elegant background for the after-church Sunday brunch crowd, mostly senior officers and their wives, music for their relaxation and enjoyment.

Carter expressed the concept in a nutshell. "These folks don't want to be distracted by loud music or intrusive action from the bandstand. Try to think of us as servants, musical servants, who don't intrude or attract attention among their superiors."

I thought he had laid it on a little too thick and I objected. "Give me a break, Sarge. Musical servants? You've got to be kidding."

But he waved my complaints aside. "Remember. Musical servants. It's just a state of mind and it works. They love it and you'll do fine, Ted. The Old Man told me you were smart, so I'm not going to worry about you."

"Servants my aching ass." But I found out what he said made sense. The gig paid well. Following his rules, you could count on good tips from the older officers.

I enjoyed working with the group, and learned a lot about music, style and people. Things were going well, but Carter had to leave soon to rotate back to the States for a new assignment. Williams and I wanted to keep the gig so we looked around for a new drummer. We found guys who talked like they were drummers with a lot of talent. We even tried a few of them in auditions, but most of them couldn't even hold a beat.

We finally tried one of our band squadron members, a new kid named Bernie, and he was a drummer, a natural talent. I brought him with me to the Officers' Club one Sunday to watch Henry Carter do his thing, to let him get a first-hand view of some excellent drum work. Carter had subtlety. His playing style was so distinctive, if you walked into a room where he was working, you could identify the drummer without a glance at the bandstand. Bernie watched him closely for the first set.

At the break, he commented to me. "He's a good drummer, cool and kind of laid back, but I don't know. He acts like he's afraid to really hit the drums."

I should have listened more closely to that remark and taken his words as a warning instead of trying to explain Carter's style and approach. We worked with Bernie in a few rehearsals, trying to calm down his forceful, heavy-handed style. He was a naturally aggressive kid, but we felt we were getting him adjusted to Sunday brunch standards. He'd begun to settle down and play clean and clear, but quiet.

* * *

The next Sunday Bernie joined us for the first time at the Officers' Club brunch. Our performance started out well. We kicked off with a medley of songs from the musical "Carousel." Bernie used his brushes with a light touch and seemed to be doing fine. He didn't sound like Henry Carter, but he fit in well, held a solid tempo and didn't stick out at all.

Then we moved to a few tunes from "Oklahoma," winding up with the title song. We did it upbeat and Bernie used his sticks and moved the old tune along nicely with clean, light, staccato work on the snare drum and the hi-hat cymbals. Coming out of the first chorus, he began working a heavier foot on the bass drum pedal, using short rolls on the snare drum. I tried to catch his eye, mouthing the words 'Sunday Brunch', but he'd gotten too busy impressing himself to look around. By the time we got half way through the second chorus, Bernie was banging away on his ride cymbal, kicking the bass and punching old "Oklahoma!" with everything he had.

We never got to the third chorus. Williams cut the rendition short at the same time the manager arrived at the bandstand. He handed Williams a neat but small stack of bills and said, "Pack it up, men. Time for you to leave."

And so our Sunday brunch gig came to an end, and it was almost the end of Bernie's ability to get a paying job on the air base. With the demise of the job with the trio, my free time increased but my income fell off more than I wanted. How could I keep building my college fund? I felt lucky to have the job at Club Tripoli. Now I needed it more than ever. I figured I'd better be extra nice to

Scarlatti and his people, and keep things working smoothly between us. I just couldn't afford to lose another gig. I looked around for something to fill in with, but the jazz people I usually worked with were booked. I had mixed feelings about my problem. Sometimes I had trouble fitting in with those guys. They always tried to convince everyone they were the coolest players around, guys like the Pres, causing contention and continuous friction when they should have been trying to work together. Except for Scarlatti, my friend Charlie stood out as the only musician I played with who seemed to understand the destructive influence of this gamesmanship. But then, Charlie seemed to be that rare bird, a quiet, conservative musician, a thinker.

* * *

One Sunday afternoon I talked to Sergeant Nelson, one of our younger NCOs about a jam session coming up later in the day. "Listen Sarge, why don't you come with me over to the Airman's Club and jam for a while? My friend Charlie is trying to put a group together. A few of the other bandsmen will be there and it'll be a good chance to see if we fit with their style. And I know he's looking for somebody on trumpet."

He stood there for a moment, with his brow in furrows, looking hesitant. "Well okay, Miller," he said. "I can only stay for an hour, maybe two. But let's do it."

I had a great time, backing up anybody who wanted to play. We had a lot of talent there, some better than others and the youngest players struggled the most. But hey, how else were they going to learn how to improvise?

Our group played to a young crowd, about ten or twelve couples on the dance floor and about that many at the tables by the U-shaped bar. The usual rowdy crowd of single men kept the atmosphere alive. I saw Dave at the bar with a couple of younger NCOs, guys I didn't know. He wore civvies, and told jokes and cracked them up. Good old Dave. Nelson worked a couple of numbers with us, playing with a solid big-band jazz sound, not the low-key subtleties of the Pres, but good confident trumpet work.

Then Charlie called for an old standard from the twenties, "Apple Blossom Time," moderately up-tempo, kind of cool. Richard on valve trombone and Charlie on tenor sax played a tight unison to establish the main melodic line. Bill Nelson worked a background ad-lib accompaniment on trumpet to brighten up the deeper, heavier sounds of Richard and Charlie. Bernie was sitting in on drums and I kind of braced myself. I looked at Charlie and he shrugged and said, "We'll see." Bernie began to kick Nelson along with insistent pedal work on the bass drum and tight pops on the cymbals and snare drums. He kept his drumming in the background, but just barely, with explosions of raw power here and there that added tension and color.

We sounded tight now, and Williams, on piano, had started talking to himself, throwing in some fuller chords and taut rhythms for the horns to follow. We rocked along with a solid and coherent sound, strong and punchy.

Now we had all three horns playing together and we were all watching each other closely. Charlie signaled to the drummer. As we came up on the end of the chorus, Bernie increased his cymbal work and started a slow deceleration of the beat to arrive at a continuous assault of cymbals and snare drum, closed at last with a tom-tom roll and a mighty slam on the bass drum.

The dancers and most of the single airmen crowded around the bandstand, clapped and cheered and shouted and whistled for a long, loud minute or more. I noticed Dave slouching on his stool at the bar. He had a sour look on his face and he stayed where he was, sitting by himself with his arms folded, not taking part in the moment. The rest of us felt our fatigue, but it looked like we'd found a showcase for Bernie, a place where he finally did fit in.

Dave still sat at the bar, shaking his head, staring at us. I walked over to get a drink for the break and he sneered at me. "Well, well. It's the Gui-tar Man, the big jazz star."

What's Dave's big problem now? I wondered. I didn't need his attitude and I didn't need his surly company either. I turned on my heel and took my drink back to the bandstand.

Packing up after the last set, I helped Bernie take his drum set apart and carry the stuff out to his van. Carrying his bass drum out through the back door, I nearly knocked Dave down. I stepped back. "Sorry, Dave." He grunted something. Since he was there anyway, I said, "We still need to talk if you've got a minute."

He lit a cigarette and stared at me. From the way he handled his Zippo I knew he was having trouble staying coordinated. A closer look told me he was drunk, probably worse off than I'd ever seen him. Drunk and belligerent.

He smirked. "So. What can I do for you, little man? Has the big star come to lecture me again? I've warned you more than once about minding your own business." He seemed to forget what he'd been going to say and he dropped his cigarette and stumbled slightly. "Like I said, I've had enough of your sneaking around and spying on me. You useless punk."

He looked like he might pass out any minute, or maybe decide to kick my butt before he did. "Dave, hang loose for a minute. You don't look too good. Tell you what. I'll go get you a drink and that'll make everything better. What do you say?"

"Yeah. I need a drink, Ted. You're a real friend, aren't you? But why do my friends always turn on me? They try to get me, screw me. Scarlatti, the Pres. And now it's you too." His face twisted up and to my shock he started crying. Then the next minute he was cursing me again.

I sighed. "Dave. I'm going to get that drink now. Be right back."

I went back inside, got him a glassful of cheap scotch whiskey, and brought it out to the parking lot. When I got back to the van, I found Dave telling Charlie what a crummy little punk I'd always been. He slurred and cursed, not making a lot of sense to anybody. Charlie turned away from him shaking his head. Dave grabbed him by the arm and whirled him around. "I'll tell you when I'm done with you, ya little son of a bitch!"

Charlie shook his hand loose. "Dave, back off. You're twice my size but you're too drunk to stand up, much less fight. Lay off. That's my last warning."

Dave's face turned a deep red and he took a big clumsy roundhouse swing. Charlie ducked and Dave whirled around awkwardly, stumbling back. Charlie stepped forward, wound up and slammed a solid uppercut into Dave's belly landing him flat on his ass. Dave looked around and tried to locate his tormentor. He'd gotten in bad shape and started fading out fast.

As he swayed and rocked, sitting there in the gravel, I held out the glass of whisky I was still holding. "Here you are, man. One scotch, as promised."

Dave took the glass and looked up at me. "Geez, Ted. You are still my best, best friend again, aren't you?" He turned the glass up and gulped a big swallow of scotch and blinked at me. He sat there swaying a little and it didn't take much longer. A couple of deep breaths and two more swigs of whisky and he sort of melted and rolled over onto the gravel of the parking lot.

Charlie stood there rubbing his hand and wrist. "He's got to be down for the count, surely. Man, that fool can put it away, can't he?"

"Yeah. He really can. Now, give me a hand with him, will you? He's pretty heavy." Charlie and Bill Nelson helped me get him into the van and back to the barracks. The evening was definitely over, and it looked like my talk with Dave would have to wait for a better day.

I felt tired and a little bit drunk. Considering Dave and the shape he'd gotten into was enough to make me think about laying off the booze for a while. But, hey, my bouts of abstinence only lasted for a day or two. Dave was the guy with the problems. I climbed the stairs, entered my room in a mild state of depression and collapsed on my bunk.

- 11 -

The next night, Tuesday, I worked on the bandstand at Club Tripoli. We played an hour of songs requested from the audience, a lot of back-and-forth with a happy, noisy crowd. At the first break, I walked over to the bar to get a drink and bumped into one of the dancers I knew. She hustled orders from a couple of oil-field roughnecks, and I watched her operate for a minute. She knew her job and kept the glasses moving, along with a few snacks, everything over-priced and nobody much caring.

Business slowed down in a few minutes and she walked back to the bar. She gave me a cool glance and leaned on the stool next to me. "Ah. Mr. Ted, *il padrone*. How good of you to visit with us in the bar, *signore*."

Oh-oh. It'd been a week or two since we'd talked, but I remembered her face. The name, what was her name? Maria? Maria di Gioia! Ah. "Hey, Maria," I said. "You're looking nice tonight. You're wearing another new dress, aren't you? I just can't keep up. You're too pretty to be wasting your style and sophistication on this place."

She responded with a brittle laugh. "Oh yeah, yeah. The prettiest girl at Club Tripoli, that's me. You tell that to all of us, Ted, but I love it. You're pretty, too!"

She sat down with a nervous look at the bartender, and darted a quick look over her shoulder. What was this? Maria looking kind of worried? "What's up, Maria? You're not yourself tonight. Did I miss something?"

She looked me in the eyes then. "I don't know. Mostly I miss Gianni. She's not here for a couple of days. Nobody know where she goes but I don't see her for a while. You don't hear nothing?"

Gianni and Maria worked together and shared one of the small, third-floor flats the club kept for employees. "No, Maria. I haven't seen her lately, haven't heard anything. I thought she'd gotten pretty close with Mr. Scarlatti, here lately?"

She smiled wearily. "You think so? Close? Mr. Scarlatti, he gets tired of her, you know? He don't last too long with any girl."

The girls at the club changed often enough that I had a hard time keeping them straight, but I didn't want to say that to Maria. "Well, maybe she quit. Or got married to one of those big boys from the oil company. What do you think?"

She grimaced at me. "You try to be funny, Ted? Or dumb, maybe. Do you ever hear of anyone who quits Club Tripoli? Anyone ever? *Idiota stupido!*"

It sounded like I really pissed her off, but from the way she talked you'd think the damn club owned her. Seemed to me if she wanted to make a living in a bar, in a cathouse, she had a problem. She didn't have to stay, did she? Or was that her point? How in the world would I know, anyway?

The conversation died as Maria sat glumly on her stool, then went over to a table to hustle a couple more drinks. I didn't want to spend my whole break listening to her complain, but I thought about what she'd said—and what she hadn't said. A few minutes later, she came back to the bar looking a little more cheerful and picked up where she'd left off.

"You ask around for me, please Ted. Ask Mr. Scarlatti or Mr. Rodrigo about Gianni. But don't say Maria asked."

"Sure. I can do that, but I doubt if they'll tell me much. I'll say I had a date with her and she stood me up. We'll see."

She wasn't angry and pouting anymore and I made my move. "What time do you get off work?" I asked.

She laughed and gave me a hug. "I don't think I get off tonight, the way it looks now. But I save you a night soon. Wednesday okay? And you bring some of the good pot. I'm always better with some pot."

Now, that sounded more like the Maria I knew. "You're on Maria."

I got another whisky and water from the bartender. We were having a quiet evening except for a pair of pilots, first lieutenants, at the end of the bar having some sort of loud, unintelligible argument about the F-100 and adverse yaw, flat-plating and some hot-shot fighter-jockey named Boyd. They went on and on, waving and wagging their hands in the air. Irritating jerks.

I walked down the hall and out the back door into the enclosed courtyard. The atmosphere in the club had been getting a little too tense for me lately and I wanted a few quiet moments to myself. I stewed and worried about Scarlatti and my courier runs. Now, he was talking about getting me more involved with moving his merchandise.

I leaned on the back wall in a niche of the courtyard, looked up at the lovely bright stars overhead. I thought about my dilemma and wished I had a Pall Mall to go with my drink.

The door to the lounge crashed open and three people burst into the courtyard, all shouting at once.

Ah, Jesus. Now what? I held still and stayed in the heavy shadows of the niche and hoped they'd go away. Bob Rodrigo and a club security guard held one of the noisy lieutenants I'd noticed at the bar. I recognized the security guard, too, a sergeant in the support squadron who'd worked at Club Tripoli longer than I had. Apparently, they wanted the pilot to leave. Rodrigo gripped the guy's big arms from behind and held him steady. I could see Bob grinning at the sergeant.

The drunken pilot tried to jerk loose. "Let go of me you son of a bitch! Who the hell do you think you're messing with?" He jerked again and managed to kick the guard.

The guard stepped in close. "Okay, tough guy." He punched him hard in the belly and the lieutenant's air blew out with a whoosh. Then he stepped back, pounded the guy in the guts, and hit him in the face once or twice. The lieutenant's head snapped around in time to the sharp crack of the blows to his face and head. Then the guard slammed his knee into the lieutenant's crotch and the poor bastard cried out, grunting from the pain.

Bob and the guard breathed harder now, as they slammed the pilot into the tile floor. I kept still, hoping they'd finished. Then the pilot tried to crawl off and the guard stomped his back. Rodrigo walked up to him, took careful, measured aim and kicked him in the face making a harsh cracking sound. The guy wailed now, squealing in a high thin voice, blood and snot pouring from his face.

Bob leaned his head back and laughed. "Listen to that. He ain't so mean now, is he?"

The guard muttered, "Huh. This half-assed punk don't know when to back off, that's for sure."

They dragged him back to the heavy door in the rear wall about twenty feet from my hiding place and threw him through the doorway into the alley. The guard came back through the door and Bob closed it and slid the heavy steel bolt home. They walked back across the courtyard, both laughing.

When they closed the door as they re-entered, I finally took a deep, shuddering breath and nearly threw up. I stood there, still hidden, tasting bile and trying not to gag. How had I gotten mixed up with these sick maniacs? Every day it seemed to get worse. I'd gotten so deep into this filth, yet there had to be a way to back off from all this. Had to be.

Getting back to the bandstand late, I felt tired and angry. Scarlatti examined me closely over his keyboard and said, "You don't look so good, Ted. Are you all right?"

"Sorry, Mr. Scarlatti. My stomach's not feeling too good, but I'll be okay."

The scene in the courtyard still filled my vision. "Sir, I just saw our security people beating the hell out of one of the guests out in the courtyard. What's that all about? Is that club policy or something?"

Scarlatti's face went hard and blank as he stared at me for a long moment. "You need to learn when to worry and when to look the other way, Mr. Miller. These things do not concern you. Security is security. Not your affair, *capisce lei?*"

Yeah, I understood well enough. I knew enough to keep my head down and my mouth shut. And I guess I didn't really expect an answer to a question like that. Not from Scarlatti. I shouldn't have asked. I picked up my guitar, checked the tuning and turned up the volume. Scarlatti counted off to the drummer and we kicked the set off with an up-tempo version of "Lady Be Good."

* * *

The next night I came by the bar after my last set. The place looked empty. Maria sat at the bar looking cute and sophisticated, but small and vulnerable sitting on the high stool.

I asked the bartender for a whisky and water, and she looked up. "Ah, it's Mr. Ted. You look like you dressed up for somebody special. Got a big date or something?"

"Yeah, Maria. I have a date with a pretty girl. Want to party?"

"Could be. We'll see. Did you get the pot—like you say?"

"Well yeah I got it… The club's best stuff."

She tossed her hair and said something to the bartender in the local dialect, something I couldn't understand. They both laughed and looked at me. *Crap! Was she jerking me around or what?* "C'mon Maria. Do we have a date or not?"

She turned to me with a wicked grin. "Oh! You jealous, maybe?" She put her hand on my leg and slowly moved it higher. "We go get high now, okay?"

I took a deep breath, got a pint of whisky from the bartender and we walked up to her flat on the third floor. She rolled a joint while I poured the drinks. As usual, I had almost no initial response to the marijuana, but she got high then higher. She grew cuddly and warm in a hurry and we took each other to bed. As always, she surprised me with her gentleness and her affection. I wondered idly if she thought of me as a pet or a sexy, stuffed toy.

Finally, the whisky and the pot got the better of her and she came crashing down. She started to cry, not much at first but it became worse. I held her for a long time until she dropped off to sleep for a few minutes.

When she woke, she seemed to feel better. She got out of bed, relit the joint and crawled back in bed. She handed it to me and snuggled up again. "What you hear from Mr. Scarlatti, Ted. Did you ask about Gianni?"

"Yeah, I did. He said she'd asked to move to his place at Marrakech and told me she'd gone there about a week ago. He said if I wanted to see her, I'd have to make the run to Morocco."

Maria looked serious and sad, like she might start to cry again. She took another big drag, held it for a long, long time and finally let it out. "Yeah. It's been a while, but the last time I lost a friend like Gianni, they found her body in the alley out back. But maybe Gianni really goes to Morocco…. Filthy little man, Scarlatti."

She wrapped her arms around me and snuggled up again. She sniffled loudly once or twice and said, "Hold me? You hold me for a while?"

I held her and petted her for a time, and soon she returned to the here and now, all hands and mouth and lips. She climbed on and rode me until I lost track of time, the room and the rest of the world, living inside a big black cloud where only we could go. It was good pot.

- 12 -

I still hadn't had my talk with Dave Walker. I'd tried to pin him down at the club and in the barracks, but he'd avoided any confrontation. If I did see him he had to be somewhere else, always in a hurry. Finally, one afternoon we'd met at the Oasis. He didn't try to get away and I didn't pull any punches. "Dave, I need to talk. There's just too much crap going on, things I don't understand. It's stuff that can affect me, too, and you owe me some explanations."

Dave stared at me for a moment. "Yeah, I know that. But I don't have any easy answers for you."

"I didn't ask for easy answers, Walker. Just answers."

He looked away. "Look, let's not talk about any of this here in the Oasis or even on base. Can you meet me at the Sailing Club? Be at the harbor at about ten in the morning?"

I thought about it. We didn't have anything on the squadron schedule then, just individual practice. Screw that. "Yeah. I can make it if you can."

"All right. See you there." He got up to go and I didn't see him again that day.

Next morning I took the bus downtown, got there a little early and sat on the harbor seawall to enjoy the cooler morning air. At the west end of the harbor, among the piers, warehouses and railway sidings, trucks and horse drawn carts were in constant motion, carrying the commerce of the port. There seemed to be a lot of action. Busy place. Now, where was Dave?

As always, getting a sailboat depended on availability. The sailing club wouldn't let us reserve one, but we were usually lucky. I killed some time checking with the manager and there were boats available. He said we could have one of the new Snipes they'd just gotten in from England. Unfortunately, Dave hadn't arrived yet. I thought maybe he wouldn't come at all.

But he finally got there. He wasn't all that late, maybe thirty minutes, enough to put me on edge. "Nice of you to come, sport.

You're a little behind schedule, aren't you. Anyway, the manager says we can have one of the new Snipes if we like," I said. "He made a kind of big deal of it, so I thanked him. What do you think?"

Dave grinned. "Yeah, sure. The new boats are going to be a lot more lively on the water. You'll see."

He added some lame excuse for being late but he muttered and I didn't catch it. No big deal. "If you say so. The new boats look just the same as the old ones to me."

We had a few minutes to wait until the boys on the dock could rig out the boat. He turned to me and asked, "So, Ted. How's the colonel's little girl? Seeing her much?"

My antennae went up. Dave being warm and sociable? *Right.* "She's all right. We went to a movie at the base theatre the other night, and we had shakes after. We enjoyed it."

"You know, you shouldn't be picking on pint-sized high school girls at your age. You should give Penny a break, and take a look at some real women."

"Oh, right. Like you do. Most of the 'real women' I see you spending time with look awful mature to me. Or is that matronly?"

He snorted. "You know, for somebody who's playing games with the dancers and waitresses, you're coming off a shade too pure, don't you think?"

Not having a strong comeback for that one, I retreated. "Well, Penny's good for me. She's pretty and funny. Smart, too. I like being with her."

Dave put his hands on his hips. "Ah, that's where it always starts, lad. But it ends in a trip down the aisle, don't you know."

"Spare me the old Irish charm, Davey boy. I've heard it all before."

He turned to look out over the harbor and became quiet for a moment, staring vacantly into the distance.

The boys finally had the boat ready and Dave made a show of checking the rigging and making adjustments here and there, carrying on a commentary to me. He always seemed like a teacher around a boat, and I made it a point to listen.

We took the Snipe out and beat our way upwind across the big harbor, tacking back and forth toward the outer seawall. Even in the moderate breeze, the Snipe seemed more agile and responsive than the others we'd sailed at the club. I gave Dave a questioning look.

He chuckled. "See, man? It's because the wood is new and still dry. The boat weighs less and rides higher in the water. Being slightly waterlogged like the older Snipes makes a big difference."

I still had a lot to learn about boats, but what Dave said made sense. I could feel the difference in performance.

The wind died off and except for an occasional puff of air we were becalmed. We could see some patches of ruffled water across the harbor, but rather than get out the paddle and try to move to the wind, we decided to relax for a few minutes. The wind might come to us. The bright, warm sunshine made me feel lazy and loose.

I hadn't mentioned the beating in the courtyard at Club Tripoli to Dave, or told him how much the casual brutality of it had bothered me. I hadn't heard anything about the lieutenant who took the beating and I didn't want to ask around. It was something I shouldn't know anything about and I feared getting involved. And there was Gianni… It all kept eating away at me, so I told Dave about it. But out here in the sunshine, it didn't seem possible for me to recapture the horror of the beating or Maria's fear.

He listened in silence as I related the almost casual progression of the assault, from their dragging the pilot out into the patio to the final kicks. Dave listened and nodded from time to time, but the story sounded pitifully short when I spelled it out.

Without taking his eyes off the small, puffy white clouds above us, Dave said, "Hey. That stuff happens. It's usually some cocky dumb-ass who's had too much beer, but he's just too thick-skulled to know when to keep his mouth shut."

I heard the echo of the guard's words in what Dave was saying. He seemed indifferent to the amusement of the attackers and the pain and damage they'd deliberately inflicted. His willingness to dismiss all of that with such detachment just came off as unconvincing.

I tried to clear my thinking. "That doesn't sound like you, Dave. I'm telling you, they enjoyed busting this guy up. Like it was entertainment. You told me the same ones are humping the Arab children working there. How can you accept all that?"

"Dammit, I don't 'accept it.' It's wrong, but there's nothing I can do about it. Or you either. Rodrigo is a mean son of a bitch, a sick creepy bastard—"

"And he has a lot of mean company at the club."

Dave moved restlessly on his seat at the back of the boat.

"Understand me, man. I can't get shook up every time some jerk decides he's a badass. If that kind of stuff starts to bother me I'll have to quit."

I paused as his phrase rang in my ears. "Well, now. There's a thought."

He inclined his head. "I'm not ready to do that. I'm not that far ahead on the money yet. But I'm getting close."

He stayed quiet for a while. Then he continued, squinting with his eyes darting in constant motion. "The guys who've been there a while, they all say it's not that easy to back away from the organization once you're involved. 'The more you know, the more you owe.' That's the way it is, and I don't get to make up the rules. The only guy I've known who threatened to quit the club went out the back door feet first. So quitting won't work. Quietly catching the plane back to the States is about the only way I know to do the job."

Dave always had an answer. Like, "It's not my fault," or "I'm just a small player." That sounded too easy and he knew it. I probed a little more. "Yeah, Dave. Yet you take the money, week after week, and close your eyes to what's going on."

Dave exhaled noisily. "It's not the money, Ted. It's making your own breaks. It's gaining the upper hand so you don't have to take the orders. So you can give them. But that kind of power takes money, and that's where it is for me."

"Well, for me it's a real problem, having to watch people acting like—I don't know—like Nazis and not even knowing they are."

Dave stared at me like I'd drooled down my chin. "There you go again, man. You take yourself way too seriously."

I looked away, out over the harbor. "Maybe so. My picture of Club Tripoli and what these people are like is getting clearer now. I'm guessing that beating out back was a minor event, just a hint of what's going on. Like that scene with you and Bob in the Souk. Remember? You've been here a lot longer than me. You tell me."

He didn't respond or even look at me.

I felt my face flush in a surge of anger. "Listen to me, Walker. What I'm trying to say is this. If we stay involved long enough, we'll become exactly like them. Harden up and never even know what's become of us. Start sodomizing the bus boys and the cleaning girls, like Rodrigo."

Dave leaned wearily back in the boat and shrugged. "Look.

Maybe it's time for you to think about backing out of this whole scene. You know, it might be you don't have the stomach for it, or you're not as tough as you thought you were, or as you need to be."

"You never heard me talk about being tough. Not me."

Dave became quiet for a moment. "That's true. I don't remember you talking tough. But you know, Scarlatti says you're getting spooky. I think he might let you go at this point, without a hassle. Maybe . . . I don't know."

He fished out his Zippo and his pack of Luckies and lit up, smoking in silence for a long minute. "Anyway, with your outlook, your negative attitude, you're likely to say something careless or judgmental around the place. I'm telling you, they don't take kindly to that kind of crap. You can lose your ass in nothing flat if those guys turn on you."

I looked closely at him. Could he be serious? "Come on, man give me a little credit. I'm not that dumb."

"I hear you, Ted. You say the right stuff, but you think you're above these guys. That's dangerous because it can make you careless. Anyway, if you're going to stick around, getting loose only gets harder and harder."

He sat there for a while and I thought he was finished. Then he said, "Me? I'm in deep. I've already gotten under Scarlatti's skin a couple of times. He's not real happy with me right now, but I know I can smooth that over."

And he thought I sounded stupid. "Yeah? Good luck."

He didn't react. "Anyway, I like him. He's basically a decent man. We've always gotten along pretty well, up to now."

I couldn't quite believe he'd said that. "Man, your 'decent' Scarlatti scares the hell out of me. I'm thinking about how I should stick with the clubs on base and forget the good life downtown—and the good money. Maybe I don't need it that bad."

"That's your call, Ted. That may be the right way to go, for you. Think about it."

"You know, I'd feel a lot better if you did some thinking yourself. I stew and worry and, for the life of me, can't see any kind of good outcome from all of this. Not for me, and not for you. This lousy club gets inside you and eats away at you, from the inside out. I mean, just look around."

Dave lit another cigarette and stared at the clouds again. Without even looking at the water, he said, "Hey, we're finally going to get some breeze." He stared off across the harbor, took a deep draw on his Lucky Strike and flicked it out over the water. Then he turned back to me and grimaced. "I hear you Ted, but I'm still not ready to quit, not quite yet."

The breeze freshened and we had good sailing for an hour or so. The mild weather made a perfect day, a day way too nice to remain in my morose, gloomy mood. I enjoyed the sailing in spite of my premonitions.

- 13 -

I took my worries back to Club Tripoli and continued to play guitar for another week. I kept my head down and my mouth shut. I couldn't make up my mind whether to hang in with the job and bank the money, or find a way to ease out of the organization and back into a safer, more sensible life. I'd preached my sermon to Dave Walker out there on the harbor, but hadn't made any kind of decision that would resolve my own conflict about working there.

I still thought of myself as a normal, reasonable human being, someone who cared about the people he worked with. The struggle wore me down, making me tired and irritable. Penny and I had gotten into an absurd argument a couple of days ago. I couldn't even remember what we'd fought about, but we parted with neither one of us backing off or apologizing.

I wasn't sleeping well, waking up too often from dark, haunting nightmares about home and my family, dreams about people dying, people weeping over graves.

One evening in the barracks, I cornered Dave in his room and tried to talk to him again about my conflict. "I'm feeling as if the money they're spreading around so generously down at the club isn't going to be of much use to a man who loses his life. Or loses his soul."

Dave put his head in his hands and muttered something. "Stow it, Ted. Spare me some of the melodramatic crap, okay? You remind me of a lousy priest I knew back in Boston. Phony prick."

"Dave, back off and try to understand what I'm saying. I'm not talking about my soul in some religious sense, not about damnation or the loss of eternal life or any of that. What I mean is—if I lose my self-respect then this thing has cost me too much. More than any financial gain from Club Tripoli is worth. Remember my talk with Maria, how she's worried about Gianni? Do you know if they actually control the girls that tightly, almost as if they owned them outright?"

Dave snickered. "Come on. They're only whores, you know? Who cares what they do or how they treat them?"

That stopped me cold because it didn't make any sense. "Dave. Exactly what big difference do you think there is—in Scarlatti's mind—between those whores and the two of us?"

Dave's eyes widened and he stared at me for a moment, then looked at his watch. "Whoa," he said. "I'm going to be late." He grabbed his hat and took off down the hall.

* * *

The next day I had to act as CQ runner, handle the morning report and pick up the mail from the main Post Office. One crummy little job led to another and kept me away from the squadron barracks until about two. My appetite was off, but I'd stopped at the Airmen's Club for a late lunch. There'd been no progress with Dave or my problems in the last day or two. It felt weird, like being suspended in time, kind of twisting in the wind. Maybe Dave was right. My life didn't make much sense to me these days. Had things gotten too melodramatic?

When I checked in with the CQ he said he'd logged a call for me from Penny. I usually returned my personal calls from the Oasis across the street to avoid providing light entertainment for the guys in the dayroom. I grabbed my leather-billed hat from the peg on the wall where I'd just hung it and headed for the snack bar.

She answered on the first ring. "Ted! Listen, there's this new movie at the base theatre, brand new and I haven't seen it yet. Can we go? Do you want to see it? Say yes. My treat."

I could never say no to Penny when she was high on excitement and wanted something badly. I resisted, knowing full well we were going to go see this movie, whatever it was. I figured I could beg off because I had to do runner duty for the CQ, but it would be easy to get somebody to swap some time for me. Maybe Richard. "Well. I don't know," I said. "I ought to stay in tonight and catch up on my letter writing to the folks back home."

"Letters! You drip. What's the matter with you? This is the first new movie we've had at the base theatre in three weeks and you're talking about writing letters home. I'll give you something to write home about if you're not careful."

"Penny! How can you be so selfish? I haven't written to poor old Aunt Emma in days and days and you'd deny her the pleasure of hearing from her favorite nephew?"

She made a croaking noise. "Bull. You don't even have an Aunt Emma. We're going to the movies and that's that! Please?"

She'd had enough of my chatter. "Course we are. I just can't resist making you fly off the handle. You're so cute when you're mad."

"Idiot."

"So, are you going to pick me up at the barracks or should I meet you at the theatre?"

"I'll pick you up. You might get lost on the way or forget what day it is or something. Make it six at the back stairway. Okay?"

"Okay, Penny. See you then."

Richard had agreed to swap me some runner-time, but he nicked me for a two-to-one trade, putting me in debt to him for about three or four hours. At six, I sat at the foot of the back stairs to the barracks waiting for Penny to drive into the parking lot. She'd probably be a little late, like always, but it didn't make much difference to me. A quick call to the base theatre had told me the movie was a romantic true-love story with actors old enough to be my parents. My enthusiasm to see this flick hadn't reached the hopping up and down stage, but it would be time spent with Penny.

She arrived at last and I got up and strolled out to her car, climbed in and turned toward her to say hello. She had that look on her face, tense but happy. She wanted me to kiss her again. I could handle that all right and slid over, put my arms around her, and kissed her thoroughly. We'd kissed before, but this was hot. I had to stop and take a deep breath and so did she. She looked at me and laughed. "You'd better move back over to your side or we're not going to see any movie tonight."

"So? I'm not all that eager to see this movie."

"Oh, no you don't. You promised to go with me and I'm holding you to it."

I watched the movie, sat through the whole thing without touching her or saying anything. She hung on every word. When the heroine died in the last scene, still the very soul of purity and virtue, she got sniffley and had to dig a Kleenex out of her purse. Enough. To me, it just didn't seem all that believable, but who knew?

We got up and made our way out of the crowd and back to her car. Penny chattered on about the heroine and the sad, sad ending, and I used my head for once and kept my mouth shut and nodded at the right times. We pulled out of the parking lot and she turned right, away from the snack bar and the BX, and drove along the beach road.

As we approached the beach pavilion, she pulled off into the parking area and stopped the car. A strong breeze blew off the Mediterranean and there'd been enough cloud cover to keep the temperature down. I thought she wanted to take a walk on the beach and I reached for my door handle, but she put her hand on my arm and tugged me in her direction. I slid over, took her in my arms, and kissed her gently. Before long, our breathing had gotten heavier and she sat up straight and tried to catch her breath. She gently pushed me away, back to my side of the car. I wanted her so much, but was afraid of scaring her away. Some of the girls I'd known back in high school didn't do much pushing, but Penny was different. Maybe it was the colonel's daughter thing, but I couldn't be as sure of my ground with her. I felt a little off balance with a girl like Penny. And maybe that's how she wanted me to feel.

But right now she was hot and I feared I might lose my self-control, maybe do something crude and ugly. "Oh, Penny, I've never had a girl who kissed the way you do. Like you're going to burn me up."

She stared silently through the windshield, took a deep breath, let it out, and turned to face me. "It's all your fault. You make me want you and I can barely hold still when you hold me. It's just too much. I know how this is going to come out, but I'm not ready. Not yet. Now. Hold me again."

I held her close and tried not to overwhelm her or cover her up in kisses, but it wasn't long before I had my hand under her skirt again, caressing and massaging. Pretty soon we were both gasping for breath and it seemed like I was finally going to score unless we took that walk down the beach. And that's what we did. We took a walk, all the way to the edge of the air base property and back to the pavilion. We'd covered a lot of distance and we both felt tired when we got back to the car. Penny held my head between her hands and kissed me as sweetly and innocently as a small girl. She started the car and turned toward barracks row. What an idiot I was! I could have had her, but no. I played Mr. Nice again. Yet maybe I'd done the right thing. Christ. I didn't know *what* to think.

And now I owed Richard about six hours runner duty on our swap agreement.

- 14 -

Charlie and I were drinking a beer in the Airman's Club bar when he told me. "The manager said they're going to close down for a week, starting next Monday."

"What? Just shut it down?"

"Yeah, that's what they said. Wiring problems, apparently. You know how we're always having flickers and blown fuses and stuff."

"Like I hadn't noticed?" I said. "The other night I thought they'd blown my amp for sure. Turned out to be the fuses, but they sure did have me worried."

Charlie chuckled. "Anyway, I guess they'll get the whole place rewired. That's great, but it means we're out of a gig for the whole week."

"A whole week?" My inner cash-register kicked in, and I shifted into worry mode.

"So, I thought I'd give you and the guys some warning. Maybe you can pick up a fill-in during the week."

I sat there and fiddled with my beer, worrying about the money. How could I make up the hit on my savings? With my work downtown, my college fund had built much more quickly than expected, but still, you hate to see money slip through your fingers. I ran the numbers out. I wouldn't be hurt too bad, but it *was* real money.

On the other hand, there never seemed to be enough time to see Penny or go anywhere. I stayed busy all week, every week, working on base and downtown and running back and forth. Not to mention my extra duties on the weekends. Why not take a few evenings off and relax. I turned to Charlie and laughed. "Hey, man. Sometimes bad news is good news, you know?" I left Charlie sitting at the bar with a befuddled expression, found an empty phone booth and dialed Penny's number. I wanted to ask her to have dinner with me at Club Tripoli. I thought she'd get a kick out of the lavish décor—the luxurious atmosphere and the elegance. It would be easy enough for us to avoid any encounters with the cruder elements of the place. We'd just have to stay out of the back bar and the game room. I planned the evening in my head with high expectations. Her phone rang about six times before she finally picked up. I had started to hang up when her voice came on the line.

"Hey, Penny, how you doing? Listen, I've suddenly got a couple of nights off from the Airmen's Club next week. It'll be a great chance to go out to dinner. You know, no big deal, just dinner and maybe see a show and have a great time. What do you say?"

"Oh. That sounds good. Where do you want to go?"

"Well, Club Tripoli gives me a big discount and we ought to take advantage of that. We can have dinner in the main salon. It's a beautiful setting with a really nice view of the harbor and the castle, and the food is great."

It was like the line went dead for a long moment. "Gee, that sounds exciting, but I don't know. Wouldn't you rather take a night off from there?"

"Well, not really. It's the best in Tripoli, you know. You really ought to see the place. The dining room is very nice. Sumptuous, even."

She kept hedging for a little longer, and finally she quit sparring with me. "Listen Ted, I have to tell you this. Mom and Dad have said Club Tripoli is off-limits to me. They definitely don't want me to go there. I'd be in deep, deep trouble if they knew I'd been to Club Tripoli."

Whoa. Maybe she understood the place a lot better than I'd thought "What's the big deal?"

She hesitated. "Dad says it's a rough place full of crude, coarse people. We've talked about it since you've been working in the band there, and he says that club is a well-decorated honky-tonk, a real dive, and not a place for a respectable woman. Not even a good place for a respectable man."

It didn't sound like I'd have much luck trying to talk her around on this one. Not with a conviction that strong. I mean, yeah, we had some whores and some drugs. And maybe they had a point. I knew my way around well enough to keep clear of that kind of stuff and she'd never even know the difference. Or would she? It seemed like a good time to back off—like it was an argument I just wouldn't win. "Your dad may be right. I guess it isn't much of a place for a nice girl, except the dining room."

I knew for sure there'd be a big price to pay if I took her there and the colonel found out about it. Then they'd probably put me off-limits, too. I shrugged. "Oh well. It's no big deal. Charlie's been telling me about a new restaurant near the old castle, called Café Venezia. We could give that place a try. I can check on reservations for Monday or Tuesday evening. What do you say?"

"Are you sure this new place is okay?" she asked. "Not some kind of joint?"

"Charlie says it's small, but pretty elegant. And it's not a honky-tonk, not even a cabaret."

She signed with relief. "Okay, then. I'll talk to the folks to be sure they're all right with Café Venezia."

A thought struck me. "Charlie's dating a girl who works at the Base Exchange, Pat something or other. I think he might want to join us with his date and we could all have dinner together. What do you think?"

There was a short silence. "Oh. You must mean Patricia Barrett. She graduated a year ago and has stayed here at Wheelus with her family. Dating Charlie, huh? I thought I knew all the gossip, but I didn't know that. I need to give her a call and do a little digging."

"Please, spare me the gossip. Anyway, how about getting together with the two of them? What do you say?"

"Sure. That sounds like fun. I haven't seen Patricia in weeks, and Charlie's nice."

So much for best laid plans, but things were coming together anyway. "Great. Let me check it out with Charlie and I'll call you back. And you check with your folks, too."

* * *

On Tuesday, Penny and I arrived early at the fountain on Castle Square, and strolled down the seaside walk along the harbor, watched the stars become brighter in the fading twilight. We had a relatively clear evening sky with a gentle wind blowing in from the Mediterranean. It was gorgeous, romantic even, and we held hands as we strolled along. We turned and walked back along the *Lungo Mare* and arrived at the old castle as Charlie and Patricia pulled into a parking place. The city traffic had died down and the evening had become as quiet and peaceful as I'd ever heard it. We could hear the muezzin from the minaret of the big mosque next to the gate into the old city, calling the faithful to prayer. The haunting echo of his eerie chant sounded alien, an incomprehensible voice from another world, yet only a block away. I'd heard the calls many times, but they always induced a shiver and a moment of hesitant pause when I heard them.

We talked quietly for a minute or two there on the sidewalk, then went on to the café. The headwaiter seated us in the bar to wait until they had our table ready and Charlie tried out his Italian on the chef and the owner.

After he had ordered drinks for everyone and we'd been served, he switched back to English. Penny and Patricia were impressed by his expertise and made a big fuss over him. Charlie tried to be modest. "Come on, it's not that big a deal. You've got to realize, a lot of what I said there was a list of standard questions and answers you'd use in a bar in any language. *Un bicchiere di vino bianco* is a glass of white wine. And so on."

Patricia laughed at that. "Oh, right. It's something you picked up hanging around bars?"

"Well, no. I've taken three semesters of Italian with Professor Bertone on base at the extension school. University of Maryland."

"But you make it sound easy," Penny said.

He laughed. "Hey. Making it sound easy is the hard part."

Charlie really was modest and he changed the subject. He asked me a few questions about my work downtown. "Are you still working with Scarlatti's quartet? You know, I've noticed a change in your playing. You're playing with a lot more complexity, getting more positive, more confident."

Everybody likes to be praised, but I'd become the postman taking a walk on his day off. "Yeah, Scarlatti's working me pretty hard, but I do feel like I'm getting better. Anyway, forget all that. It's my night off, right?"

He folded his arms and leaned back. "Peace. I'll lay off."

We sat and listened to the girls for a moment, talking about fashions and sororities and other alien crap, like they had their own private language.

"My mom and I are planning a trip to Rome so I can do some shopping before I leave," Penny said. "I wanted to go to Paris but Mom says things are too expensive there. Like Rome's going to be cheap?"

Pat laughed. "At least she doesn't say you have to use your own money! My mom does."

Charlie just chuckled and I gazed out over the harbor, enjoying the calm reflections of the evening light from the water, shining like a sheet of old ripply glass.

The headwaiter showed up then to tell us our table was ready. When we were seated, Charlie ordered us an antipasto with small dishes of pasta, linguine in a delicate seafood sauce. The main course was leg of lamb, the recommendation of Signor Bertone.

We worked our way through the meal with enthusiasm. Charlie leaned back in his chair and sighed. "What do you think, Ted? It was good, right? Not up to the Al Nahklah, but not a bad meal, overall."

The girls looked blank and I tried to fill them in. "Charlie's talking about a Libyan restaurant he and I went to a couple of weeks ago. You know Charlie. He got to ranting and raving one night about how tasty and healthy the Arab diet is, on and on. I tried to jerk him up short and told him he didn't know what he was talking about. But Charlie never backs down, you know. He called my bluff and we went to this restaurant near the base, called Al Nahklah. And of course, the food was great and I lost another bet to him."

Patricia wanted to know all about it. "You never told me about that, Charlie. You have to take me there now that I know about it. Come on."

She'd put Charlie on the spot. "I don't know, Pat. I think the Arabs might be offended if we bring women into the place. I can check with the owner but I have my doubts. I don't remember seeing any women there at all. Do you, Ted?"

I didn't, but I wasn't sure. Had there been Arabic women there? I shrugged. Charlie gave me a dirty look, raised his hand to bring our waiter over. He got off that hook in the distraction of splitting the check with me and preparing to leave.

* * *

The next day Penny and I had lunch at La Loggia. She asked me about the apartment upstairs. Charlie kept a tiny apartment on the second floor above the restaurant for a getaway when he wanted to escape the air base. I had a key and helped him with the rent. I didn't use it a lot, but it was a great place to get some privacy and some peace, away from the base and Club Tripoli.

It seemed that Penny and Patricia had been talking and Penny mentioned lunch at La Loggia. Patricia asked her if she'd seen the cute apartment upstairs. When Penny said no, she asked her why not, so Penny told me she had to see the place the next time we had lunch downtown. I took her upstairs and she looked in every nook and cranny of the apartment, exploring the closets and cabinets like she was going to rent the place. I watched her rambling around and finally she seemed to be satisfied. "It's a nice place, Ted. It's clean and neat as a pin. It's just precious."

I never heard anybody call a cheap little apartment precious, but it was neat, small and clean, with lots of light. I got a bottle of wine out of the cabinet and poured us a glass and we sat at a little table in front of the tall French doors that opened out on the tiny balcony.

Late afternoon light poured in and a full, steady breeze blew through the open doors. We went out and leaned on the rail of the balcony, watching the Arabs' lateen-rigged fishing boats moving through the harbor and tall clouds building out over the sea. After a while, our conversation turned to my working at Club Tripoli.

"It's good and it's not good," I said. "It's a great place, the coolest club around here. And the pay's good. That's the good part, but most of the people who work there are really tiresome."

Penny's eyes narrowed. "I don't get it. If you enjoy what you're doing there, what's the problem? It's not as though you're trying to make friends there or spend a lot of time with them."

I shrugged. "Friends? Not likely. But if you're around the club at all hours and in the back rooms you see and hear things that can curl the hair on your head."

She shifted her hands on the balcony rail, hesitating. "But you keep telling me that you're not involved in the sleazy part of the business, right? So why is that a problem? You're not making sense, not to me."

"Listen, you don't know what it's like down there sometimes. It can be a mean place with hard, ugly people. There's stuff going on there that's illegal, or at least immoral and dishonest. It can be dangerous to be around some of that."

She watched me closely, impatiently. "Can you get to the point?"

"I'm trying, I'm trying. That's why the money's so good. They pay us to take risks that are hard to know about ahead of time and hard to control. They throw money at us, a lot of money, and that's supposed to make it all right."

Penny stared at me as though I were a stranger, like she didn't know me as well as she'd thought. She stood up straight. "Try to be consistent, will you?" she said. "If you're telling me what you're doing is dishonest or unethical or immoral, then the money can't possibly be good enough for you to compromise yourself."

"I don't know. It's just—"

"If it's bad, then you need to get out of it. Forget about sending home a hundred a month or whatever it is. It's not worth it." She swung her ponytail roughly.

That was blunt. She had unerringly come to the crux of the problem. She couldn't see how the money could have any influence on my decision, but now she sounded like she was lecturing me. The whole thing was getting pretty tiresome. "Listen. You told me your dad is paying for your college education and you don't have to sweat it. It's like right there, waiting for you. So just how are you going to understand my problems—or me?"

Penny's face hardened around the eyes. "What? Am I supposed to apologize for my father? Is it the officer-airman thing again?"

"No. That's not the point at all. It's just that I'm fighting, struggling to get enough money together to walk away from the Air Force, to find some way to make a decent living as a civilian. So how can you tell me what I ought to do when you've never been in my position?"

She took a deep breath. "Don't talk to me like I'm a child. I'm not your little girl or anybody else's."

"I wasn't—"

"Simply because you need the money more than I do has absolutely nothing to do with whether it's right or wrong to take it, or to work in a place for people doing immoral jobs!"

I leaned back on the railing of the balcony. "Yeah, well, those are easy words for somebody born with a silver spoon in her mouth. Penny, if you see it *that* plainly then the question has only one answer. It boils down to doing the right thing, doesn't it?"

"Yes. Exactly."

"Well, it's not that simple, not as easy as you'd like to think. Somehow, it's hard." I tried to marshal my thoughts, to say what I meant without sounding stubborn or condescending. "It's hard—really—to just walk away from the answer to all my problems. But it's killing me to stay."

I needed a break from all this yammering and bickering. Both of us were close to losing our tempers. Enough. We could finish this argument some other time, but for now, I needed to cool her down. I turned away from her and stared out over the harbor.

"What a mess," I said. "You know, if you hang around the wrong people, the ones with the easy answers, you finally start to think the way they do. Or not think at all."

She sniffed. Her face and her dark eyes had lost none of that sharp, hard expression she'd taken on. "Listen to me, Ted. This is important. I need to believe you care what I think. Don't say pretty words to make me feel better. And don't start that 'Aw, shucks' crap again."

Penny could read me and sometimes knew what I'd say before I did. I slipped an arm around her and held her hand. "It is important, important to you and me both. This whole situation with Scarlatti and the club has to be resolved. I have to get my problems cleared away and start working to find a school that will accept me. You can see that, can't you?"

She listened closely, so I went on. "Everything doesn't have to be bought and paid for when I leave here. Once in school, I can find a group to play with, join the union and get a regular gig."

She smiled—her first in a while. "That's a lot better than getting messed up by Scarlatti and his gang."

She had begun to hear some of what she wanted to hear, even if she hadn't heard quite the right words. I held my silence for a long moment and deliberately took the next step. "Penny, I was raised to do the right thing, but I need someone like you to remind me what the truth is. You're good for me."

Had she bought it? She cupped my face in her little hands "Oh, Ted. Let me help. If we work together we can solve your problems."

She put her arms around my neck and snuggled up to me. I sighed, knowing how much I needed her. What I was actually going to do was still up in the air. But I knew I'd deceived her. She kissed me then and my doubts faded into the back of my mind.

She'd told me she had to meet her mother for some baby shower or bridal thing, so it was time to head back to the base. The issue about working and staying involved with the club had to be faced. It would be faced, but the first step had to be a talk with Scarlatti.

* * *

After another week, I sat down with Scarlatti at one of the booths in the back bar of the club. It was a quiet night and he ordered each of us a glass of his personal stock of Marsala. While he lit a cigarette, I took a big sip of the wine and rolled it around in my mouth. Whew. The wine had strength and body and tasted more like a brandy than a table wine. Sitting in the quiet bar I felt tired, worn out from trying to keep up my pretenses with him, searching for the courage to tell him what bothered me.

I had to get to the point. I blurted, "Sir, I'm spread way too thin, working for you three nights a week and Saturday afternoons. At the end of my eighteen-month tour over here I'll return to the States and get into an engineering school. To make that work, I need to take some courses at night at the university extension on base—"

"Ted." He gave me a weary smile as he tapped the ash from his cigarette. "You're a good kid and smart, too. I think going back to school is the right thing to do. But take your time. Think about it."

He seemed to be relaxed and taking things calmly, so I went on. "Sir, I don't have a lot of time."

He frowned. "Yes. Hard work does take time. But it is the most important thing. And you surely know that you're like family to the organization and me. We need bright young men like you to work your way up and help the business."

Work my way up? That didn't exactly fit the message I wanted to deliver. "Mr. Scarlatti, you know I enjoy working here and playing in the quartet, and the money's great. But even so, I'm to the point now where I don't have any time left for a personal life."

Scarlatti tilted his head and raised an eyebrow. "A personal life? Well."

"I'm dating this girl on base. She's become very important to me. But I worry about her. I'm afraid if I don't start spending more time with her, I may lose her. I need time off, time for myself."

Scarlatti mashed his cigarette in the ashtray. "And I—I need you right here, right now, to take on an additional task for me. I need a man to put my confidence in, to take over deliveries here in the European sector of Tripoli and in the port facility as well."

"Sir, I—"

He talked right over me. "We move a lot of valuable merchandise through the port and distribute the goods at about ten locations here in the city. That is a big job, and you need to take it on for me. I can provide a couple of men to help you with this, but I need you, Ted, to take the responsibility. It pays an extra two hundred a week so it's a big move up. As I have told you before, there is great opportunity here for a smart young man. You know you are needed and welcome here."

I sighed in frustration. I didn't like or respect this man. I feared him, and I couldn't seem to make any headway at all. My familiarity with the place gave me a clear idea of what kind of merchandise he meant. I didn't want to go that far. Then he backed off a little. "But there is time to think about it. I know it's a big move." We talked some more and he agreed to let me think about the new job over the next few weeks.

At that moment, another Italian, an older man, walked up to our booth. I'd seen him around from time to time, but I didn't know where he fit into the hierarchy. From the way he walked right up and started talking to Scarlatti in rapid Italian I figured he must be family or a business partner, or both. Pretty soon they were going at it, speaking rapidly in a dialect I couldn't keep up with. I couldn't catch more than a word of it, now and then. Their voices rose until Scarlatti stood with a shout of laughter and clapped the other man on the shoulders, saying, "*Si. Signore, si!*" The older man smiled broadly, clicked his heels and stalked off. Scarlatti chuckled and turned toward me. "My brother. A brilliant businessman but a little excitable. Anyway, see me on Monday evening. Meanwhile, you have improved enough with the quartet that you deserve an extra fifty a week as a raise," he said.

In spite of myself, I did the math. I could send home an extra two hundred a month and a lot more than that if I accepted his new offer. But I knew this extra responsibility wasn't any part-time bandstand gig. It meant heavy involvement in the real business of Club Tripoli. It meant work that could eventually put me in a cell at Fort Leavenworth. Or maybe get me killed. Everything pointed in the same direction. It was time to reduce my activities at the club, not increase my involvement with Scarlatti. Another offer and another temptation. I tried to not think about Penny at all.

* * *

On Sunday, I didn't have a gig on base and Penny wanted to get out of a social thing her mother had gotten tangled up with. She called me at the barracks.

"Ted. I told Mom that you and I had a date to see an afternoon movie in downtown Tripoli. I need to pick you up at two, okay?"

"What movie? I don't know anything about movies in downtown Tripoli."

"I don't either, but it'll get me off-base and out of having to go to another baby shower."

"Oh. Okay. Where do you want to go?"

"La Loggia. It's our place, you know."

"Yeah. Maybe I can get you back upstairs."

She chuckled. "Promises, promises."

"Well, I'll see you at two, then."

For a change she arrived early and I found her waiting in the parking lot when I walked out. I trotted down the steps and got in the little Ford coupe. She leaned over and kissed me on the cheek, put the car in gear and headed for the main gate. We got to La Loggia in time for a late lunch and dawdled over our salads and pasta. I ordered another glass of wine and Penny took another sip of hers. I thought maybe she drank wine just to be polite, but I didn't ask.

We took our coffees up to the little apartment, sat at the table by the balcony and enjoyed the breeze. Penny seemed restless and tense and I asked her. "What's wrong? You seem to be strung tight today. Did I say something? Or do something?"

"I'm fine."

She was quiet again. Then she stood and came around the table and bent to kiss me. What started as a sweet gesture of affection turned into another of her aroused kisses. I rose, held her tightly, and kissed her again. She walked inside, stood by the bed and began pulling back the bedspread. I knew she'd finally made up her mind that she wanted me. Then and there. I was all thumbs and stumbles as we undressed and held each other close. She kissed me again and climbed onto the bed. We lay there in the strong breeze off the harbor, caressing and petting each other. We made love until I barely had the strength to move. Then we made love some more. I felt like an intruder in a place I'd never been—a place of warmth and tenderness, of aching desire and fulfilled love.

Penny fell asleep with her arms around me. I finally had to move and stretch my muscles. She woke when I sat up and stared at me for a long moment, an intense stare that gradually melted into a happy smile. "Come here, Ted. Come over here and hold me."

I'd become tongue-tied again so I just kissed her mouth and nose and eyes. My breath was becoming heavy again and she raised her eyebrows. "Good heavens, you can't want me again already. Yes, you're—"

"Yes I am."

"Oh, Ted. Please. I'm supposed to get home sometime this evening and if I leave it up to you who knows when I'll make it."

"Okay, you're right. You are. Ah Penny. You're so wonderful and I want you so bad."

She sat up and rolled off the bed, pulled her scattered clothing together and took possession of the bathroom. When we were back in the car, she kissed me again, started the engine and turned toward the air base.

I rode along in a dreamy silence, thinking about her gentleness and her small, strong hands and her tender, demanding insistence as I tried to be more careful and cautious with her than she needed and wanted me to be. *Ah. Life is good,* I thought.

And it came creeping back into my consciousness, my constant problem. If I could just figure out how to escape the horrors of Club Tripoli I could be a happy man.

- 15 -

Monday morning dawned cloudy. The Old Man had scheduled our rehearsal a little earlier than usual, and then cut it short. Sergeant Andrews caught me as I was wiping down my guitar "Stick around, Miller. The Old Man let us go early so we can go out to the firing range. I guess he wants to see if you know which end of a forty-five to poke the ammo into."

"Gee, Sarge, I thought they came from the supply room already loaded. But I guess I can handle it, and maybe get in a little practice."

He chuckled. "You'll do okay. I'm a little rusty myself, but there's only one cure for that, so come on. We'll draw weapons and ammo from supply."

Sergeant Wallace, our squadron supply-sergeant, issued us two forty-fives and 200 rounds of ammunition. He muttered as he rummaged through a drawer. He laid a pair of small packages on the counter and said, "Here. You men need to take these ear plugs out to the range with you. You got to take good care of your hearing. You don't appreciate it till you lose it. I ought to know."

Sergeant Andrews sighed, took a pair of plugs from him and handed me a pair.

Mr. Mackey, the Old Man, showed up as we gathered our equipment together, wearing his own forty-five Colt on a web belt. "All set? Let's do it."

We climbed into the Old Man's Jeep to ride out to the range. When we arrived, the parking lot was empty except for an Air Police Jeep. Mr. Mackey introduced us to Captain Jerry Myers as we all got out. "Captain Myers is my favorite Air Policeman, a model for the younger men in the squadron." Myers gave him a weary look and muttered something I didn't catch. "He works for the Provost Marshal. When he works," he told us. "And he shoots on the base pistol team with me."

The captain greeted the first sergeant and turned to me. "I see you in the Oasis eating doughnuts, twice a day. Terrible habit," he said, as he patted his belly. I recognized him from the snack bar.

I started to salute but he waved me off. "Save that for the parade ground, Miller. We're here to shoot."

I took my weapon from the First Sergeant. Captain Myers appointed Sergeant Andrews to act as range safety officer. I removed my forty-five from its holster, checked the chamber and ran the safeties through their paces. Everything worked, right down to the predictable rattling of the slide and slight movement of the barrel when I shook the pistol.

Captain Myers saw me shaking my head. "What were you expecting, Miller, a precision instrument? That's typical of the standard-issue weapons we all have to use."

"Yes, sir, I know. I guess I've learned to deal with the problem." What was I supposed to be? The new kid? The rookie?

We each loaded two full clips of seven rounds and fired at will as a warm-up. Somehow, the results didn't surprise me too much. On the second clip the Old Man shot a 67 out of 70, the first sergeant and Captain Myers had 64 and I managed a 55. I'd have to do a little better or they all surely would treat me like a rookie.

Such a low score made me miss my old German 9-mm pistol. I'd bought a Walther P38 double-action, semi-automatic at a gun shop in Laredo. It was the standard German officers' sidearm during World War II, inherently accurate, made with tight tolerances and using a high velocity 9 mm cartridge; and it wasn't worn out from years of rough use. It could beat one of these GI forty-fives hands down. When he left Laredo to come to Tripoli, Dave Walker bought it from me and he still had it.

Captain Myers studied my target. "Your pattern's low, Miller," he said. "Pull your image up an inch and to the right a little bit. Look at what you're doing and think."

The captain pissed me off because I knew I could shoot as well as anybody here. And I would. We set new targets, reloaded, and fired off another clip. I concentrated and shot a respectable score. The Old Man said, "Looking better, Miller. You should get a bench rest setup and get those sights zeroed in. Of course, Sergeant Wallace almost never gives you the same weapon twice, so it may not be worth the trouble. That's why I have my own. If you get serious about shooting, you'll want to have one, too."

"My own match-type weapon? Yes, sir, that sure would be nice, wouldn't it? But I think that's a little too expensive for me."

"Nonsense. You can afford one. Keep on playing guitar at that downtown whorehouse and you can buy yourself one next Friday."

Ouch. I looked at the Old Man to see if he was joking, but he looked serious enough with clamped jaws and narrowed eyes.

He said, "The crew at the American Express Office say you're making steady deposits. Good money."

What? How could he possibly know about that? "Sir, that bank account is my business. My private business. How can you know about it?"

"Miller, I have friends where I need them. Friends who can help me do my job. And that means knowing what my men are up to. Get it?"

I got it, all right. The officers—*the gentlemen*—running the show didn't have to obey any rules and an airman didn't have any rights. Like always. Bunch of pricks. And it looked as if I'd have to put up with another full-scale lecture on my offbase activities.

Sure enough, Sergeant Andrews picked up the script and fixed me with a hard stare. "You need to take a careful look at what you're doing and where you're going, Miller. I know Walker is an old friend of yours, but you have to remember that people change, and they can change for the worse."

"I—"

"Walker and Rodrigo have been hanging out with a mean bunch of folks at that club," the sergeant said. "They see a lot of rough action down there and they may be starting to think rough and mean themselves."

The Old Man shifted his stance, stepped back and put his hands on his hips, picking up where the first sergeant left off. "I'm telling you, the people at that club are not interested in doing the right thing for some nice guitar-playing kid. They're trying to get you involved, get you roped into their organization. Why do you think they pay you so well? Because they like you?"

I tried to interrupt him. "Sir, I—"

The Old Man was just getting warmed up. "You'll find out soon enough. They'll start using you for dangerous, dirty work. What do you do then? Walker and Rodrigo didn't do you any favor when they recruited you to work there. But then, who knows what kind of pressure they were under."

Here we go again, I thought. It seemed like everybody had sound advice for me. Penny, Dave, Scarlatti. Now the Old Man and the first sergeant rode my butt. I'd developed a bad case of the red-ass thinking about it. At the same time, I certainly didn't want to get these people angry with me. They were my direct military supervisors and could make my life totally miserable with practically no effort. I turned to Sergeant Andrews. "Why are you telling me what to do, telling me what to think? You're talking about my personal life, Sergeant, and that's not something you're in charge of. I'm a man and I can make my own decisions about my own affairs."

He narrowed his eyes and took a deep breath. "Miller, life's never as simple as you'd like it to be. This situation you've gotten yourself into is no exception. You are a man. You make your own mistakes or the right decisions because you have to learn. But sometimes, like here and now, the stakes get too high and the wrong decision may be more than a learning experience. It might end up in a prison term. Or worse."

Captain Myers had been hanging back from the discussion. "Your top sergeant's right and you know it. We've had our eye on the operations of that club for months now, and we know the business they're in. And there's a pattern to it. Air Force men going missing for a day or a week were last seen at Club Tripoli. A few have disappeared entirely. Deserters? Dead? We don't know. But most of it's beneath the surface, more suspicion than fact."

I turned away from them and tried to calm my thoughts. The eerie feeling that they could see over my shoulder at the club or look inside my head just wouldn't go away. They'd described my situation with Scarlatti's organization accurately, as if they'd seen it all through my eyes. And yet, I didn't want to let them interfere.

I took a deep breath. "Sergeant. Mr. Mackey. You may be right about this, but I have to try to work things out for myself, my way. It's complicated and difficult." I held my hands out, palm up. "Look. What about some help? I'm worried. Worried and not sure what to do next. Can you help me? Is that what you're saying? Can we talk about all this?"

The Old Man let out a small sigh. "Absolutely. That's why we're here. We want to offer you a way out of this quagmire."

Captain Myers took the lead again. "My office is running an

investigation of Club Tripoli under the Provost's authority. I expect the OSI is involved or soon will be."

The OSI? What! Where was this going? I wondered. Were these people going to throw me to the dogs? Dave always said airmen don't count much in the Air Force view of things, like we're both disposable. Is that what they were saying here? Was Dave right?

The captain continued. "Our problem is we don't have a clear picture of what's going on inside the place, just unrelated bits and pieces we pick up. And that's where you might come into the picture. How long have you been working down there?"

I thought back. "It's been about three months, sir. Give or take."

"Then you must know your way around pretty well; know the layout and the basic operation of the staff and crew, right?"

"Well sir, yes and no. I'm just a guitar man with Scarlatti's jazz quartet." I didn't intend to mention my courier run out to Homs. No way.

The Old Man shifted from foot to foot and glowered at me. "But you have eyes and ears, Miller. You probably know a lot more about the operation down there than—"

Myers cut him off. "We'll get into the details later. Right now, I want you to think about what you do down there, what you see and what you hear. I'll set up a meeting with the upper level staff at the Provost's office. They'll want to spend some time with you. In the meantime, just keep doing what you've been doing and keep your eyes open."

That didn't sound like they planned to get rid of me, but maybe they'd just use me up and spit me out. They'd hit me cold with all this and I was shocked. I wasn't anybody's criminal, but their treatment made me feel like one. Enough was enough.

"Don't I get any say in this? Any choice?" I asked. "You talk like it's all settled and I'm already some kind of spy. What's going on? Are you going to charge me with something, some crime, or am I already convicted?"

I struggled to remain calm. "Do I get legal advice? A trial? Or is this some kind of railroad? A kangaroo court?" I took a deep breath. Captain Myers' eyebrows had climbed a lot and I decided to take that as a warning sign. I lowered my voice a notch. "Sir. We do still have a Uniform Code of Military Justice, don't we?"

The Old Man's face hardened up as he squinted at me. "Now you listen to me, Miller—"

Captain Myers moved in with authority. "Take it easy, Airman. You're going to be thoroughly briefed about your situation and your rights—"

"Sir—"

"Let me finish, Miller. I'm sure there's going to be a discussion about immunity if you're interested in working with us, but that's going to be handled above my level. You'll be well-treated and handled in a proper and legal manner. I'll go back to the Provost's Office and get the arrangements started. You'll hear from your first sergeant."

They were moving way too fast for me. I could be one of the good guys or just another target for the OSI. Would I have any choice in this or was it cooperate or go to jail? Man, my thoughts raced like a rabbit trying to outrun a long-legged dog.

We went back to the shooting. In my mind, I went over the months since my arrival at Wheelus. My relationship to Club Tripoli had seemed harmless enough at the beginning, but had gradually changed, along with the atmosphere of the club. Light-hearted was not a part of the description anymore. I felt trapped, like I'd walked into an ambush. And now it looked like my life might get pretty rough before it got any better.

I finally began to concentrate on the shooting and held my own on the scores. Then Captain Myers went over to his Jeep and got a heavy canvas case, olive drab with black metal snaps, out of the back. He brought it over to the firing line and laid it down. The canvas case contained a grease gun, like the ones I'd seen during the Wheelus orientation lectures. And again—on the road from Homs.

Myers asked, "Did you ever fire one of these babies?"

"No sir," I said. "I've only seen one once at a perimeter defense drill. And not close up at all."

He took me through the safety procedures for clearing the chamber and inserting and removing the clips. Then he handed me the weapon along with a full, thirty-round clip.

"Here. Try it, but be ready. Get a good solid stance and expect a strong kick. The gun is light, and the recoil is a little high in your hand. It'll try to climb the muzzle up, so hang onto it. Go for it!"

With the clip installed and one round manually loaded into the chamber, I took the safety off, got a good grip, and held my breath.

One firm pull on the trigger and the grease gun started this big popping rip. By the time my finger came off the trigger, about ten rounds were gone and the last round fired almost straight up in the air! I took a deep breath, got set again, and fired a few short bursts, about three or four rounds each. This time most of my shots stayed under tight control.

I removed the clip and locked the trigger safety with my hands shaking a little. Now I could better understand how that maniac on the road to Homs could have missed me. Maybe he'd never fired a grease gun before.

The captain chuckled. "That's a lot of firepower, isn't it? Quite an experience. I've got two more clips loaded. Go ahead and fire them off. That'll give you a lot better feel for the piece."

He was right. By firing short bursts, I could hold decent aim and chew the center out of the target—more or less.

I cleared the breech, locked it back and handed the weapon back to Myers. He laughed like a boy with a new toy. "Ain't that something? Does that get your pulses going? Man! I love that little devil. You'll get used to the grease gun with a little practice, but that's enough for today. You're getting the feel of it. With a few more sessions I can get you qualified on the weapon. And like they say, you never know what the most important tool in the bag is going to be." He slid the weapon back into its case, snapping snaps and looking busy.

Mr. Mackey picked up his cue. He said, "You think about what we said, Miller, you hear me? Remember, we need you and you need us. The captain's plan is your way out of this hole you're in, and it's a way to solve a lot of problems for the Air Force and your fellow airmen."

"Yes, sir," I said. "I—I'll remember that." They seemed to be laying it on a little too thick. I mean, it was baseball practice back in high school. I had this nagging eerie feeling. All this crap about keeping my eyes open and helping the Air Force—and practicing with the grease gun. All the encouragement and the pep talks sounded like a sign of what was coming. It seemed kind of overdone, like they were prepping me to be used by the Air Force in ways that I hadn't signed on for. What were these people going to do with me?

- 16 -

After lunch, we got the military marching band together and worked through a lot of standard marches and ceremonial maneuvers. It was hot, sweaty work, even though the clouds still shielded us from the harsh sun. Following the workout, we took a break, cleaned up, and changed into fresh class-A uniforms to march down to the flagpole for a retreat ceremony, formal and military. The parade flights for the formation met us at the assembly point near the main gate and we formed up in order for the march down to Wing Headquarters. We played a couple of Sousa marches on the way, halting vehicle and pedestrian traffic. By the time we got to the flagpole we had a fair-sized audience assembled, mostly military men with a sprinkling of civilian employees and military dependents.

Bob Rodrigo played the old bugle call, "Retreat," on the trumpet with crisp precision and a gradual ritardando at the end, followed by an arrangement of the "Star Spangled Banner" that Mr. Mackey had written.

The full band played a soft, harmonically complex, contrapuntal accompaniment to the melodic line carried by Bob and Bill Nelson on trumpets. The melody alternated between echoing trumpets and simple harmony following Bob's lead. They played their duet with remarkable care and timing and the Old Man directed the band with hands and baton, keeping us subdued but tightly linked to Bob's timing and phrasing right up to the end.

The flag security detail brought down the colors as we finished. The crowd around the Wing Headquarters building was hushed and still. For people who spent their days on a military base, they seemed moved, transported by the solemnity of the formal ceremony.

Rodrigo gave Nelson a quick nod at the end and Nelson smiled. Bob always caught me by surprise when he performed in such an impeccable way. For a guy who acted like a deliberate prick most of the time, he could do a tremendous job in his role as a senior musician in the squadron, as if he actually cared. Life might be simpler if he'd just be consistent and act like a jerk all the time. Oh, well. We marched in a subdued silence to the precise beat of a solo snare drum, back to the squadron barracks. Mr. Mackey stopped the band with "Squadron, halt!" and said, "Well done, men."

Sergeant Andrews saluted him, did an about-face and called out, "Dismissed."

Everybody talked at once as we went to the assembly room to put our instruments away. We were through for the day. Some of the guys were going down the street to the Airmen's Club for a beer and they asked me to come along.

* * *

The next morning we had mail call after the big band rehearsal. The mail clerk called out, "Miller!"

I shouted, "Here!" The clerk handed me a letter from home and I tucked it into my hip pocket. My superstition about opening mail in front of anybody else stemmed from experience. It seemed like every time I'd ever done that, the news was bad. Better to open this one later, in my room.

As mail call ended, the first sergeant called my name. "Miller. Front and center. I need a word with you in my office." I heard a couple of the men laughing, delighted to see me being called on the carpet, or maybe just delighted it was someone else. I felt worried out of habit. I couldn't remember many times when I'd reported to the front office and things turned out in my favor. Oh, well. Mine not to reason why.

The formation broke up and I stood at attention in front of the first sergeant's desk. Tradition and custom prevailed while he sorted through his mail. At least he didn't read it all and make me stand there through the whole process. He picked up a piece of paper from his desktop. "Says here you need to report to the Provost's Office at 1400 hours, today. No purpose stated, just be there. Report to Master Sergeant Wilson at the front desk. He'll take it from there."

"Yes, Sergeant. 1400 hours, report to Sergeant Wilson."

"I think you know what this is about, but I'm not to mention any of that. Neither are you. Not to anyone. Clear?"

"Yes, Sergeant."

"Dismissed. And Miller, clean up. Get rid of the fatigues and put on some fresh class B's. Try to look sharp over there."

"Yes, Sergeant!"

It was almost noon so I decided to grab some lunch across the street and come back and clean up. I wanted to call Penny. I hadn't seen her or even called her in three, no, four days, but I'd thought about her. A lot. I decided I'd better stick to business. There wasn't a lot of slack in my schedule.

A couple of guys I knew were in the Oasis and we killed a few minutes talking. Then I hurried back to the barracks, shaved and got out a fresh uniform. My shoeshine looked dull and scruffy, so I took some extra time to work on my low-quarters. By the time I finished that, I had just enough time left to walk over to the Provost's office.

I got there a couple of minutes early, found Sergeant Wilson's location in the anteroom of the commander's office and walked up to his desk. I stood at attention and waited for him to notice me. After a long minute or two, he looked up and said, "Well?"

"Sergeant Wilson, I'm Airman Miller, reporting as ordered."

He scrutinized me from head to foot with a stern look. I was glad I'd spent the extra time spiffing up. Sergeant Andrews would have been proud of me. And Sergeant Wilson looked like he'd have torn strips off my ass if I'd come in front of his desk looking unprepared or unkempt.

Finally, he said, "At ease, Airman. Have a seat over there and I'll see if we're ready for your appointment."

I sat on one of the hard, straight, oak chairs against the wall to the side of the sergeant's desk and I was back in high school, waiting with dread to talk to the assistant principal. At exactly 1400 hours, the sergeant called me over and took me down the hall to a room near the back of the building. He opened the door. I entered and he closed it.

I stood in front of a small desk and Colonel Crawford sat behind it. I snapped to attention and made a sharp salute, held it, and said. "Sir. Airman Miller reporting as ordered."

He sat up straighter at his desk and returned the salute. I dropped my hand to my side, and remained at attention.

He looked me over and I thought he suppressed the slight flicker of an incipient smile with a stern look. "At ease, Airman. I didn't know a bandsman could look that sharp in a military situation."

"Yes, sir. We're trained for ceremony and appearance," I said. "We're supposed to know all the moves."

"Apparently." He indicated a small, straight-backed chair by the side of the desk. "Sit down, and let's get started. Where did you leave off with Captain Myers yesterday?"

"Colonel, he explained to me about the on-going investigation of the nightclub, Club Tripoli. He said something about the OSI, but mostly he talked about the work being carried out by the Provost's staff, your staff, and the need for somebody on the inside."

"Right. And of course you currently work at the place, as a musician, it says here." He was shuffling through a small stack of three-by-five cards. "It also says you're doing a little more than just playing in the band. We'll get into that in a minute. Right now I need your initial reaction to a straight-forward proposal."

I'd broken out in a light sweat in spite of the coolness of the room. His remark about doing a little more than just playing sounded ominous. "Yes, sir. What's the proposal?"

He put the cards down. "Simply stated, I need a man inside the club who knows what's going on and can keep his eyes and ears open to the nefarious side of the nightclub's business. I need facts. Names and numbers in as much detail as possible about what they're up to in gambling, prostitution, drugs and extortion."

"Sir. That's a pretty tall order."

"It's not an order, Airman. At this point I'm asking for a volunteer. There are others who might fill the shoes, but right now, it's between you and me. You're my first choice."

"Why me, Colonel?"

"Because I know something about you. I know you've worked there for a couple of months now, and I have information that says you're involved with illegal activities inside the organization—"

"But, Colonel—"

"What you're doing down there is against the law, and in violation of Air Force regulations as well. I figure we have a good chance of being able to direct and control you, to rely on you to do as you're told. I can't make myself much clearer than that, can I?"

"Sir. . . That sure does sound like a threat."

The colonel smiled for the first time since I'd entered the room. "Of course it does, Miller, but I think what we're talking about here is a negotiated arrangement. You give me what I want and I'll see that you get a clean slate, no charges and no record. As if nothing ever happened. Now, what's so bad about that?"

"Sir, for starters, what you're asking me to do is hard-down dangerous. Those people down there are ruthless. They beat people. They abuse them, torture them and they kill them, mostly for business reasons, but sometimes just for amusement. Yet you want me to sniff around, ask questions, and make notes on a clipboard? Jesus, sir, I'd be dead the first day."

He shook his head. "Whoa, Airman. I'm not new to the police investigation business. I know the dangers and the risks a lot better than you think you do. You can get me a substantial amount of information if you just watch and listen in the course of your normal activities down there. In fact, if you'll spend some time racking your brains you'll find you already have a lot of valuable data stored away. Just needs organizing."

"So you're not talking about me following people around or asking weird questions? Or openly spying on people?"

"I'm not trying to get you killed, Miller. No profit in that."

"That's comforting, sir. Thank you." *Big hearted prick.*

The colonel looked stern. "Miller, I need you to continue to function in your present position with that club, on the bandstand and off, and I'll need regular reports and updates. We'll set up a contact system and require verbal reports from you to one of the men in my office, one of the younger officers. In the course of following my orders you'll come to view these reporting sessions as interrogation. Can't be helped. The interrogator is trained to glean information from the most ordinary of events, and he'll ask you all sorts of questions that seem irrelevant, but he knows what he's doing."

"Mine not to reason why, Colonel. I hear you loud and clear, but I'm only a guitar player. I don't know much about Club Tripoli and I don't commit any crimes."

He narrowed his eyes and regarded me for a moment in silence. "I know—for a fact—that's not true. It's your activities off the bandstand we're talking about now. Think about doing hard time at Leavenworth and at least be honest with yourself. And think about the question of aiding and abetting. We both know that mild sins are graduated to the felony level as quickly as they can move you along. At some point, they own you outright. Understand me, Airman?"

I didn't want to hear what he said. I didn't even want to think about it. Still, he was right—he'd struck to the heart of my predicament. I'd gotten in deep enough to be in big trouble, and he knew that. I let out the breath I didn't realize I held. "Colonel, I do understand, and you don't leave me much choice. Who is this younger officer I'll have to work with?"

He picked up the phone on the desk and dialed. "Sergeant Wilson, send Lieutenant Gibson in. Yes. Now."

We sat in silence for a moment, waiting for the lieutenant to arrive. The colonel looked me over carefully. "You're the bandsman, the guitar player my daughter Penny has been dating, aren't you?"

"Uh. Yes, sir. I am. She told you about me?"

"Of course she did. There's not much that goes on in my family, or on this base for that matter, that I don't know about. She talks about you. And I'd advise you to be very careful with her. Make certain you don't expose her to any of the rotten crap associated with Club Tripoli. Understand me?"

I tried not to look as guilty as I felt. "Yes, sir!" I said. "That won't happen, ever. I think too much of her to put her into any kind of danger."

"Just watch your step. That's a thoroughly despicable outfit you're dealing with."

At a knock on the door, Colonel Crawford called, "Come in!"

A young second lieutenant came through the door and snapped to attention in front of the colonel. "At ease, Lieutenant. This is the airman we discussed this morning. You and he will be seeing a lot of each other over the next few weeks."

We regarded each other in wary silence. I said, "Lieutenant Gibson, the colonel says you know your stuff. I don't think I'm going to enjoy your company all that much, but he says we'll have to work together."

The lieutenant gave me a seriously hard look. "That's about it, Airman Miller. Let's hope it goes well and we get the job done quickly. The survival rate is a lot better if we don't expose our informers any more than is absolutely necessary."

Informer, I thought. *This son of a bitch is talking about me!*

Colonel Crawford cleared his throat and we both looked around at him. He stood up. "That does it for me, today. I'm going to leave you two here so Lieutenant Gibson can get to work on the initial interview. Gibson, see if you can bring the file up to date. You'll need a couple of hours at least. Call Sergeant Wilson if you need anything like writing supplies or coffee. Oh, and call over to the band squadron and tell them that Airman Miller is helping you on a special assignment. Talk to Mr. Mackey. Be vague, but let him know Miller will be here the rest of the day. At Ease," the colonel said and left us.

The lieutenant sat down behind the desk. "Miller, we'll arrange to meet at other locations for our future sessions. We can't have you coming and going at the Provost Office like you worked here, you know. We might as well put up a sign, or hang one around your neck. I'll contact you through your first sergeant and he'll let you know where and when."

He pulled a pad of paper out of his briefcase. "Now, let's get started."

It was a long afternoon.

Walking back toward my barracks, I shivered for a moment in spite of the heat of the afternoon sun. I felt out of step, out of balance with my world. The colonel had turned me into an informer. He'd up-ended my life and changed how I felt about myself in just a few minutes. It made me feel unclean, misused. Me, Ted Miller. They were using me, exploiting me, but despising me for being exploited at the same time. There was nobody to talk to about it, no one. And no way to complain or even try to come to terms with this new situation. I was totally spooked.

- 17 -

Our squadron had to load the aircraft for the flight to Aviano Air Base in northern Italy. We had a two-week tour coming up, scheduled and arranged by the First Sergeant, and a lot of gear to organize. My eyes burned from the hot, gritty air, heavy with the kerosene smell of jet fuel. A pair of F-100s taxied out for takeoff. Their powerful engines screamed as they streaked down the main runway. They lit their afterburners and boomed so loud I felt it through my back and chest.

During their takeoff the first sergeant suspended his instructions about loading. We stood there in the brassy North African sunshine of a hot June day. Sergeant Andrews had delegated this work detail to our staff sergeants. "You men get this operation organized. We have a flight to take and a tour to make, and we can't do it with everything sitting here on the runway. And the men sitting here on their butts. Move it!"

He gave these four-stripers some command experience and the rest of us an opportunity to get jerked around. I saw what was coming. "Richard, I know they have to start training these guys sometime, but I'll bet you twenty dollars they'll make a huge mess of the whole operation."

Richard snorted. "Man, I won't take that bet. What do you think? I'm some kind of fool? No way."

The operation started badly and got worse. With all the equipment piled up in the same area, it seemed the entire squadron rooted through the heap at the same time to check on their gear.

No arrangement or system existed, nothing. Sergeant Nelson tried to get it all organized, but he competed with three other sergeants for the men's attention.

Finally, Sergeant Andrews came over and put his hand on Nelson's shoulder. "Nelson," he said, "You're the senior staff sergeant out here, the one with the most time in grade, so you get these guys off the dime and get this crap aboard."

Sergeant Nelson grinned and said, "Yes, Sergeant!" The other staff sergeants backed off and he turned to us and shouted. "Charlie, Richard! You and Miller get in that heap and drag all the instruments off to the right so we can see what we've got."

Richard grabbed me by the arm. "Come on, Ted. That's the first sensible thing anybody's said yet. Let's do it."

We waded in and pulled out every musical instrument and grouped them in their dull black cases by section. Trumpets, trombones, reeds and rhythm. We had the sections formed, lined up and countable. Anyone could tell at a glance we had all of the instruments there for loading.

Nelson looked around. "Now, pull all of the AWOL bags and suitcases out and line them up over there by the tail, so each man can see if his gear is there or not." Then Sergeant Nelson pointed at me. "Ted. You and Dave get up in the Gooney Bird and they'll hand the equipment up to you. Get it stacked where the loadmaster wants it and get it tied down."

We got it all inside and stowed, then handed down the parachutes and the life preservers. At last, we all climbed aboard the airplane, dropped the long retractable metal bench-seats of the C-47 down at the sides of the cargo bay, and belted in. As we sat on the runway and the sun rose higher in the sky, the old Gooney Bird began to heat up. By the time the rest of the flight crew got there we were soaked in sweat. Richard wanted to get up a pool on how high the temperature would go, but we didn't have any way to measure and Richard was just guessing at it. Finally, Sergeant Nelson said, "Richard. Shut the fuck up." And he did.

When we landed in Italy we played our first performance, a dress rehearsal, at the base theatre at Aviano Air Base, with a full house. It went all right. I heard a few rough spots, minor problems the section leaders could work out during breaks, or some time before our next performance.

Before we packed up for our long road tour we had to make a quick side trip with concerts in Pordenone and Udine, and around the tip of the Adriatic for a pair of concerts in Trieste. Trieste was a big, old city, with a complicated kind of international history. It had been owned by a lot of people—Austria, Hungary, France, Italy and Yugoslavia— and had been the Free Territory of Trieste after the big war. But now, according to our guides, it belonged to Italy again, since 1954. It seemed to depend on who you asked. I looked forward to the visit because I knew I'd never have another shot at the place. And I knew I'd need to spend some more time in the base library when we got home, trying to figure out what I'd seen and where I'd been.

We arrived at the theatre in Trieste in early afternoon and we set up for the afternoon gig, a matinee for school kids. The Old Man wanted to make sure the rough spots he'd heard in Aviano were cured and behind us. Within two hours we were free to wander around the city on our own. That night we set up for our main show in the *Teatro Verdi*. The place was huge. I sneaked a look at the edge of the curtain and saw a packed full house. They looked like a young, restless, noisy audience and I warned the guys. "We'd better be sharp, tonight. That's a hungry bunch out there."

But it went great. We started off with a Glen Miller medley, a surefire crowd pleaser and eased into some Count Basie numbers and a couple of my favorite Kenton arrangements. Loud and louder, the brass, four trumpets and four trombones, blowing all out and riveting the audience. They loved it!

We finished the book the Old Man had called up, and they wouldn't quit. "Encore! Encore!" On and on. What? We finished up with Basie's *April in Paris* and did the "one more time" tag about five times. Sergeant Nelson's trumpet over-ride at the end got a little weaker each time, and I didn't think he'd make the high notes again. The First Sergeant rescued him and had the theatre crew close the curtain during the final signature theme of April in Paris, with the trombones in high harmonic fusion. We packed up the music and the instruments. Everybody likes an enthusiastic audience, but these fans were maniacs.

When we tried to sneak out the back door into the alleyway, they found us again and drowned us in showers of confetti and noise. It was frantic! It looked like we had every screechy teenager in Trieste out there, male and female. Every last one of them had a scrap of paper of some kind, notes or concert programs, and they all wanted autographs. It took us about twenty or thirty minutes to get everything and everyone back on the bus. Man I was tired. I mean it had been a long day and these kids didn't want to quit.

* * *

We returned to Aviano and transferred everything to the big, dark-blue Air Force bus that became our home for the next two weeks. Sergeant Andrews had our itinerary and the roadmap and sat up front to direct the driver. The rest of us read, watched the scenery or tried to get some sleep.

The tour became a routine of concerts, late night jam sessions, and long slow bus rides. Seemed like we ate too much, drank too much and never got enough sleep. The jam sessions were the most taxing part of the routine. There was always some local bar where the area's musicians and the girls hung out and we'd go there after our concert. Sometimes we'd just have a drink or two, but more often than not, there'd be a pretty good local group on the bandstand and they'd invite us to sit in. The girls always hung around the Americans and we thought we'd discovered gold. Or maybe it was pyrite, but we were all studs.

Some of the older guys in the squadron would hang around for a half hour, then slip out and return to our hotel. And they were the ones who'd laugh at the rest of us as we nursed our hangovers through coffee and breakfast. Then we'd try to make up the lost sleep on the bus ride to the next stop. The fatigue was cumulative so the situation was self-correcting. After a few days of jamming all night, I had to drop out of the enthusiastic group and get a good night's sleep. The names in the sessions changed or rotated but the spirit stayed on. Man, we were swingers, the coolest jazz musicians in Italy. Or we thought we were.

* * *

We finally finished the official itinerary of our tour and we made a two-day stopover at Rome to wait for our old C-47 to take us back to Tripoli. Before the first sergeant let us get off the bus, he lectured us. "I want you men to have a good time in Rome, but remember this. The bus leaves for the airport at 0530 on Friday. Be in the hotel lobby at 0500 with your luggage."

He ignored the ragged chorus of "Yes, Sergeant," and checked his watch. "We've arranged a tour bus for today, and it'll give you a chance to see the city. The bus leaves here in twenty minutes. So get out and mix with the natives. Have a good time and I'll see you all back here on Friday morning."

The guided tour sounded good to me. I showed up with my camera to board the bus and heard Charlie call, "Hey, Ted! Wait. Wait up."

He came running up, puffing and out of breath. "Let's skip the bus ride, man. We'll just end up hanging around with the NCOs, with them playing their asinine rank games. Who needs those guys to see the city? Plus, this'll be a great chance to practice my Italian. We can take a few hours and just hang out on the Via Veneto, soaking up atmosphere. What do you say?"

"Yeah, you're right." I stepped out of the line. "It's a great chance to escape the Air Force chicken for a couple of days. Let's go."

We took off with our guidebooks. We had two days to see the city and the old Roman landmarks so we couldn't expect to do much more than hit the high spots. I couldn't match Charlie's fluency, but I'd tried to learn some conversational Italian back in Tripoli. I knew a little bit, even though my grammar was atrocious. Most of the Italians tried to help me along when I couldn't think of a word in Italian or used a Spanish word instead. Charlie tried not to groan too much and I had to put up with a lot of incredulous facial contortion from him. With Charlie's skill, we made our way through Rome. We got lost once or twice and got on the wrong bus once, but the people we met always helped us out.

We spent the second day acting like tourists again, but we spent more time in the sidewalk cafes than we had the previous day. After a good dinner, we got back to our hotel at about nine. I saw Dave sitting on a sofa by the main door into the lobby. He seemed to be waiting for someone. I waved to him but he didn't notice. Charlie and I went to the desk to ask the bell captain some questions about the sights we'd seen during the day. I looked around the lobby, empty except for a few business types in suits.

Dave stood by the main door out to the street now. Bob Rodrigo walked up to Dave and snapped, "Where are those guys? And where's your briefcase? Walker, do I have to do everything myself?"

Dave shook his head. "Everything's cool man. Here's the briefcase and it's not time for them to be here yet. Calm down, Bob."

"Don't be telling me what to do, Walker"

Dave sat down on the sofa again. They both watched the door in silence, checking the people coming into the lobby.

I nudged Charlie. "In case you never noticed, Bob can be a real jerk sometimes. Look at those guys. What are they up to? They look like a couple of pall bearers waiting for the hearse."

Charlie stared at them. "Looks like they're waiting for somebody, all right." He started to walk over to the door where they hovered and fidgeted.

I remembered my experience with Dave in the back bar at Club Tripoli. I grabbed his arm and stopped him. "Wait, man. I don't think they want any company right now. Just a hunch."

Charlie looked at me with elevated eyebrows. "Huh? Come on. This is weird."

Just then, two dark, well-dressed men came through the door, the smaller one carrying a large briefcase. They stopped just inside and the one with the briefcase changed hands and flexed his fingers.

They walked up to Bob and Dave and grunted something unintelligible. No handshakes, no smiles. Dave reached down and came up with his own briefcase. He set it on the small table by the sofa and the two swarthy men watched as Dave flipped the case open. The two men crowded up to the little table, blocking our view as they muttered to each other. After their close inspection, the bigger one said something in Italian I didn't understand and Dave snapped the briefcase shut.

The smaller man handed his heavy case to Dave and he and Bob began a careful examination of the contents. Bob hefted the case once or twice as if he were trying to gauge its weight. He said something to Dave, who hefted the case himself. Dave shrugged. Bob turned and mumbled a few words to the two dark men and handed Dave's briefcase to the smaller man. Then both swarthy men left the hotel lobby.

Charlie looked wide-eyed now, and I must have appeared as perplexed as I felt. "What did the big guy say?" I asked.

"He said, 'This better count out right.' He said something else I couldn't catch. Maybe numbers. Big numbers. Millioni something."

Dave and Bob crossed the lobby, glanced right and left, and went straight to the elevators. They caught the first car up and disappeared. It had all happened while Charlie and I stood by the bell captain's desk. I spoke first. "Charlie, I don't know any more about what they're up to than you do. Looked spooky, didn't it?"

He shrugged. "It was way over my head, man. If I didn't know better I'd say it looked like some kind of deal. A transaction, maybe. Man. I don't think I want to know."

"Yeah. I don't think they were buying souvenirs. I'm about ready to give up on those guys. Even Dave."

* * *

The next morning, Sergeant Andrews got us on the bus to Ciampino airport. He'd planned for an early start on the trip back to Wheelus. We assembled on the flightline at 0600 with our gear grouped according to plan, and waited for our C-47 to arrive from Evreux.

After an hour had passed and our gooney bird hadn't arrived, Richard muttered to himself. "Man. Looks like another case of hurry up and wait."

Sergeant Andrews went into the terminal to see if he could get any information and I went back to sleep on our pile of luggage. I slept until Dave came running up to our group.

"Hey! Wake up, you guys, wake up! There's a brand-new Boeing 707 passenger jet parked on the other side of the terminal building. It's the biggest, smoothest beauty you've ever seen."

On the bus, I'd been telling the others what I'd read about the coming revolution in civil aviation. Dave said, "Come on, Ted, you've got to see this. You, most of all."

Charlie grabbed his Leica and he and Dave took off across the flightline with Richard and me at their heels. The plane was a beauty, all right. It took my breath away. Charlie talked the Italian guard into letting us take a bunch of pictures of the plane and a couple of group pictures of us in front of the Boeing 707.

As we wandered back to our heap of equipment, I wondered, perplexed—why can't you ever depend on people to do what you expect? Only yesterday I'd written Dave off as a no-good, crooked as a dog's hind leg. Yet, here he had handed me a chance to walk all around the world's first practical, sucessful jet transport. He acted like he'd invented the whole occasion as a gift to me from a generous, innocent Irish kid.

I still couldn't figure the guy out. He reminded me of a moving target, an illusion, changing style and color all the time. Seemed like I couldn't get a handle on who he was or what he stood for. One thing for sure. When we got back to Wheelus, I would have to tell Lieutenant Gibson the whole story about Dave and Bob and their weird transaction in the lobby. Telling Gibson about the club I could handle. Ratting on Dave was something else. Like turning your brother over to the cops. I didn't think I could handle that.

- 18 -

Our plane landed at Wheelus about mid-day. We were all tired of riding the bus, tired of flying and glad to be back. The airmen loaded all the equipment and luggage on the truck, with suitable direction from the junior NCOs, climbed on and rode back to the Squadron assembly room. We stowed all the gear and piled the luggage in the middle of the room to let each man take care of his own personal gear.

I called Penny from the dayroom when my turn on the phone came up. Hearing the sound of her voice again made me grin like an idiot. "I've got the day all planned and everything's ready to go," she said.

How I'd missed her during the trip to Italy. I struggled to keep from pouring out my feelings to her right there in the dayroom in front of all the others. I took a deep breath. "I hope that includes some food," I said. "I missed breakfast and we had nothing on the plane but C-rations."

She laughed "Hungry as always. Lunch is packed and waiting. Fried chicken all right?"

My stomach growled. "Oh, man, that sounds great. I'll be ready."

"Good. I'll pick you up behind the barracks in ten minutes and we'll head for the beach. Don't forget. We'll have supper at my house with Mom and Dad and my little sister."

"Oh, yeah." I hadn't forgotten about the dinner with her family, but I dreaded it. Maybe I could put it off for a few days, or a week. "You know, this whole family dinner thing is really bothering me."

Penny's voice hardened. "Oh, stop. You know Mom's had this arranged for weeks now."

"Penny—"

"It's only a couple of hours and you'll do fine."

I hesitated again. "I don't know."

Penny persisted. "Come on Ted. They're anxious to meet you."

"Yeah, sure. What do you think they'll call me? Airman Miller?"

"Please," she said. "You have to do this for me. I've gotten them all warmed up for this and you just have to come."

I knew a lost cause when I saw one, and resigned myself to getting through the evening. I couldn't explain to Penny what bothered me the most. How could I look the colonel in the eye and pretend to be just a guy who dated his daughter. The colonel would take the lead, but I felt pretty sure he wouldn't want to expose his family to our real relationship. Surely my work on the investigation by the Provost Office or my immunity arrangements wouldn't be talked about in front of the family.

This evening promised to be awkward at best, or a real case of walking on eggs. I expected it to be tense and didn't want to look like a lout to Penny's mom, but my mother's early training in good manners and the social graces ought to get me through. Mom didn't raise any roughnecks. Still, I didn't look forward to the dinner. Or tiptoeing around the colonel all evening.

* * *

Penny picked me up at the barracks. We stopped at the Airmen's Club to buy some cold Cokes and headed for the beach. She parked the car near the pavilion and chose an area on the beach which she claimed with her big, red-striped blanket. I lugged beach gear and the huge picnic basket she'd packed. She stopped to say hello to several kids she knew from Wheelus High School. They exchanged greetings, chatted for a moment. I felt as if they were sizing me up but I tried to be polite as she introduced me. Had I seemed that young just three years ago? They parted with a rousing "Uaddans forever!" Honest. . . .

We ran to the water and crashed through the light surf until we stood waist deep. Patches of seaweed swayed in the water and lined the beach. The rich, salty smell of the weed as it dried in the sun took me back to the beach in southern Virginia, my beach, and the odor evoked a poignant longing for home. We cooled off in the water a while, then walked along the shore, away from the pavilion.

When we were out of sight of the others, we waded out to the first sand bar into chest-deep water. We hadn't been together in over two weeks and we needed to hold each other. We created a vertical tangle of arms and legs and searching hands as we stood kissing and gasping for air. We waded back to shallow water where we lolled in the surf and relaxed. It was an intimate, hypnotic interlude, holding onto each other there in the gentle waves, with the ebbing warmth of our excitement still coursing through our veins. I wanted her desperately, but I knew I had to be cool. The beach attracted people from all over the base—and the colonel's daughter would be a target of gossip in a heartbeat if I didn't behave myself. Finally, we broke apart for the walk back, hand in hand as the strong sun warmed our bodies.

Penny distracted me from my desire. "I can't believe summer is going by so fast," she said.

I sighed. "Yeah, I know, I know. Summer never lasts."

"It never does, but this summer is really flying."

I laughed. "It is for me. I expected to be bored, but—"

"Just think," she said. "I'll be leaving for the States to go to school in less than six weeks."

I looked over at her. "Is everything all set?"

Penny sighed. "I guess so, but I'm not sure what to do or if I even want to go. Why does life have to get so complicated? Will you miss me?"

I squeezed her hand. "Yeah, I'll miss you. You know I will."

"But now I feel all confused," she said

I thought about her complaint. "Simple and uncomplicated. That's what I had before you showed up that day at the sailing club. I'm telling you, I wouldn't go back to that on a bet. I wouldn't trade that day, or the days since, for anything."

Penny stopped and looked out over the blue water in silence.

I put my arm around her shoulders and kissed the back of her neck. "I've never known anyone like you. I've never cared about anybody as much as I care about you."

She checked up and down the beach, then put her head on my chest and snuggled up close. We kissed again and held each other. I felt sentimental and mushy as I held her and felt the need to back away before I made myself look foolish. I stepped away from her and gave her a big grin. "So there," I said. "I'll miss you and I love you. What else could a girl ask?" She looked a little put out by my maneuver to break the mood. We walked on down the beach, back toward her striped blanket.

I bent, picked up a small shell, tossed it into the gentle surf and changed the subject. "So. It's Agnes Scott, huh?"

"Well, I guess so. Daddy went to LSU but Mom insisted on Agnes Scott. I just don't know."

"What are you going to study there? The two schools don't seem much alike, do they? One of them has to be better for what you want to major in."

Penny laughed. "If I knew what I wanted to major in, I guess it would be easier to choose."

"What? You don't know?"

"No, I don't." She shrugged. "I'm not sure what I want, literature or business or journalism. Anyway, I don't plan to work too hard the first year."

I looked at her in wonder. "You know, what you need to do is put school off until you know what you want. Get a job for a while and think about what you want to do, or what you want to study."

"I don't think so," she said. "That would mean staying here, staying home with the family and working on base. But I want to get out on my own, you know?"

"Think about it. It would mean staying with me. Giving us a chance to know each other better."

She turned her head slowly. "I know, I know. That sounds great, but my mother would kill me if I even mentioned doing anything like that."

"You won't know if you don't ask."

"I know how she feels. Still, I never thought I'd be standing here on a beach in North Africa, happy and confused—in love. I'll think about it, but don't make any big plans for me. Not yet."

How could I not make plans, one way or another? I thought. I couldn't just turn off my mind and my dreams, and I couldn't bear to think about breaking up with her.

Back at her red and white blanket, we unpacked the lunch. The cold Cokes made little trickles of condensation as we had a couple to cool off. Penny spread our lunch on the white towel she'd packed with the food. She'd brought fried chicken, deviled eggs, fried sliced potatoes and apple pie—enough for three or four people.

"Good lord, girl, what are you trying to do? Fatten me up?" She didn't know all my little secrets and didn't realize that I fought a constant battle to keep my waist and belly from ballooning out.

"Oh, you're too skinny. You can afford to gain some weight."

"I'm not going to walk away hungry, anyway," I said. I tried the chicken. "Man, this is good chicken. Did you make it?"

She rolled her eyes. "No. The maid fixed everything here. But Mom's taught me how to cook. Some."

She watched me reach for another piece and smiled. "You do like it, don't you?"

I had so much chicken in my mouth that I couldn't speak. When we finished the lunch I felt full and lazy, too stuffed to move. I lay back on the blanket and moaned.

Penny looked at me in feigned disgust. "Up! On your feet! We'll have to walk some of that down or you'll never be able to eat enough of Mom's dinner."

I staggered to my feet and groaned. "How can you even mention another meal to me so soon?"

She shoved me toward the water. "Come on, you lazy lout. Walk. Walk!"

I slogged along for a while and soon began to feel better. We went west, past the wing commander's mansion. We strolled along and enjoyed the sight of the big imposing house. We stopped and kissed again and held each other tightly.

"It's good to be back, Penny. I missed you."

"Me too."

We picked up the pace on the return walk, then gathered our gear and headed for the car. Penny drove me to the barracks.

"I'll see you at six," she called as she drove away.

* * *

I went up to my room and laid out my best civvies, my tropical-weight, navy blazer outfit with my conservative dark red tie. I took a quick shower and got dressed. Then I walked down the hall to see Sergeant Wallace. He had seemed a little down today and I thought maybe I could cheer him up. He'd gotten a letter from home, from an older brother, and acted gloomy, more melancholy than usual.

"Seems like everybody back home is getting older or getting sick and dying," he said. He thumped one fist into the other hand, absently and rhythmically. "You know? It almost makes you wish they wouldn't write if they don't have something better to talk about than doctors and funerals."

"Yeah, Sarge. I know. Some days I wish I hadn't read my mail at all."

He sighed heavily and sat down on his footlocker.

I went back to my room and poured each of us a drink of whisky. I figured he could use a little cheering up and I needed something to bolster me for the long evening at the Crawford home.

I took the drinks back down the hall and handed one to him. "Here you go, Sarge. Doctor's orders. Two aspirins and one big whiskey. The aspirins are optional. Here's looking at you."

Wallace managed to work up a smile. "Now that's my kind of doctor, Dr. Ted. You've got to have a date or something, dressed up that nice with a coat and tie. What's the occasion?"

I told him about the dinner at the colonel's house, me meeting the family and all. He laughed and his eyes took on a faraway look. "I miss the pretty girls, you know, but I sure don't miss being grilled by their families. It's been a long time, but I can still remember the nervous conversation and wishing I didn't sweat so bad. Better you than me, boy, better you than me."

"Come on, Sarge. No fair gloating. Anyway, I'll get through it all right. How bad can it be?"

Old Wallace started laughing again so I changed the subject, wanting to talk about something I felt better about. "You know, I'm trying to get Penny to consider staying at Wheelus for a while. What I'd like to happen is for her to stay here long enough for me to go home with my release from active duty. Maybe even a letter of acceptance to a good engineering school."

Wallace looked at me for a moment, shaking his head. "That sounds like a tall order to me. Didn't you say she's already been accepted at some girl's college?"

I took a good swallow of my drink. Sergeant Wallace didn't miss much and he had me on the defensive. "Uh, yeah. She has. I'm still not sure she'll stay. Says she's thinking about it. To tell you the truth, I might be having a case of wishful thinking." Conversation slowed down. I finished my drink and wandered down the hall.

I felt resigned to the dinner at Penny's house, but still dreaded an evening with the colonel on his own ground. I wondered how you spent a social evening with a man who could put you in prison unless you did his dirty work for him. I'd have to pussyfoot my way through the whole visit. I knew I couldn't afford any show of anger or rebellion.

- 19 -

I had about decided to catch the base bus over to Penny's house, but I remembered my last ride on the rickety old shuttle. The old busses weren't air-conditioned or even well ventilated and I'd be a mass of sweat and stringy hair after the long slow ride to the Crawford's house. I got lucky. I found Richard hanging out in the dayroom, and he said he needed to go to the Base Exchange and could drop me off at Penny's house, so I wouldn't have to take the bus in my coat and tie. As we approached, I could see Colonel Crawford's quarters weren't as grand as the Base Commander's, but they were a lot bigger and neater looking than the old war-surplus trailers for the enlisted families who lived down the road. He had a great view of the Mediterranean, and the whole layout looked way up scale from anywhere I had ever lived. It looked nice—nice enough to make me feel nervous and out of place.

Richard stopped his evil-looking '52 Mercury coupe in the street to let me out.

I stepped back and gave his car the once-over as I put my coat on. "Thanks for the ride, man. And, hey, the lowering job you got is cool. Makes the car look mean, like a North Carolina moonshine runner. Tough."

Richard beamed, pleased with the car and himself. He looked at me and chuckled. "Now, Ted, you better remember your manners when you get in there, you hear? And be nice to the colonel's ladies." He chirped the back wheels as he pulled away and I felt a hint of butterflies in my stomach. *Thanks, Richard*, I thought.

I checked my watch. It showed just past six and I walked up the drive and knocked on the front door. I waited for a moment as my nerves stretched tighter over the whole prospect of spending a long, tense evening with Penny's family. Finally, the door popped open and a girl with a dark suntan and dark brown hair looked at me intently for a moment. Her resemblance to Penny startled me. She was a very pretty girl, a younger copy of my Penny.

"Oh, you must be Ted," She said, and called back over her shoulder. "Penny, your boy's here." She turned back to me. "I'm Sandra, Penny's sister, but everybody calls me Sandy." I guessed her age at about ten, maybe twelve. She had the poise and self-assurance of an older girl. A gentleman's daughter if I ever saw one, a member of the privileged class. Having subjected me to a thorough examination, she asked me in.

"Penny's running late as usual. Mom said I should entertain you until she comes down." She cocked her head to one side. "Do you like tropical fish? My dad has some neat ones in his aquarium. It's right over here. Let me turn on the lights. See?"

"Wow. That's pretty," I said. "Look at all those colors. I don't know anything about tropical fish. What's this one?" I pointed to a tetra, the only thing I recognized in the tank.

"Oh," she said quickly, "That one's a tetra. A tetragonopterus characidae."

I wondered if she was pulling my leg. "You know, I'd never remember that technical name," I said. "Things like that don't stick with me too well."

Sandy smiled, or maybe she smirked. "Oh, that's all right. If you can remember tetra, everybody will know what you mean. Funny. That was Cynthia's favorite, too. She liked bright things." She looked at me with a sidelong glance and turned a little red.

I didn't want to leave her hanging there looking embarrassed, so I said, "Oh. That sounds kind of like Cynthia. What little I know. Penny was talking about her the other day." Sandy's eyes widened and I said, "I guess she didn't have a very happy life, did she?"

She stared at the floor. "I guess not. But she always seemed happy when she and I were together. Not sad or unhappy at all. I guess I shouldn't be talking about her. Mom never mentions her name anymore. Like she was never here...."

My heart went out to her. Such heavy words from a young girl. "Well, Penny talks about her. What about your dad?"

"Oh, Daddy does, too, sometimes. He asks me to remember her in my prayers. He said he always does and it makes him feel better. And I feel better, too."

"Your dad's a smart man. I guess I'd do the same as you. I come from a family with lots of kids, but I've never had to face losing anybody. It makes me sad just to think about it."

Sandy took my hand. "You'd be all right. What you have to do is remember the good times you had together, the happy times. You can't sit around and feel sorry for yourself. Death comes... to everybody, Daddy says. So you have to learn how to deal with it. But it is hard."

Sandy had upset my sense of balance. Here I stood with a twelve-year-old girl trying to comfort me and educate me about loss, sorrow and death. I felt years behind her, and maybe I was.

Then she gave me a big, beautiful smile, and turned to the fish tank again. I played it straight as she identified and named most of the fish in the tank. "I'm impressed, Sandy. That's a lot of fish. Which one's your favorite?"

She pointed to the most brightly colored fish in the aquarium. "This one. I've named her Cynthia. But don't tell my mother. She'd be pretty upset, I think."

I had to agree with her, about the fish and her mom, too. It was the prettiest one of all. We talked for a few minutes about my music and her school, and Penny finally came into the room. She wore a full-length black skirt with a loose, soft-looking cream-colored blouse that emphasized her dark coloring and her dark brown eyes. A golden necklace and earrings made her look more grown-up than I'd ever seen her. I couldn't take my eyes off her. I reached out and took her by the hands. "Umm, you look gorgeous."

She gave me a big smile and squeezed my hands. "And you look nice too. I don't think I've ever seen you in a coat and tie." Sandy excused herself and slipped out quietly. Penny walked across the room to a set of French doors. "Come on. Let me show you the patio. It's the prettiest part of the house, and the coolest this time of day. We'll be much more comfortable there."

We went outside and the transformation stunned me. They had furnished their patio in wicker and bamboo, with straw matting and a small, gurgling fountain in the middle. A large red, white and green awning above the fountain sheltered part of the patio.

Their gorgeous view of the sea impressed me most of all. "Oh, man. This is like a Florida beach resort. What a nice breeze. What a great view!"

Penny took my hand. "This is the best time of the whole day. The family lives out here during the evening. My dad designed the whole thing and had it built. He'd seen something like the fountain and awnings in Morocco."

"It reminds me of the souk downtown, remember? Especially the awnings."

"It gets too hot out here during the day," she said. "Thank heavens we have an air conditioner unit in the game room. We hide in there when the heat gets to be too much, but then you don't want to leave the room. You can't win."

I opened the buttons on my blazer. "We sure don't have any air conditioning equipment to worry about at the squadron. You ought to spend a day in my barracks or try marching on the flightline during a nice Saturday base parade."

"No, thank you. Daddy's told me how the troops drop like flies out there, standing at attention. He says he's never seen a bandsman keel over from the heat. Why's that?"

I glanced behind me then whispered to her, "It's a secret, you see, but I'll tell it to you if you swear not to divulge this to anyone."

She rolled her eyes and groaned.

"The answer is simple. We *don't* stand at attention. Our knees are bent and we move, constantly, never standing still. We flex and sway. We rock on our heels and wiggle our toes in our shoes. That way, we keep our circulation going and our breathing rate up, and we naturally stay cooler and more alert."

"I heard all that, young man," Penny's father said as he and her mother entered the patio. "But you never see the Air Police collapsing on the flightline, either. I don't know who invented that technique, probably the Roman Legions, but it works."

I stood up. "Good evening, Colonel. Thanks for having me over, sir."

Penny made the formal introductions and I shook hands with both parents. I felt a sense of relief to see the colonel wearing civilian clothing. "Welcome, Ted. I've heard a lot about you," he said.

I cringed and hoped it didn't show. Remembering our real relationship in his investigation of the club—and the defiantly aggressive behavior of my high school days— made me feel out of place, like some kind of ruffian. I struggled on. "Thank you, sir. I hope it was all favorable comment."

The colonel served us drinks with lots of ice and not much whisky, and mild screwdrivers for the ladies. Mrs. Crawford picked up the conversation and asked me about the band.

I told them about the TDY tours we did, our interactions and personnel trades with the bands in France and Germany, and the trip the band had made to Italy. "We always have lots of volunteers to go from Tripoli up to France and Germany, but not many of their people want to come down here to Wheelus."

The colonel laughed. "Imagine that! Amazing."

The Crawfords had visited the old Roman ruins and the Italian restorations at Leptis Magna here in Libya, out near Homs. Mrs. Crawford led the discussion, and I thought about Sergeant Wallace's remarks about trying not to sweat. They'd seen the big amphitheatre and all the statues and were impressed with the ancient city.

I loosened up a little and listened to their descriptions closely. "I haven't been out there yet, but you've convinced me. I'd really like to see it all."

"It's best to go in the winter months if you can," Penny's mother said. "It's so awfully hot out there in mid-summer. I'm told even the Arabs won't go out there then. If you're going, try January or February."

"That sounds like good advice. You know, the next time we take our rock-and-roll group out to the tank base at Homs we ought to stay over and visit the ruins the next day," I said.

Penny huffed with undisguised impatience. "No, no. Let me take you. I have the car and I'd make a great guide because I've been there before. Please?"

That would work for me. With her involved, I knew I'd find the time to go and finally see the old seaport.

Her mother fiddled with her watch. "John, it's time for dinner. Let's get organized and go on in."

She turned to me. "Actually, Ted, we're using the game room for dinner because of the air conditioning."

"That sounds good to me, Mrs. Crawford."

* * *

We gathered around the table and Sandy and Penny sat on either side of me. Dinner was roast beef left slightly rare, with peas and whipped potatoes and small green salads all served by their maid. The colonel poured wine. Its mellow smoothness surprised me a little. "Now that's a good wine," I said. "What is it?"

The colonel smiled, looking pleased. "It's one of the great secrets of Italy, actually. I think the only Chianti they export is the raw red wine that comes in the straw covered bottles you see back in the states. You know, the kind you stick a candle in, when you've drunk it all. This is a Chianti classico from Tuscany. It's made to strict standards, using the Sangiovese grape exclusively. It's one of their excellent table wines, up to the standards of the better known and much more expensive French table wines."

He sounded slightly smug, a little like a lecturer, but I agreed with him. It had a rich, warm taste, smooth and a little bit tangy. I was surprised to find an air policeman with his knowledge and a taste for good wine—but I decided against saying that.

The food tasted good, even though I felt too tense to eat a big meal. I tried to stay loose and relaxed and things were getting better, but now and then I'd catch Penny's mother studying me. If I looked straight at her she'd smile, but I felt as though she was observing me, judging me. She made me uncomfortable, but I couldn't do much about that. I tried to enjoy the meal and Penny's sophisticated appearance. Sandy helped, trying to guide the conversation a little more in my direction, asking me questions about the band and our trips.

* * *

After dinner, the colonel and I walked out to the patio, while the ladies stayed behind to clean up. Since the maid owned the kitchen, it seemed an obvious maneuver to allow the colonel to talk with me in private.

I had dreaded this part of the evening the most. The real relationship between the colonel and me made the idea of a light conversation between us seem like a farce. We took our wine glasses with us and the colonel brought the bottle along. I hoped we could just relax and not try to keep up a façade, but Colonel Crawford seemed to be genuinely interested in my plans.

"Penny says you're thinking about engineering. Any school you're looking at in particular?"

"Yes, sir. There's Georgia Tech and a few other schools. Some of my high school classmates and guys from my neighborhood go to the Virginia Polytechnic Institute. But I'm not sure. I need to take a closer look."

We sat down in the wicker chairs. "Where's your home? You can save a lot of tuition money where you're an in-state student, you know."

"Yes sir. I'll be eligible for in-state tuition in Georgia since my folks moved there last year. In-state status at Georgia Tech could save me thousands of dollars over four years."

The colonel crossed his legs and looked at me as if I'd surprised him with my response. "Nothing wrong with Georgia Tech's engineering program from what I hear."

"No sir, but the thing is, they have tight admission standards. If I decide on Tech, I'll be required to do a battery of prep courses. But that's a good idea anyway. I know I'm rusty on all the basics, especially math and science, and I wouldn't want to jump back in without some kind of a warm-up."

"You should be doing some of that right now, using the University of Maryland program here on base. They surely offer some basic math and science courses you could use." The colonel put his chin in his hand. "Or maybe your off-base work doesn't leave you time for that sort of thing."

Fact was, my frequent TDYs with the band made that a difficult undertaking. I decided saying so would sound a little too much like an excuse, so I cut to the core of the problem. "Colonel, without the money I can take home from my off-base work, the question of college is kind of like moot, don't you think?"

His eyebrows climbed and we stared at each other for a moment. He cleared his throat. "Well. We have graduate engineers right here on base. You may want to sit down with some of them and talk. Most people like to talk about what they do. Don't let the time slip up on you, though. It takes a while to be accepted to any school. There's a lot of paper work that has to go back and forth."

He got up and poured us some of the remaining wine and sat back down He straightened his tie and took on a more serious expression. "How's it going with Lieutenant Gibson? Are you making any progress?"

"Yes, sir. You were right about the lieutenant. He pulls thoughts and memories out of me—things I didn't even know I knew."

"Hmmm. The situation with the club is still fluid, still in the planning stages. We may have to limit your activities to reflect your actual training in the Air Force. Fortunately, for us at least, the experience and certifications you got in Texas as an auxiliary Air Policeman will cover most of the legal requirements for your involvement in the investigation."

I thought his comments sounded a lot like C.Y.A. or maybe cover the boss, but decided I'd better leave that unsaid. The colonel sipped his wine. "You'll continue to work with Lieutenant Gibson for now, but you're the one who knows the most about how they work down there so I'll want you to take part in the planning when we get into that, particularly in the timing and the risk-taking. For better or for worse, you're too valuable a resource to ignore."

A resource? I shifted in my chair. "Sir, when will we start? Waiting is the hard part for me. Waiting and not knowing is killing me."

"We all have to wait, Miller. But don't make light of your contributions. This whole thing is going to come out better as a result of what you can tell us about Club Tripoli."

"I believe that, Colonel. Yet my situation gives me the jitters. Going to the club and pretending nothing's changed. I swear. I get the feeling people are staring at me, like they know somehow. I'm getting spooked. But I can't afford to act strange or unnatural. How much longer do I have to play this role?"

"I can't give you a hard number on that. But I expect to have everything in place within the month. Maybe sooner. It depends on the wing commander and on the Libyans. And it depends on when I decide we're ready to move." He leaned back again from the edge of his chair, clearing his throat. "Try to stay loose. Take it one day at a time and we'll get it all in order. Remember, getting jumpy won't help. Be cool, as they say in the band squadron. We're nearly there."

"Yes sir. But I need a better idea of what's expected of me. I don't have combat experience like you and a lot of your men. Can you trust me to do okay in a fight? Will there be a fight? Will I be in it? Will—?"

"Easy, Miller. Take it easy. You can leave those questions up to me and my officers and NCOs. Like you said, we are experienced and we'll make the proper judgments when the time comes."

I wanted him to tell me straight out how much they expected me to do. I wanted to insist on answers. Now, not two weeks or a month from now. But just then Penny and her mother came back out to the patio and sat down. Just as well. She probably saved me from overstepping the bounds, and I couldn't afford to alienate the colonel or anybody else.

The conversation returned to lighter topics, and Penny and I got ready to leave.

Her family followed us out onto the driveway and I thanked them for a pleasant evening and a great meal. They thanked me for coming and Penny seemed too quiet. Maybe she just felt relieved to have the evening behind us. I know I did.

As I shook hands with her dad I said, "Colonel, I'd like to continue our talk. In the part about planning and risk-taking, I'm sure I can help. Later in the week?"

The colonel hesitated. "Yes. Good. You'll hear from me."

"Thank you, sir."

Penny gave me a questioning look and I wondered how in the world I could ever explain my situation to her. Somehow, my life became more and more complicated. Maybe the colonel would save me the trouble of trying to explain. I'd become a man on a tightrope. I wanted a chance to climb down and live like a normal human being again. Yet that certainly seemed unlikely just then.

- 20 -

We walked out to the car. Penny started the engine and turned toward the main part of the base. Brilliant stars and a nearly full moon made using the headlights seem unnecessary. She drove slowly and as we approached the beach pavilion she pulled into the parking area. The windows were down and a good breeze blew through the car. We sat for a moment, enjoying the beautiful night.

Penny turned to me with a soft laugh. "Now that didn't really hurt much, did it?"

"No, I guess not. I survived the evening, didn't I? Your mother seemed tense, though. She examined me all evening. I felt kind of like something on a laboratory table, or a microscope slide."

"Oh, she wasn't that bad. Mom's always slow to warm up to people. She'll come around. I think they like you."

I sighed. "Well anyway, that's behind me now. But your dad did quiz me pretty good. And he does have some pretty strong feelings about Club Tripoli, I can tell you."

Penny's impatience began to show again. "I've already told you how he feels about that. He thinks you shouldn't even go near the place. He's talked about putting it off limits."

Crap! "If he feels that strongly about the place, then yeah, why not put it off limits? Let him put his money where his mouth is."

She looked down and hesitated. "Well, he planned to do that when we first got here, but the pilots and senior officers all complained. They went to the wing commander and cried on his shoulder until Dad had to back down. But, now he's thinking of making the place off limits to the enlisted ranks."

"Are you serious? Penny, most airmen can't even afford a drink there. How much sense does that make?"

She glowered at me. "Maybe he wants to protect some enlisted men from their own stupidity. Ever think of that?"

Oof! I'd been hit below the belt. The conversation wasn't going my way at all and I decided it needed a shift in direction. I moved over, put my arm around her, and held her hands. She tilted her face up and we kissed for a few long moments. She moved away from me and started to get out of the car. "Come on. Let's walk up the beach. I know you want to get into the heavy necking, but you won't want to stop. You never want to stop and you think I'm not being fair."

What could I say to that? This was the same girl who'd been so passionate in the apartment above La Loggia. I didn't understand women, but sometimes I could tell when to back off. "Okay," I said. "You're right. I guess a walk is what we need right now."

We took off our shoes and strolled on the beach with the gentle waves lapping at our ankles. I sensed Penny wanted to have a serious talk, but I wasn't ready yet. I put my arm around her shoulders and stared up at the moon and sky and talked about trivial details of my life in the squadron. She patiently waited me out, then shifted the conversation to her going to school back in the States. "I still don't know what I'm going to major in when I get there. It all seems so unnecessary somehow. But I'll think of something. Besides, you can always change your major, later."

Her uncertainty about how to plan her life was clear enough, but I thought she avoided her real problems. She didn't even know why she wanted to go to college. We'd covered this ground earlier, and she sounded just as vague about her goals as she had before.

"What do you want to get out of college? Why are you going?" I asked, interrupting her monologue.

She threw up her hands. "There you go again, the great analyzer! You have to have everything figured out and nailed down tight, don't you? Listen, I don't take college as seriously as you do. It's a thing you do. Can't you see that?"

I tried to interrupt, but she was wound pretty tight, and she talked right over me. "You go to school to get away from home, to get some freedom, to have a chance to think and breathe, instead of being told what you can do and when, and where you can do it, and why. It's a place to meet people who haven't been military brats all their lives and a place to go to parties and raise hell and have fun."

It seemed like I'd hit a nerve. "I can understand that. I know I sound like a scratched record, but I've been at the bottom of the heap for the last three years and it's taught me lessons that you won't get in a classroom, or as a colonel's daughter."

Her eyes narrowed. "Huh. Like you know something about being a colonel's daughter."

"I know you, don't I? Listen, I don't intend to go through the rest of my life as part of the rank and file. I won't do that. So we see this from different points of view."

She folded her arms, and looked at me like a patient mother. "Oh, Ted. You're way too sensitive about being an airman. It's the officer thing all over again, isn't it? That has nothing to do with the real you."

I looked down at her. "You still don't understand that, do you? You always want to oversimplify the facts." I didn't seem to be able to get around the fixed, idealized view she had of military life. She'd grown up as an officer's daughter and that protective elitist atmosphere had distorted her vision, impaired her ability to recognize the real world when she saw it.

We walked in silence for a few minutes. "I hear you saying you want to live a new, freer life, but that doesn't mean we can't go ahead together, does it?"

She didn't answer. We watched the luminescence of the foam on the light surf. I knew it was time to back off, but there were questions that needed asking, even if I didn't like the answers. "Look, why not stay here for another year while you decide? It would take the pressure off and give you a chance to get to know me better. By then, I'd be ready to return to the States and get my discharge. Maybe we could go to the same school."

She stopped and looked at the waves for a moment and turned back to me. "I *said* I'd think about it, Ted. I mentioned to Mom this afternoon about maybe staying here for a year, like Patricia did, but she didn't want to hear about it. Her mind is made up. It doesn't matter what *I* think or want. To hear her tell it, I'm going to college this fall. End of conversation."

I stepped back a pace. "I see. Maybe that's why she seemed so tense and hostile toward me. She really was looking daggers."

Penny started walking up the beach again. "Anyway, that's

where we are now. She won't soften up right away, but she'll talk to Dad about it and I can handle him." She laughed. "We'll see. I can tell him you've proposed to me."

"What?" Proposed! I didn't know how to respond to that, but it didn't sound funny, not to me. "Penny, please. Don't be making jokes. My life is hard enough right now. I love you and I need you. And I need to know how you feel and what you think our future ought to be."

Penny put up her hands in mock surrender. "Ease up a little, Ted. I'm not sure what I want to do, not yet. Can't you please wait for an answer? Let me think about it. But I love you. I do."

I took her in my arms and we held each other. She loved me. That might have to be enough for now. It was getting late, so we walked back to the car.

We sat for a moment and looked out over the moonlit sea. Penny turned to me and put her arms around me. She squeezed me and kissed me hard on the mouth. Now what? I didn't understand women at all.

She started the car and turned toward the barracks. I studied her as we drove along the beach. "Do I have any chance with you the way things are?" I immediately regretted my impatience.

She gave me a weary smile.

I turned away from her. "Sorry. I don't have to have an answer tonight. But please, think about it. I need to know what to expect. How to plan."

We drove across the base in silence and she avoided looking at me. When we got to the barracks, I got out of the car and left her with a simple good night, and began my slow climb of the stairs to the third floor.

I sat on the edge of my bunk, staring at the high windows along the opposite wall, trying to sort out my problems. Maybe the best thing for me to do, right now, is to break up with her, to just walk away. Forget the true love story and start trying to arrange my life. I needed to work on acceptance to an engineering school and getting myself on track for an early-out from the Air Force if I could. Anyway, about all I could offer Penny Crawford was a Spartan, serious regimen of work and study on a limited budget. I tried to picture her in my Mom's role, scrimping and saving, keeping a household together when there wasn't enough money for necessities, let alone luxuries. The colonel's daughter? Not the sort of life she'd been raised to enjoy. Not by a long shot.

And yet. I'd never known a girl like Penny. She could do anything she decided to do. She was determined, hardheaded and smart. A winner. And I'd never felt as close to anyone in my life. I couldn't simply walk away from her. There had to be some way to make it work, to make it all come together.

I felt dog-tired, but as late as it was I couldn't get to sleep. I got my big towel and clogs and started down the hall. Sometimes a long hot shower helped. On my way down the hall, the unexpected sound of conversation startled me. As I approached Sergeant Wallace's room, the voice became more distinct. I peeked in his door and he was sitting there on his bunk, looking straight at the wall behind his footlocker, drink in hand, carrying on a quiet conversation with somebody I couldn't see. It was spooky even though the guys had forewarned me. Wallace was talking to his buddies again, the ones who didn't come home from the Pacific. They were there for him, sitting on his footlocker, even if no one else could see them.

Without making a sound, I went on down the hall and showered until the hot water ran out. Maybe my problems weren't so big after all. Some guys were a lot worse off than me.

I still couldn't sleep, feeling like a mule in a sugar cane mill, plodding along in my endless circular rut. When sleep finally came, it brought vague dreams of struggle and exhaustion, and more nightmares about my family.

- 21 -

As I struggled to come awake I found myself preoccupied with Penny. I could see her face before me and felt waves of guilt pressing in on me. We'd met just a few months ago, but I felt closer to her now than anyone, closer to her than my family or any of my friends, past or present. Last night, she'd told me again that she loved me and sounded like she meant it, but somehow that left me confused and dangling. What did I need? She trusted me to be straight with her, to tell her the truth, but she didn't comprehend the huge number of lies and half-truths she'd listened to. It had been going on for a long time.

I lay there worrying, trying to ignore my guilt. Surely a simple attempt could be made to do what was right. Made and stuck to. She needed to know the truth about Club Tripoli and my commitment to Scarlatti. The last time we'd discussed my involvement with the club, I'd deliberately misled her, lied to her about going straight, getting clear of the place and away from Scarlatti. She thought I believed in her, agreed with her. Actually, I believed in the money I made and sent home. Plain and simple.

My work for Scarlatti had continued, on the bandstand and off. The run to Homs every week when I moved the money for him and exchanged the briefcases went like clockwork. Money or goods involving who knew what illegal, immoral operations. I'd agreed to accept his offer of more money on the bandstand, and now he pressured me to make a greater commitment to the real part of my job, the disreputable part. I couldn't face Penny with that. I couldn't look her in the eyes and tell her the truth. She didn't know about my deal with the colonel, and what would she think of me if she did? I didn't have the guts to try to explain that to her. My life had gotten so complicated I didn't know where to turn. Getting straightened out had to be a priority. To cut loose from Scarlatti and his organization. That was critical.

Yes. The need was as simple as that, wasn't it? I wished the solution, the answer was that easy, but along with my obligations to Scarlatti, I now had a deal with Colonel Crawford to spy on the operations at Club Tripoli. So what could I do? Get loose and clean up my act? God! One thing at a time. Quit first and then explain it to the colonel. Or try.

The first step would be to arrange a meeting with Scarlatti, somewhere away from his club if possible. He had an aura of command there in Club Tripoli that made opposition to his wishes almost impossible. At his club he dominated every conversation. If he'd agree to meet me at one of the sidewalk cafes, or here on base, it would be much easier. I needed to tell him I couldn't work for him and the organization anymore. The words seemed easy enough, but not easy to say to Scarlatti.

At last I forced myself out of bed, into uniform and down to the orderly room to check the duty roster for the day. Individual Practice; Concert Band Rehearsal at 1000 hours; Section Rehearsals at 1300; Retreat at 1700. A pretty full day.

During rehearsal, my mind wandered away from the music and back to my problems, back to Penny and Club Tripoli. I missed chords and lost strict meter. During one number, the Old Man stopped the band and looked at me. "Miller, we'd certainly appreciate it if you joined us here. If it's not too much trouble."

My worries were already bad enough without the Old Man getting on my case, so I tried to finish the rehearsal without messing up any more. The discipline I'd learned working in music for the last ten years allowed me to pull it off without additional screw-ups. We finished the rehearsal after we worked on another two pieces. The Old Man stepped down off the podium and stared at me for a long moment. He looked away and walked down the long hall to the orderly room. He'd let me off light and I appreciated it.

At lunch, I called Scarlatti's office, remembering the commitment I'd made to Colonel Crawford with a twinge of guilt and a sense of mixed loyalties. Scarlatti was out and not expected back until 2:30. Another try after the section rehearsal caught him in the office. "Sir, can we meet at the Airmen's Club one night this week?" I asked.

"That's out of the question," he growled. "I can give you a few minutes before we begin playing on Tuesday night."

Arrogant ass. I started to hang up on him but thought better of it.

"I'm too tied up Tuesday afternoon. I'll be hard pressed to make the first set on time. How about later, after we finish?"

His attitude grew cooler. "I can give you a few minutes after our last set. A very few." He hung up. It was a rough start, but at least we'd set a time.

After my phone call to Scarlatti, uneasiness set in. My brief flush of victory at arranging the meeting on my own terms faded in a fog of gloom. Yeah, the meeting was set up, but I couldn't stop worrying about the outcome. Persuading him to listen to me in the past hadn't been one of my great successes. And this time I had to convince him that my needs were more important than his. My expectations for success weren't high, but there wasn't much to lose. For once, he might see it my way. Maybe.

But I still had the other layer of complication to worry about. Watching the activities for Colonel Crawford. How could I hope to get loose from Scarlatti and satisfy the colonel's needs at the same time? Maybe I could get enough information for the Provost's investigation and still get away from the place. The hole I'd dug for myself required me to divide my obedience, my service, between Scarlatti and Crawford, but I wanted to satisfy my own needs first. I staggered along with a four hundred pound backpack. The whole situation made me feel like an idiot, like a helpless puppet jerking around at the end of everybody else's strings. How could I go on doing this and hope to get anywhere, much less regain my self-respect?

* * *

Lieutenant Gibson had scheduled another meeting a few minutes from now for his daily brain-picking session, this time at my barracks. I crossed the street to the snack bar before the meeting and felt my dread slow my steps. Captain Myers had a table so I got my coffee and my jelly-filled doughnut and walked over. "Mind if I join you, Captain Myers?"

"Sit down." He watched me fidget with my coffee cup and spoon and said, "You seem kind of keyed up today, Miller. Restless, on edge. Is everything going all right?"

"Well, Captain. I've been talking to Colonel Crawford and I've spent a lot of time with Lieutenant Gibson. They've been trying to extract information out of me that I didn't even know I had. It's effective, it works, but it's kind of like pulling teeth. Mine. There's another meeting with the lieutenant in a few minutes and it's not much fun."

"I wouldn't think so. Talking about Club Tripoli, right? I get the feeling, from what's being said around the coffee pot, that the problems at that club may be coming to a head. Maybe you won't have to stay involved down there much longer."

I stared at him. "Captain Myers—that would be about the best news I could hear. I've been talking to Mr. Mackey and Sergeant Andrews again about my support from them. I told Colonel Crawford about that—how I needed to find a way to make an orderly exit from the club and its activities. It sounds like the colonel wants me to keep watching. But Penny Crawford does not approve my working in a whorehouse."

He watched me for a moment. "Miller, I'm going to level with you. This is off the record, a hundred percent, like you didn't hear it from me, got it?"

What? "Yes, sir, Captain Myers. Off the record."

He put his hands flat on the table. "All right, then. Everything I hear about that miserable club tells me things are starting to move. All the studies and investigations and opinions are lined up in a row and they all point in the same direction. I mean, minds are made up. Decisions are being finalized. What that means for you is your role in the investigation is about over."

"Captain, I hear you. But when? When can I get out of there?"

"I can't tell you that. I don't mean I won't. I just don't know. But hear me. Don't take any chances or run any risks. It won't affect the outcome because their minds are already made up. Son—keep your head down and your mouth shut. A few more days and you'll be out of this mess."

I heaved a big sigh and felt a little better.

Myers stirred his coffee. "Maybe the colonel thinks he needs your view of the place right now, but my guess is he's just hedging his bets. Do yourself a favor, Miller. Look out for number one. Get out of that snake pit as quick as you can."

I stared at him for a moment. "Thanks, Captain. I appreciate that, but it's not going to be easy. Things have gotten way too complicated."

I finished my coffee and donut and we talked about the weather—hot and hotter. Then I got up and headed for my meeting.

Events were moving like a train picking up speed. I didn't want to be on board. She rocked and swayed like an old car on a bad piece of track, but I didn't know how to get off. It scared the hell out of me.

- 22 -

On Tuesday evening, the downtown bus took me to Castle Square, arriving about twenty minutes before my first set. I walked down to Café Venezia, went into the bar and ordered a glass of wine. After putting Scarlatti off about an early meeting, it wouldn't do to just show up ahead of time. I killed a few minutes reading the latest copy of the *Sunday Ghibli* and trying to make out the headlines on the local paper, *La Corriere di Tripoli*. The Italian idioms were worse than usual and defied translation.

Charlie told me the problem was connected to the inclusion of Sicilian forms by the local writers. Their form of the language differed from the northern dialects on which the "official" form of the national language was based. His professor, Signor Bertone, referred to Northern Italian as the pure form, but then he was a northern Italian. Our local journalists didn't always share this opinion.

I gave up the struggle. I finished my glass of wine, got up and walked down to the club, arriving with just enough time to set up on the bandstand.

We kicked off a fast paced set of tunes featuring several long ad-lib solos on the guitar. Scarlatti pushed me harder and harder, calling "Tempo! Tempo!" about every eight bars. Then he began throwing in alternate chords for me to follow. Some were so dissonant I couldn't tell what they were. I wasn't helped much by the bass man. He missed more chords than I did. After about four or five of these difficult pieces Scarlatti laughed and slowed down for a couple of numbers.

At the first break, he said, "Perhaps I have taught you too well, my boy. There are not many guitar players in Tripoli who could handle what I just put you through. You are getting good, Ted, but don't get overconfident." As he frequently did on breaks, Scarlatti moved to an out of the way table with one of his managers for what appeared to be a grueling business discussion. I pitied the guy, but for me it meant a long break—a welcome one.

We worked through the next couple of sets without the hostile feeling I'd sensed through the opener. Scarlatti called for a balance of songs and moods, and more of the tunes the quartet were accustomed to doing. Near the end of the last set, we did a couple of numbers that he had adapted from traditional Italian music.

The last set ended with a sanitized version of my recently completed "Driving down the Highway." I played and sang a folk-music version with some clean walking-bass runs and talking lyrics, key of C, 4/4 time.

> I was driving down a black-top two-lane highway,
> Past worn-out farms and towns without a name;
> I could see the used up homesteads on the byway
> And the swayback barns a-leaning in the rain.
>
> Old out-buildings peeling paint, a-reeling in the wind,
> Worn-out tired and ready, just to lay down on the ground.
> Time to give it up because they knew they'd never win,
> And couldn't even hope that they'd survive another round.

A couple of Guthrie fans in the audience thought it was all right and told me so.

* * *

After the last set, we'd often go to the late-night bar in the back. That night, we went to Scarlatti's office at the top of the tower at the western corner of the building. He explained to me that the tower had been built in the mid-thirties with the original hotel building. When he'd taken over the business from his father a few years ago, in the late 40s, he'd had the tower modified and updated as his personal office suite. The view was a panorama including the sweep of the well-lighted avenues around the harbor and the broad boulevards running beyond the old city of Tarablus.

I'd never been there before, and the views and the fine old furnishings of his office suite impressed me. He even had a small elevator tucked into a corner, blending into the rich paneling of the wall. The display of wealth and good taste intimidated me, and I guessed that was Scarlatti's intention.

Scarlatti let me look around for a few moments. He seemed

pleased with himself and proud of his private suite. He gestured toward a pair of chairs and got down to business. "So, Ted, what is so urgent that you need a meeting with me?"

I hesitated and sat down. "Mr. Scarlatti, there's a problem I need to discuss with you."

He folded his arms. "I thought your situation here was going well. Perhaps the money is not adequate for your college plans, or perhaps the hours you're putting in here are too long? We can work with such problems and make necessary adjustments."

I took a deep breath. This had to be done right on the first try. I chose my words with care and precision. "I wish it was something simple and easy to handle, but my problem is more complicated."

He uncrossed his arms and dropped his hands on the arms of his chair, making a muffled thump. "Come, come Mr. Miller. Speak your mind."

"Sir, I've requested an early-out from the Air Force and an early return to the States. That's the only way for me to get into school for the fall semester. In the meantime, I'm going to ask a girl to marry me and go back home with me." Scarlatti had no way to know I stretched the truth to strengthen my argument, and I didn't feel obligated to be honest with him.

He watched me with a patient look and a hint of a smile, but said nothing.

"What this means is I have to quit working for you now if I'm going to get this all pulled together. There's a lot to do and not much time."

Scarlatti's face darkened and the veins on his forehead grew prominent as he rose from his chair. "That is not good. That will not work for me."

"Mr. Scarlatti—"

"I depend on you to keep doing the things you're doing." He leaned over me with a tautly strained smile. "Get out of the Air Force, yes! But stay in Tripoli and work for me. I can offer you so much more here. I guarantee you. You'll make better money here with me than if you go back to the States."

"Mr. Scarlatti, I can't—"

"Listen to me!" He paused and settled himself on the corner of a table. His voice dropped back to his deep, bass rumble as he continued. "What I tell you now is a long story, an old story. My family came to Tripoli in 1912, when Italy recovered the Roman provinces in Africa from the Turks. My grandfather settled here with my father and his brothers. They worked hard and prospered. I grew up in North Africa. It is my home. And now, after the war and the misjudgments of Il Duce, we are ruled by the Arabs!"

He was silent for a moment and then he sighed. "But still we prosper. Through our hard work and our ingenuity, my brothers and I maintain our power and our strength. Someday, before too long, you will see. We will regain control of our own destiny here in Africa. My organization in Tripoli will grow and become stronger with the right people in power."

He rose from the desk and stared out through the big windows overlooking the harbor. Scarlatti's eyes were bright and his voice had risen in pitch as he began pacing up and down, breathing harder. "You will stay! And you, too, will benefit from these changes. I can promise you and the others who stay with me, power and wealth, position and prestige. Look out there. This city will be our city, its people will be our people. It is our destiny to prevail!"

I understood what he offered and was more frightened of him now than ever. With such ambitions and his frenzied belief in the destiny of himself and his people, he couldn't be bothered with considering the needs and wants of people like Dave or me. We were his pawns. We existed to serve his vision and neither of us was of real importance to him. In this dawning clarity I knew the time had come—somehow, I had to break away.

I steeled my nerves. "Mr. Scarlatti, I respect your vision. I admire your abilities and your power. But that's your world and your dream. Not mine." I had to make him understand! "My future lies in America with my own family, my world and my people. I can't stay here and pretend to be someone I'm not. I'd disappoint you more by staying than by leaving. It will take a clean break from Club Tripoli, and it won't get any easier. I need to do it now, tonight!"

I heard the increasing agitation in my voice and couldn't quite conquer it. "Don't misunderstand me, sir. I'm grateful for everything you've done for me, for all you've taught me, but I'm not part of your family or your traditions and history. I never can be."

Scarlatti stopped pacing and faced me, his stance rigid and tense. His eyes bored into me as his eyelids drooped slightly and his expression changed to a dark, hooded glare. "I didn't ask you about your gratitude, Mr. Miller," he said in a tight, strained voice. "And I don't care to hear about your world and your people. You owe me, not them. I have given you much and you remain in my debt. I will not free you from that debt, and you will continue to serve me. You will stay until I release you from your obligations. There is no leaving!"

His ranting speech stunned me. The son of a bitch thought he owned me. Me! Did he think I was one of his whores? "I am not—"

"Silenzio! You will do as I say, or you will come to understand the power, the true discipline of my organization. No one quits Club Tripoli. You will be here at the business office on Saturday for your courier run to Homs. Is that clear?"

It was clear, all right. The most ruthless son of a bitch I'd ever known had threatened me, screamed at me. I'd had enough of Scarlatti and his club. After all of the anguish and misgivings, the endless lying to Penny, I felt free. My elation faded with an inaudible thump as the hard truth soaked through my thick skull. First, I had to figure out how to survive quitting his employment. How to stay alive in the process. I took a deep breath.

I tried to look as if he'd shamed me, twisting my hands together, hanging my head and staring at the carpet. With a huge sigh I looked Scarlatti straight in the eye.

"All right, then. I'll see you on Saturday afternoon, sir."

He stared at me for a long moment, shaking his head. He cleared his throat and said, "Good. I will see you on Saturday."

* * *

I let myself out of the office and headed for the back door of Club Tripoli. Escape was my only thought. I cut through the late-night bar where Maria worked and she stopped me. "Ted, I need to talk."

I glanced around. Everything seemed calm. No phones ringing. But I felt scared and jumpy and Maria stood between the door and me. "It's good to see you, Maria, but I'm in a big, big hurry. I've got to meet a guy back on base and I'm late already."

She glanced over her shoulder and shivered. "No. Wait. This is important I think."

"What? What is it Maria?"

"It's about Mr. Walker, Dave. You helped me, so I help you. I hear Mr. Scarlatti talking to a guard, saying bad things about Dave.

Something like 'He not cheat me again!' He is in trouble?"

Now what? "Maria, I don't think so, but I'm not sure."

"Then you tell him what I say, okay? Tell him be careful."

Scarlatti had already spooked me and now this. I didn't know what to tell her. "Listen, Maria, I've got to run, but I'll talk to you tomorrow night, okay?" And I bolted for the back door.

I wanted to get back to Wheelus, back to safety and protection. There wasn't much time to sort this all out, but maybe my ploy with Scarlatti about the run to Homs had bought me a few days to figure out a way to escape from the club and his grasp. Or maybe not. I trotted down to Castle Square and grabbed a cab.

As we drove through the empty streets toward the base, my thoughts returned to the talks I'd had with the colonel. He'd told me about the ingrained evil of Scarlatti and the ruthless determination of the people at Club Tripoli. He warned me of the serious risks of getting in too deep. He'd talked about how difficult it might be to crawl back up to the daylight again. "Risks to your spiritual and physical health" were the words he'd used. I remembered being amused by the old-fashioned sound of his warning. Yet now my amusement had been replaced by fear. I couldn't remember anything funny.

- 23 -

That night I tossed and turned. I crawled out of bed and walked the halls. I climbed the steep stairs to the flat roof of the barracks, sat there and watched the bright stars and worried. The temperature dropped until I became aware of the chill. I shivered a little, and couldn't decide if my problems or the forming dew made me tremble there on the roof. After a while, I could see the earliest faint light of dawn out over the runways to the east. I got up and paced the roof of the barracks from end to end. The only sensible idea I had was to get some help. Trying to stonewall Scarlatti and his whole organization on my own made for lousy odds. The only other answer—go to the Old Man and the first sergeant—made good sense. I decided to see Sergeant Andrews first thing in the morning. As soon as the decision was made I went back to bed and fell sound asleep.

On Wednesday morning I killed time waiting in the day room until the first sergeant came in. Scarlatti's threat and the deadline coming up in four days worried me as I turned the situation over and over in my mind. Dave needed to know what Maria had said and how my problems had ballooned, but I couldn't find him in the barracks. The CQ told me he'd signed out on a three-day pass.

I filled my coffee mug in the dayroom and checked on the first sergeant again. I could smell his pipe smoke as I stepped into the orderly room. He looked up from studying his morning report and saw me standing in his doorway. The tension and worry must have shown on my face. He took his pipe out of his mouth and raised his eyebrows.

"Sergeant Andrews, I need to talk," I said. "My situation's going bad. I need help."

He got up, walked to the door and called to the CQ in the outer office, "Hold calls and visitors, understood?"

"Yes, First Sergeant."

Sergeant Andrews went back behind his desk and told me to sit down. He looked me over, shaking his head. "You don't look too good, Miller. Like life's going downhill, maybe. Better bring me up to speed."

I sat down and took a deep breath. "First Sergeant." I cleared my throat and tried again. "Sergeant, last night at Club Tripoli, I tried to quit my job. Mr. Scarlatti refused to let me do that. He said if I didn't continue to cooperate and obey his orders, I'd be punished or worse. I tried to reason with him, but he only became more insistent. He acted crazy. He's intends to have me killed. I'm sure of that. And I'm scared. What can I do now, Sergeant?"

The first sergeant stared at me for a moment. "Miller, I knew you were involved down there. Like you were in pretty deep. But what you're talking about now sounds out of proportion. What, exactly, are you up to?"

I hesitated.

"Come on, boy. Spit it out. I may not be able to help you very much, but I sure can't if I don't know what the situation is."

It was time to own up. "I've been making a run for him. A courier run to pick up and drop off, at the inn out by Homs on Saturdays."

"Drop off and pick up what?" he demanded.

"Money. From their operations at the remote site, Sergeant."

"That's pretty heavy activity, son. Drug money. Or more likely drugs and money. Has to be. You didn't have any qualms about that?"

"I don't know anything about any drugs. They didn't say and I didn't ask."

"So, you're telling me you didn't know. How much does it pay?"

I shifted in my chair and tried to look him in the eye. "Two hundred dollars a run."

"Well, then, you did know. You didn't have to ask."

He had me. "I guess I knew it was drug money, or gambling, Sarge."

Sergeant Andrews' scowl deepened. "So how long have you been doing this? A week? A month?"

I thought back and realized that I'd been driving the road to Homs for over four months. Maybe twenty runs, about four thousand dollars. Over three years' pay for an airman second class.

I sighed. "For about four months, Sergeant. I've made about four thousand dollars."

He pushed his chair back from his desk, looked at me with a slightly opened mouth and leaned forward. "You sit there and tell me that you've put your life on the line for a few thousand dollars. For the price of a new car? Is that what you think you're worth?"

He made me sound like an idiot and that pissed me off. "Sergeant, I never thought of it as risking my life for the money. Still . . . there was one time when I had to run a roadblock. Some Arabs set it up on the road back to Tripoli. They were armed. Automatic weapons."

He sat there and stared at me. "I think I've got a clear enough picture of what you've been doing. It does sounds like Scarlatti's ready to kill you. Think about it. In his terms you've betrayed his trust."

"Sergeant Andrews, that's what I've tried to tell you—"

"He paid you several years' salary in a few months and thinks that's enough to buy your loyalty. I'd guess he sees you as setting a bad example for the other men, especially the other Americans working for him. Now he's probably worried about a breakdown in discipline. I agree. You've got a problem, Miller."

"At least we agree on that much, Sergeant."

He fussed with his pipe for a moment and relit. Then he picked up his phone and dialed. After a moment, he said, "Sir. Sergeant Andrews here. The problem with Airman Miller. The situation just broke wide open. Yes. He's here in my office now. Can you come over, or should we come over there? Yes, sir."

"The Old Man is coming over in a minute," he said as he hung up the phone. "Let's get a cup of coffee while we wait. I have a fresh pot on the table there, so we won't have to drink that crap you have in the dayroom. Do you take it black?"

He poured two mugs of coffee, and he was right. It was a lot better than the coffee that simmered all day in the big urn in the dayroom. We made a halfhearted try at some conversation, but I felt tense and irritable. The small talk faded out quickly as we waited for the Old Man.

Mr. Mackey knocked and walked in with a mug in his hand. He went straight to the coffee pot behind Sergeant Andrews' desk. He looked at me as he dragged up a chair.

"Sit down, Miller. I think we'll be here for a while."

He turned to the first sergeant with an impatient wave of his hand. "Okay, Ed, let me have it. Where do we stand?"

Sergeant Andrews gave the Old Man a quick briefing, explaining what I'd told him. "He says he sends about a thousand a month home by American Express."

The Old Man cocked his head to one side. "That's even more than I thought. I guess Scarlatti thinks Ted, here, has been bought and paid for. And now he wants out." He turned to me. "Miller, that's what I meant when I told you that Scarlatti wasn't simply being nice to a talented young guitar player. I should have been more blunt."

This prolonged lecture wore me down. Enough. I tried to look serious and resolute, but didn't quite make it. "Sir, sometimes you see and hear only as much as you want to. Sending home all that money dazzled me. I didn't try to think it all through."

Mr. Mackey ran his hand over his head, where his hair used to be. "As you know, Walker and Rodrigo are into this mess at least as deep as you, maybe worse. I've been talking to the Judge Advocate General's Office about their involvement and yours. It turns out the Special Investigations people, OSI, have had that club under surveillance for about a year—but then you already know something about that."

He reached for his coffee, took a sip and put the cup down. "I've worked with the JAG and Colonel Crawford to try to protect you men, to find some way to get you out of this mess with your hides intact. The colonel tells me you've been cooperative, but there may be more coming. It's not pretty. You'll not only have to provide information as you're doing now, but you'll give testimony when the time comes."

That didn't sound good, not to me. "Wait a minute, sir. Are we talking about the deal I've already made or are you changing the rules as we go?"

Mr. Mackey's expression turned hard and cold. "You guys aren't in a very strong dealing position, Miller, but the Provost's office needs the kind of inside knowledge you have. They intend to bring down Scarlatti and his family, and they'll look to you men to help and cooperate. You've done that and that's good. And we know how to proceed from here."

He pulled off his glasses, rubbed his eyes and turned to the first sergeant. "Some days being a Commanding Officer is a lot less fun than other days." He took a deep breath and let it out, "Ed, unless you've got another suggestion, I think the next step is to talk to Colonel Crawford."

The first sergeant nodded emphatically. "Yes, sir. I don't recommend trying to handle this at the squadron level. We need to see what kind of break is possible for all our men, but we can't risk tripping up a major investigation in the process."

Mr. Mackey faced me. "You see where it stands and where we're headed? I trust Colonel Crawford to do the right thing. If he said you have a deal then you're already set, but there may be more to come and you don't have any options on this, Miller. I have to make this phone call."

"Yes, sir." Guilt and regret weighed me down. I'd lost control of my life. They wouldn't give me much of a choice, but maybe if I worked with them and tried hard it would help pull me out of this jam. I needed all the help available.

Mr. Mackey reached for the first sergeant's phone.

- 24 -

The Old Man dialed the number for Colonel Crawford's office and we could all hear Sergeant Wilson's abrasive response. I fidgeted as Sergeant Wilson put him through to the colonel.

"Yes, Colonel Crawford, this is Mr. Mackey. I'm afraid we have problems. It's the Club Tripoli investigation and the involvement of my airmen down there."

I was just a bug on the screen. They discussed me as if I weren't there.

"The situation's about to break wide open. Airman Miller has tried to resign from his job in Scarlatti's organization and the band there and it's not going too well."

Mr. Mackey's understatement irritated me and I fought the urge to grab the phone out of hand his and talk directly to the colonel. But I knew I had to sit there and stay calm. It wasn't easy.

"He's been told he's not allowed to quit and Scarlatti has made some heavy threats if he even tries. Yes, sir. Yes, sir. Should we come over to your office now? Oh. All right, we'll sit tight. Thank you, Colonel."

He hung up the handset and turned to the first sergeant and me.

"The colonel's on his way over here. He wants to continue to maintain a low profile and keep Miller out of the Provost's Office as much as possible. It'll be a few minutes."

The speed with which everything moved made me feel helpless. And yet, I knew things could get worse instead of better. *What about Dave?* "Mr. Mackey, where does Dave Walker fit into this plan? Will there be any provision made for him to clear himself?"

He stared at me with a stiff, unreadable expression. "Maybe, maybe not. It'll depend on where he stands, on what he thinks or wants. Maybe the colonel knows more about that than I do. We'll see when he gets here."

Sergeant Andrews suggested we take a break. I walked down the hall to the latrine. The colonel's visit made me uneasy. My situation seemed pretty clear, but I wanted to hedge my bets if I could. Using an open, honest approach with the first sergeant and the Old Man might keep them in my corner—maybe.

I ran into Charlie as I came back up the hall.

"What's up, Ted?"

For once in my life, I thought ahead and kept my mouth shut. "Not much," I said. "I've got to make a couple of phone calls. Have you seen Dave today? I need to talk to him. It's important."

He shook his head. "Haven't seen him since yesterday, but I haven't been looking for him."

"If you do see him, tell him I need to talk to him—right away."

"Okay, man. I'll tell him," he said.

I stopped by my room for a moment and hustled on back to the Orderly Room. We sat around with cups of fresh coffee, not saying much until the colonel arrived. He slipped through the door from the CQ's office.

"At ease, men." He closed the door and sat down. "All right. Help me out, Mack. What's the situation?"

Mr. Mackey gave him a quick review of my problems with Scarlatti. My feelings of being invisible had returned while they discussed me, and when the colonel turned to me, I wished I really could just disappear. "Now, Airman Miller. What can you add to what your CO has already told me? I thought we'd agreed that you'd sit tight at the club. What happened?"

"Sir, Scarlatti was pushing me hard, trying to promote me to managing all of his drug distributions in the city. I'd finally hit my limit. I just couldn't go that far and I said so. From that point things went downhill in a hurry. My problems are coming to a head, mine and Dave Walker's. I feel like I beat the odds just by being here this morning. I didn't expect to get out of there alive last night, much less make it back to the base."

I paused and took a deep breath. "Looking back on last night's disaster, I should have tried to see Mr. Mackey or you right away. I'm convinced Scarlatti intends to kill me, and probably Dave too. He's a complete maniac! That's why I asked to see the first sergeant this morning. Sir, I'm scared."

He stared at me for a long moment. "Oh. So now you're scared."

"Yes, sir."

He turned to Mr. Mackey and Sergeant Andrews. "This is

awkward, men. I need to go off the record for a couple of minutes with Miller. Can you excuse us, please?"

Andrews's eyebrows shot up but the Old Man kept a straight face. They stood and walked out.

The colonel faced me, with a red face and knotted jaws. "How much does Penny know about this? Have you told her about your criminal activity, or have you lied to her as I suspect you have? Well?"

I had to struggle to go on. What could I say? There weren't any answers. "Colonel, I know that an apology is inadequate for what I've done and—"

"You got that much figured out right!"

I stammered. "I—I can't apologize, but try to believe me about what's happening now. I went to Scarlatti last night to quit. I did it for Penny and me."

"Well aren't you generous. Did it for her. I'll bet. I ought to pull you out of that chair and teach you a lesson you won't forget."

"Colonel—"

"Don't 'Colonel' me, boy. You're not fit to kiss the hem of her skirt and airmen like you don't have the right to associate with decent people."

The colonel was struggling for control. He stood and walked to the door. He stopped, cursed under his breath and slammed his fist against his palm. Finally he turned and came back to stand over my chair.

"Sir. What can I do? How can I make it better, or make it up to you and Penny? What are my options, Colonel? Tell me what to do."

He sat down behind the desk, breathing slowly and steadily. "I'll have to stick to business and you'll have to handle your own problems. So will Penny. She's nearly grown and out on her own, and I can't make her decisions for her and I can't order her around. I can't tell her how to think."

I blurted out, "Like Cynthia, you mean."

The colonel got up and stood towering over me. "What did you say?" he demanded.

"Sir, I'm sorry. That just slipped out. I meant no disrespect. Please accept my—"

"Boy, you are way out of bounds. You think you can mess with one of my daughters and wag your insolent tongue about the other one? Have you no respect at all for anything?" He turned his back to me. He took a deep breath. "Boy, you listen to me. I've been tolerant about Penny dating an enlisted man. Perhaps too lenient. Maybe partly because of Cynthia. A man can't just keep on making the same mistakes. But you hear me good. You tell her the truth about yourself and that miserable club, or so help me God, I'll take off my insignia and make you wish you'd never met her. Clear?"

"Yes, sir, Colonel. That's clear."

He turned and stared at me for a moment, then walked over and stared out the window for a minute or two, hands behind his back, rocking on heel and toe. When he turned around he took another deep breath and his face gradually relaxed. "All right then. I can't tell you much more than I already have, but we're close to taking strong action against Scarlatti and his people."

"Where do I fit in, sir?"

The colonel folded his arms. "I'm going to use you, Miller. We're preparing an informal presentation of evidence and findings about Club Tripoli and their activities for the Prince and the King's Council of Ministers. What you've seen there will make a useful contribution for that presentation."

He looked at me with narrowed eyes. He had my complete attention. "Yes, sir," I said. "I want to help."

"Then get your thoughts organized. I'm convinced that anything you can say about the exploitation and dissolute abuse of the women and children who work at the club would impress them. That can make for a good, effective talk. Straight from the horse's mouth. Use the same plain language you would use with me. Think about it. The rules of evidence for a presentation like this are not as strict as those of our military or civil courts. They're more or less what the King's council says they are, so don't worry about 'hearsay' or 'prejudicial language.' Be direct and clear."

"Yes sir. I understand."

He sat on the edge of the desk. "I'm going to work with you on this. Review it with you and make sure you don't screw it up, understand?"

"Yes sir!"

"If things go right with the council—if they allow us to gain any degree of control of the club—I may want to use you to help plan future actions. I think you'll get your chance to help, Miller."

I didn't understand where he was going with all this, but I decided not to ask. Not now, anyway.

He stood. "All right. Now, go out and ask your CO and top sergeant to come back in. You're restricted to the base until you hear otherwise. I may want to move you to the stockade for protective custody depending on developments. Move it!"

I stood and saluted the colonel. "Yes, sir."

He looked at me sternly, then returned my salute. "And for your own good, keep your eyes peeled even here on base. Stay alert . . . . Dismissed."

I'd wanted to ask the colonel about Dave Walker, but couldn't figure any way to do that. He had all but kicked me out of the office. I'd need to check back with the Old Man or Sergeant Andrews. But for my first move, I had to find Dave, and somehow explain the situation and what his options were. I had to convince him to come in and talk to the first sergeant or the Old Man, to ask for help.

* * *

The colonel's orders left me free to go to the mess hall, the Oasis, the theatre, and maybe even see Penny. I couldn't go downtown, but Tripoli had lost its charm for me in the last day or so. I reported to Sergeant Andrews, turned in my class-A pass and asked him if he had any additional restrictions in mind.

"No. The colonel said he told you to watch your back. If I were you, I'd keep my head down. This is a pretty open base so don't get careless or over-confident."

His expression softened and his voice lost some of its stern tone. "And Ted, I'd find an opportunity to talk to your girlfriend real soon. If I know anything about women, you're in for a rough time with her. You'd better start mending your fences, if you can. But I know I'm wishing you better luck than you're going to have."

His softening demeanor seemed to offer my best opportunity to try to get him on Dave's side if I could. "First Sergeant, what about Dave Walker?"

"Miller, neither Walker nor Rodrigo has talked to me or anyone else up to this point. Right now, they're a part of the problem and they're going to be treated as offenders."

A small chill ran across my scalp and down my back. Thanking him for the advice about Penny, I walked across the street to the Oasis, picked up the phone and started to dial Penny's number. I stopped. Could I find the nerve to explain what was going on?

Somehow I'd have to make a beginning, to face the problem, but my confidence had deserted me. With a coffee in front of me, I sat at one of the tables, stewed and worried, played with the cup and spoon and fidgeted. After at least three coffees, I managed to force myself to walk back over to the phone booth.

Her mother answered. "Hello, Mrs. Crawford. This is Ted. May I speak to Penny, please?"

"You missed her," she said. "She's gone to meet someone for lunch."

"Oh. Please tell her I called." She said she would.

I walked back to the dayroom to see if Dave had shown up. What with Scarlatti's threats and Maria's warning, my worries were getting out of hand.

Richard sat on a couch in the dayroom. He held a grubby coffee mug and flipped through a copy of *The Stars and Stripes*. I asked him about Dave. He shrugged. "No. Haven't seen him all day."

"Well, I need to talk to him."

"CQ said he'd be back tomorrow," Richard said. "Try Club Tripoli. Give them a call there."

"Yeah. I'll do that. Thanks."

As I left, Richard called out, "By the way, the Pres was looking for you a while ago, but I told him you weren't around. You know he's cool and all, but sometimes he's kind of spooky."

Now what? "The Pres. When was that? Just now?"

"No, maybe an hour ago."

I went back to my room and sat on my bunk, trying to decide how to tell Penny what was going on, how to explain the whole big mess to her. I had to let her know, but I was afraid of losing her in the process. There was no way to make the situation sound any better than it was. I was afraid she'd boot me right out of her life. Anyway, maybe that was what I deserved.

Now Rodrigo was looking for me. Since the time he'd kicked the teeth out of that drunken lieutenant, I'd avoided him as much as possible.

A chill swept over me making the skin over my temples tighten and tingle. Dave and I had both fallen from grace with Scarlatti, and Rodrigo was one of his hard, mean toughs. My sense of security from being on base crumbled. Uneasiness seized my guts and my imagination ran wild. But maybe I was jumping out of my skin about nothing.

I'd turned spooky, afraid of shadows, afraid of the dark, like a little boy. Yet the feeling of no longer being safe wouldn't go away. Well, maybe being uneasy was the right thing, right now. Hadn't the colonel and the first sergeant both told me to be on my guard? They had said to be alert, watch my back and keep my head down?

I sat on my bunk, wanting a smoke. Then there were footsteps coming down the hall. The sound stopped outside my door and I waited. Nothing. Opening my wall locker, I reached for my bayonet.

- 25 -

My hand tightened around the rough, knurled handle of the bayonet. Whoever was out there rapped on the door. "Are you there, Ted?"

The voice sounded muffled, strange somehow. Who was it?

"There's a call for you on the dayroom phone."

Was it Don, the CQ runner? "Yeah, I'm here," I said, cracking the door. "Who's calling?"

There stood Don, not the Pres, standing in the hall with a note in one hand and a bag of popcorn in the other. I started breathing again. He looked at the note and read, "Penny Crawford? Yeah, that's what she said."

I walked back to the dayroom with Don and picked up the phone. "This is Ted."

"Hi. It's me. What's up?"

As much as I had wanted to hear Penny's voice, now the words just wouldn't come. With a great effort I said, "I really need to see you. Can you come by here and pick me up?"

"What is it? You sound weird."

"Look, we need to talk. Can you come by? Please?"

Tenseness crept into her voice. "Yes. All right. I'll be there in a few minutes. Meet me at the back stairs."

I sat on the lower landing of the barracks stairway in the relative coolness of the shade, trying to decide what I was going to say to her. When Penny pulled into the back parking lot, I got up, walked over to the car and climbed in beside her. She took my hands in hers and looked me over.

"What is it Ted? You sounded so worried. What's wrong?"

She kissed me and held me tight for a moment or two. I pulled away. "Oh Penny, I don't know how to start. I still love you, I do, but things are closing in on me. I need to tell you what's been going on."

Her eyes widened, but she crossed her hands in her lap, leaned back and waited, uneasy yet giving me her full attention.

I began telling her the story, the full, shabby history of my involvement downtown. The activities I'd seen, the drug drops, the shooting on the road to Homs, the beating at the club. The cruel treatment of the Arab kids working there, the harshness of the security guards. I didn't include every dirty little detail, but it wasn't necessary. She understood well enough.

She sat there in silence for a long minute. She started to speak. Her voice caught and she stopped and sat, staring through the windshield. Finally she said, "All this time. I thought you were avoiding the terrible things they do down there. I hoped and prayed you'd quit and get out. Instead, you've gotten in deeper and deeper. And now, what? Are you confessing to me? Are you asking me to forgive you? Oh, Ted—how could you do this? How could you lie to me, day after day, week after week?"

"But I didn't lie to you. I didn't tell you everything, but—"

Penny's eyes flashed and she threw her hands into the air. "You've lied to me! You made me believe you were doing the right thing and cleaning up your life. Now you tell me it's worse than I ever feared. You idiot!"

God help me. I could lose her. Think. Say something! How could I explain how miserable and ashamed I felt about lying to her, betraying her love?

"Please. Listen to me, Penny. This is the truth. I've quit the job. I'm out of that place. Please, trust me."

Penny just stared at me and shook her head. "Trust. That's a funny word for you to use. Do you have any idea how much it hurts to know I've been wrong about you? Oh, please, I can't stay here. I can't bear to look at you. I can't stand to hear your voice. Get out of the car now. Get out."

"Penny—"

"Get out!"

I got out, closed the door and stepped back. Penny backed the car around and stomped the gas, kicking up gravel as she sped out of the lot. The tires screeched as she turned the corner. She didn't look back.

* * *

I walked to the Airmen's Club and ordered a hamburger and fries. Then I sat there, just pushing the food around on my plate, sipping some Coke. I shoved the whole mess away from me, put some money on the table and left. I walked down to the beach, out beyond the pavilion and the housing area and down past the trailer park, all the way to the east end. I found a big piece of driftwood and dragged it into the meager shade of a pair of palms. I sat down and stared out over the water.

I'd done it now. Things were falling apart and I had to do something. But what? How? How could I have been that cocksure, to believe I'd just handle everything and everybody and have it all go my way? I thought I was so cool, but I was too dim-witted to know what was going on. Me, the smallest player on the field, and the most inept. They had played me as casually as you'd play a card in a hand of penny-ante poker. They'd used me. Used me for a fool. And here I was, the cool man, too dumb to find my butt with both hands. I'd lost my self-respect and the only girl I'd ever loved in the process. I sat there, stunned, feeling sick and weary. I yearned for life as it might have been or could have been. Ah, if only.

So how did it happen? One foolish step at a time. I got mixed up so deep working in a cathouse and fooling with drugs, working with the dealing and the money, the whole thing. More to the point—how could I get out of this deep, deep hole I'd dug for myself?

The temperature had dropped a little and the first hint of the evening sea breeze began to disturb the palms, rattling the fronds. If I squinted, my surroundings looked like the southern beaches of Virginia, and they reminded me of how I felt as a kid with the long days of another summer at the beach stretching out ahead of me. Those were carefree times. And now—now my dreams, my family standards, everything I'd been taught to believe in and uphold lay in a rotten pile at my feet, stinking to high heaven. Where could I start? How could I fix all the things I'd broken and thrown away?

Well, Dave still needed to be brought up to date. And I'd promised to make some notes for Colonel Crawford. If I worked for the Provost's Office on this presentation and did a half-decent job, something good might come out of my clumsy mistakes after all. One thing for sure—it was time to get up and get on with it. Dave had to be warned and maybe told about my agreement with the colonel.

Whoa. There didn't seem to be any way to do that unless I knew where he stood. If he decided to stay with the club and Scarlatti, then our friendship would surely have to end.

I rose from my piece of driftwood, shook myself and brushed off the sand. Walking back up the beach toward the sunset, I felt empty. Not very hungry, but there it was. Even when I felt so down, the world still intruded and nagged for attention.

I looked up from the sand. Someone walked toward me, silhouetted against the golden sky. I shaded my eyes with my hand and squinted. Maybe Dave. Or Rodrigo. As the distance between us narrowed, it looked more like a woman from the motion of the body, smaller and lighter. It was Penny's sister, Sandy. Unable to think of anything to say to her, I stood there in silence.

She walked up to me and stopped and stared. "Penny came home this afternoon all upset. She cried and cried. I asked her what was wrong and she wouldn't say. Just 'It's Ted.' And 'I can't talk about it.'" Her voice had an edge to it, tight and strained. "What happened, Ted? I thought you two were so special, and, you know, in love and all."

She looked so sad I felt terrible. "Sandy, I'm not sure I know, or understand what happened or what it meant. Or what's going to happen next. We had a big argument. About my job off base. And some other stuff. I don't know."

"Your job downtown? At the honky-tonk?"

"At the what?"

"That's what Mom calls it. That or the cathouse."

I felt my jaw drop. "Sandy, come on. It's just a job playing guitar in a band."

"Then why do Mom and Daddy argue with Penny so much about it? It can't be 'just a job' and have everybody upset all the time, can it?"

Here she was again. A twelve-year-old seeing right through me and getting to the core issue without hesitation or confusion. Just a simple, rational evaluation of the obvious.

I took a deep breath. "Yeah. It's not just a job. But it's complicated, and like I told Penny, I'm getting loose from the place. That's not as easy as it sounds, but I'm doing it. You'll see. Things will get better between Penny and me. It'll be okay. At least I hope it will."

Sandy looked up and tried to smile. "I hope so, too. She says she loves you—and I like you too."

My tension eased a little. "Thanks, Sandy. That makes me feel better. I need a friend right now. And I don't want to lose Penny over this mess."

She narrowed her eyes. "I hope not. But Mom is upset about all this. She can't wait to get Penny packed up and off to Atlanta. So I'm going to lose another sister. I mean, it'll be kind of like when Cynthia left. But not that bad. I think. Oh, I don't know. Why do they have to make things so complicated?"

I took her hand. "Sandy, one thing you can count on. More and more as you get older. Things will be too complicated, because most people don't know what they want, or if they do, they don't know how to make the good things happen. People make mistakes, then they pay for them. And everybody around them has to pay for them, too. It's just not as simple as loving your sisters and being happy. Things keep changing, and people keep screwing things up. Not a pretty story, is it?"

She cocked her head. "You make it sound like it's hopeless, Ted."

"No, no. Never hopeless. You just have to learn how to enjoy the good times and struggle through the bad parts. That's just the way life goes."

Sandy sighed with an air of great drama. "If you say so. But I hope Penny quits acting like some movie starlet. She came home and wouldn't talk to me, or Mom. She stormed off to her room and as far as I know, she's still there. Crying."

I stood there shaking my head. "I know. It's hard, hard to explain. Things are messed up between us. And bad for me. I'm in a jam."

"What have you done?"

"Well, it's the job. At the honky-tonk. Your dad and I have talked about this and he thinks I may be able to help him. I think he could explain it a lot better than me. I've been lying to Penny and—"

"That's what she said. Then she clammed up and locked herself in her room. I'll talk to Daddy."

As she started to leave I held onto her hand. "Tell Penny I love her." I turned and started to leave.

"Ted, you need to tell her that, yourself. Really." As Sandy walked on down the beach, I turned in the other direction, trying to marshal my courage to face the mess I'd made of things.

It had been a long, painful day and my spirits were all the way down. I walked back toward the barracks and my worries returned uninvited. I thought, *Maybe Dave's back from his three-day pass and I can persuade him to talk to the Old Man. He's got to do that.* I quickened my pace.

- 26 -

The streetlights were coming on by the time I got back to the barracks. A quick glance at the back lot showed Dave's Jeep parked in the glow of the floodlights. I hurried upstairs but didn't find him in the dayroom. The CQ, Sergeant Nelson, said Dave had signed back in from his three-day pass so I walked down the hall to his room. I knocked on his door, listened and knocked again. After a couple more tries, muttering and bumping noises told me he was in. Dave opened the door, blinked and rubbed his eyes.

"What? Is it morning already? I feel like I barely had any sleep. What's up?"

"Dave we've got to talk. I've been trying to chase you down for a couple of days now, but they said you were on a three-day pass."

"Yeah, I was. What's wrong? Is it something at the club?"

"It's Scarlatti."

Dave rummaged around on his table, located his cigarettes and Zippo, and got his first smoke going. I felt a strong, momentary twinge but didn't ask him for one. He puffed for a minute or two as he sat on the edge of his bunk while I waited in his chair. At last he looked awake enough to pay attention to me, and I tried again. "It's about Scarlatti. We had a talk after we got off the bandstand last night. I told him I needed to quit working for the club."

Dave's chin dropped and he stared at me. "Oh, man, you didn't—did you?"

"Yeah, I did. Dave, listen. You had to be there to believe him. He acted weird, crazy, almost out of control. He paced up and down, seethed and raved about the glories of the past and his family. He offered me wealth and power. Scarlatti is nuts. The guy's a lunatic."

"Yeah. Yeah, I've seen him like that, spooky and strange. Sometimes he's pretty hard to take."

"Scarlatti gave me an ultimatum for the run to Homs on Saturday. Said I'd learn about the power of his organization if I didn't show up for the run. He threatened me, the son of a bitch."

Dave was shaking his head, but I continued. "He said crazy stuff like 'You are in my debt and you must serve me,' as if he owned me, like he could treat me like one of his whores or something. The time had come. I decided to quit."

"You did what? What did he say?"

"Well, I didn't tell him outright. I promised to make the Saturday afternoon run to Homs. But I won't be there."

"Really. That's when they'll try to kill you. Don't you know that?"

"I figured my only hope was to get help from the Air Force. Protection. We're trying to arrange something here on base. It'll work out all right. It has to."

Dave shook his head again and muttered to himself.

"What about you, man?" I asked. "You've talked a lot about friction with Scarlatti for weeks. And Maria said she heard Scarlatti and the security guys talking about you, how Scarlatti had decided you weren't going to cheat him anymore or something."

Dave had that old stubborn look on his face, like he was pissed at the world. "Come on, man. What the hell can Maria know? Damn dumb whore."

"Maria doesn't always get her facts right but this sounded bad to me. Has your situation sunk that low? My feeling is that you may be running out of time, too. You'll have to make up your mind."

Dave shook his head and stared at the floor. "I don't know. It's not time to give up yet. And I think you're definitely asking for trouble."

"I'm working on it, I told you."

"I don't know, man. Who are you talking to?"

"The Old Man, the first sergeant. Colonel Crawford. Those guys have enough clout to do some good. Especially the colonel. He can make things happen."

"Yeah? Maybe so, but I think you've overestimated what the APs or the Air Force can do for you—or what they will do. I know for sure, you're underestimating Scarlatti's organization."

"How so?" I asked him.

"When you go up against those maniacs, they're thorough—and ruthless. If you don't show up on Saturday, they'll put the word out on you and it's over. Who knows? They may already have done that and you don't know it yet. Walking around good as dead." He paused for a long moment, studying the smoke from his cigarette. "Richard told me the Pres was looking for you. That's a bad sign. Said he asked about me too."

"What do you think I've tried to tell you, Dave?"

He raised his eyes. "Ted, the best way to handle this is for you and me to go down to the club tonight and make a big presence in the bar and maybe the dining room. You know, a happy, cheerful appearance, just like old times—like we're great team players."

He got up and began to pace the floor. "What do you think? Then on Saturday, you make the run and move the money, business as usual. One more time isn't going to matter much. You've—"

"Dave, you're kidding yourself. Scarlatti is getting ready to wipe us out. Both of us. You just don't want to face the facts."

He acted like I hadn't said a word. "Look, if you make that run, then you gain a whole week to figure out how to get loose, instead of a couple of days. In that length of time, you can try to work something out with the Air Force. Lean on your girlfriend's old man and get some protection or some kind of break. Maybe for both of us."

"Listen to me," I said, "you need to sit down with Sergeant Andrews or the Old Man and talk about this. I think they'll help if you if you ask them. Talk to them, man."

He looked at me with his eyes wide and his mouth open. "Ted, those guys can line me up for a trip to Fort Leavenworth without even trying hard. No sir, I won't volunteer to do any hard time. No way."

I could see him chewing his way to a bad decision. What more could I say? I thought about going downtown with him. I didn't have a class A pass anymore, but I didn't know how to tell Dave that. Still, we could wave to the APs on the way through the gate, and nobody would ever be the wiser. Security could be a lot tighter on Wheelus. But my real problem was fear. Fear of the club and of losing Penny. I thought about that, hesitated and looked up at Dave. "You have to understand. If I go back there again, I'm going to lose Penny completely. She's not going to forgive me for that."

He stopped his pacing and stared at me. "What are you talking about? Here you are, in danger of getting killed by these maniacs, and me too, probably, and you're sitting here talking about girls and true love. Ted, you are one dumb bastard." He sat down again, shaking his head and swearing at me under his breath.

I didn't know what else to say. I couldn't talk about my agreement with Colonel Crawford and the Old Man or convince him that the Air Force was willing to go up against Scarlatti's organization. Without exposing the colonel's investigation, there was no way to persuade him to talk to the first sergeant. If I ran my mouth and developments didn't go right I could end up totally on my own, with no help from anybody.

It came down, finally, to an appeal. I had to beg him to see it my way—on faith. "Dave, trust me on this. I can put together a deal here on base that will save our butts."

"Bull." He sucked on his cigarette and stared out the window. "Are you coming with me? Do you have a better plan?"

"Listen to me. Let me try my way first. That's my better plan. Can't you give me a day at least?"

He lit another Lucky. "Look, I've got to go downtown and defuse this mess," he said. "I can show up at the bar, party with the staff and the girls, and put on a show. But, what about your Homs run on Saturday? Could I do it for you?"

His eyes narrowed. "Yeah, maybe that'll work. I could say you're sick. I know the men who work out at Homs. That's the answer, the short-range answer. We still have to convince the Air Force that our lives are in danger and we're worth saving. But we'll have some time to work on it."

I'd run out of ideas. "I just don't like the idea of you going down there and trying to do a snow-job on Scarlatti. I've got a real bad feeling about it. If you go in there, you probably won't come out. Come on. This is only Wednesday night. We have a couple of days left. Let me try to make a deal."

Dave threw up his hands. "Man, you don't have a couple of days with Scarlatti. I know the crazy son of a bitch a lot better than you do. I'm going down there now and try to make peace. You stay here and see what the Air Force wants to do."

Dave began to dress. He reached into his wall locker, hesitated for a long moment and came up with his old nine-millimeter Walther P38, the one I'd sold him. He stared at the pistol in its big ugly black holster for a long moment. "Ted—I thought about taking this with me, but I'd never make it past the club guards with a gun under my coat. I know you're worried. Me too. You take this and hang onto it for a while. Use it if you need to. If you see the Pres around here, be ready. Put it in your locker or under your pillow, where you can get at it quick."

I accepted the offer. I wrapped the gun in a towel, carried it down the hall to my room and stashed it under some blankets in my locker. When I got back to Dave's room, he'd started out his door. "Don't, man," I said. "Don't do this."

He didn't even glance at me. I walked down the hall with him and out on the top landing of the stairs looking out over the parking lot.

"Good luck," I said. "You'll need it."

He gave me his big Irish grin and patted me on the shoulder. "See you, Ted."

As he trotted down the stairs, I remembered back to the day he'd met my plane, and wondered how we'd both gotten so far into this mess since then. At the edge of the pool of light from the floods, the dim outline of an old low-slung Citroen sedan loomed in the shadows beyond Dave's Jeep. It looked familiar and I had a premonition. The door of the Citroen opened.

"Dave! Look out!"

- 27 -

The harsh barking of a rapid-fired forty-five drowned out the sound of my voice. The engine of the Citroen roared and Sergeant Nelson came running down the hall.

"What going on out there?"

"Sarge, call the APs—and the medics! Hurry. Dave's been shot!"

I ran down the stairs and into the parking lot. My heart was pounding and I felt sick, sure of what I'd find. I couldn't see Dave so I ran straight to his Jeep. I looked around and heard moaning coming from behind it. Dave was struggling, trying to crawl. When I reached him, he rolled over.

"Ah. Man, it hurts. The Pres shot me. The bastard. Oh Jesus, Joseph and Mary. Ted, help me. Don't let me die here. Don't leave me. . . " There was blood on his slacks and blood pumping into his lap, a lot of it. He groaned.

"Hang on, Dave! I've got you. Help's on the way. Just hang on!" I held him while we waited for the medics.

"Oh, Jesus. I'm so cold. Don't let me die, man. Help me. Please."

I heard the sound of sirens getting closer. "You hear that, Dave? They're coming to take you to the hospital. You're going to be all right."

Dave stopped talking and his breathing slowed down. I shook him. "Hang on, damn you!" I couldn't think of any way to help him. I held him, but he got quiet and he just slipped away from me. He died there in my arms.

I stayed until the medics and the Air Police arrived. One of the medics knelt down and felt Dave for a pulse or a sign of breath. He shook his head.

"This one's dead," he called to the other medic. He turned back to me. "How about you? Were you hit?"

"No." I didn't have anything to say. I just looked at him.

One of the Air Policemen came over and looked down at us.

"Get up and stand back. We'll handle this."

I did as he told me. The other medic came over with a stretcher and they rolled Dave onto it. I dropped to my knees beside it, tears rolling down my cheeks, and the AP grabbed my collar. The medic intervened and said, "Whoa. Give him a minute. Let him say goodbye." That's the last time I ever saw Dave Walker.

The medics covered him with a blanket. "Easy, now," the first medic said as they lifted the stretcher to carry it to their ambulance. "All right." They carried him away. The ambulance slowly crunched over the gravel as it left the parking lot and turned toward the base hospital. Dave was gone.

Sergeant Nelson led me back up the stairs and I started shaking. *If those guys decide they want me, they'll come right in here and get me. Just like that*, I thought.

I wanted to call the colonel and tell him what was happening. Now I was scared. Not worried, but plain, skin crawling scared. How could those guys attack someone right here on the air base? Yet, they had.

They'd murdered Dave Walker less than fifty feet from the back door of our barracks. And I was next.

- 28 -

I sat down with Sergeant Nelson in the orderly room, shaking as I tried to explain to him what was going on. "Sergeant. Dave's dead. Rodrigo shot him in the belly. He's gone. They took him. Took him away. And I'm next."

Judging from the look on Nelson's face, that hadn't made much sense to him. "Look, Ted. You're too messed up to help me on this right now. Go to your room or go talk to Sergeant Wallace, but try to get calmed down while I make a couple of calls. I need to talk to the APs and get the Old Man or the first sergeant up to date on what's happened."

I felt useless and confused and tried again to explain how things were, but he told me to clear out. I got up and went down the hall to Sergeant Wallace's room.

Wallace took one look at me, opened his locker and poured me a drink of straight whiskey. "Here. Sit down and drink this, man. What in the world's going on around here? What were those gunshots?"

I sat down and sipped some of the whiskey "Sarge, I don't know how to explain this. It's complicated. A big mess."

He reached for his own drink. "And the gunshots?"

"It was Dave. Dave's been shot. Killed."

"What? Why? That doesn't make any sense."

"I know. That's what Nelson said. He's called the APs to ask for a guard for the barracks."

"They ought to send a whole team. At least till they figure out what's going on."

"Well, Nelson talked to them. Dave's been shot, Sarge. He died, and he's gone."

Wallace stared at me for a minute "Kid, Take it easy. I know you've lost a friend, but right now, you're not doing too well. Finish your drink and we'll go talk to Nelson and see if he needs any help."

We went down to the orderly room. Nelson was hanging up the phone. "The APs are sending a guy over here for guard duty. I asked if they could send two or three. He chewed me out and said, 'That's our decision.' Cocky bastard. How can you secure a three story building with one lousy guard?" He turned to me. "Ted, keep your eye on the door and let me know when the guard arrives. Bring him in here. I'll talk to Sergeant Wallace and get him up to speed. Anyway, the situation seems more stable now. I think they'll get this sorted out. I'm counting on it."

I went into the outer office and kept my eye on the hallway toward the street-side stairway to watch for the AP's arrival. The door swung open and he came marching down the hall. I waved him down as he was about to pass the orderly room. He looked me over, "Who are you and what are you doing here?"

"I'm Airman Miller," I answered. "Our CQ said you had a man coming over here. I was waiting here for him, for you."

The AP said, "OK, Miller. Let's get to the orderly room and not be standing around. I don't know what's happening here and neither do you. Move it."

I led him into the orderly room and introduced Sergeant Nelson. The AP looked around the office. "I'm Sergeant Taylor, Air Police. I have instructions to secure this area and make sure we don't have any intruders or outsiders in the barracks. What's the layout here? How many doors, how many ways in or out do you have here?"

"There's the end doors, Sergeant. At the street-side stairway and the other end with the stairs down to the parking lot. The only other door is at the central stairs for the building."

"We need to secure that central stairway," the AP said. "I want to isolate this floor. Can we keep that door padlocked?"

"Yeah," Nelson said. "It just leads down to the finance section and the support squadron on the other two floors. We can lock that one if that's what you want. Oh, yeah. There's a stairway to the roof but I don't think that's a threat, is it?"

Taylor grunted "No, but you get that central stairway secured. Then get back here. Do you have access to weapons? I want you on guard at the back door down to the parking lot, and I want you armed."

"We've got sidearms and carbines in the supply room," Nelson said. "Sergeant Wallace can equip me."

"Good," the AP said. "Get a forty-five and a couple of clips. I want you on that door or on patrol in this main hall. I'll take the orderly room and the door at this end. Now, what's the situation with the men? How many people are in the barracks and where are they? Well?"

This Taylor was coming on strong and Sergeant Nelson frowned. "Sergeant, most of the squadron are still out for the evening, but the barracks is calm enough right now."

"Okay. Now, get your weapons and check this floor. I've got to report our status to AP HQ. Then, check all the rooms and tell everyone you see to report to the day room."

He looked at me. "Airman, you go with Nelson. Four eyes are better than two. We don't know what's going on, so look sharp."

We followed Sergeant Wallace down to the supply room. "Okay, Nelson. Here's your forty-five with a web belt, holster and two clips, Load 'em up and sign here." He plopped a box of ammo on the counter, and Nelson filled his clips while Wallace scratched out the paper work. Wallace relocked the supply room and Nelson and I began checking the floor and all the rooms.

We found Don, Bernie, and a couple of others and sent them to the dayroom. They looked jumpy but pretended to watch TV. Sergeant Wallace had returned to his room. Leaving Don and the others in the dayroom, Nelson and I went back to the orderly room. Sergeant Taylor was getting off the phone and he asked, "Well?"

"There are a few men in the dayroom," Nelson answered.

"I'll talk to the men," the AP sergeant said. We went into the dayroom. He looked around. "Is this all?" he asked.

Nelson nodded. "I told you most of the guys are still out. The only other man on this floor who's not here is Tech Sergeant Wallace. He issued me this rig," he said indicating his web belt with a holstered forty-five and clips. "He's in his room now. Drinking. I guess he's upset."

The AP gave us a hard, tough look. "I'll talk to him later." He turned to the men in the dayroom. "Listen up. You men have the option of staying here, under guard, or staying in your rooms. But make up your mind what you want to do. No wandering around in the halls. Got it?"

Don said, "Screw this, man. I'm locking myself in for the night." The men glanced at each other and looked over their shoulders as they left the dayroom.

* * *

Sergeant Taylor had Nelson patrol the hall to pick up anybody returning to the barracks so he could relay the instructions to the latecomers. He kept me in the orderly room to act as a runner if he needed one. Our guard set up his post at the CQ's desk in the anteroom and I took the runner's desk up against the wall.

It had gotten late, nearly midnight, and the barracks was quiet. The AP looked bored. "Do you have a radio around here? I could use some music."

Music? Man, this guy knew how to relax. Maybe he'd seen a lot of murders in his job, but he didn't impress me. "What did they tell you was going on over here?" I asked. "Did they explain our situation to you?"

He leaned back in his desk chair. "I've been briefed. They said it was some kind of shooting disturbance. That's about all I know. I'm here because I'm on the OIC's shit-list. He told me to get my butt over to the band barracks for guard duty. So here I am."

I tried to tell him what was going on. "A man was killed here tonight—"

"Look, kid, you do your job and I'll do mine. Do you have a radio or not?"

"No, I don't have a radio. The first sergeant doesn't allow radios in the orderly room."

What a jerk. I dropped the conversation and dug around in the desk, found some typing paper and started to put my thoughts together about Club Tripoli. It didn't look like I'd get much sleep tonight. The situation made this a good time to organize the information the colonel had asked me to present at his meeting with the Libyans. My talk with Penny in the front seat of her car was a good enough beginning so I used that as an outline and got started with my narrative.

Had we talked only this afternoon? It seemed like a week ago. My mind began to wander back over the events of the day. It all seemed disconnected and blurred. A jangling, nervous unease washed over me, but beneath the pain, there was a numbness I couldn't shake. Dave dead. And Penny lost to me. I couldn't believe it was real.

I shook my head, tried to go back to my notes and not think about my last conversation with Dave. If I'd told him about the colonel's investigation and my agreement to provide evidence, Dave might be alive now. If only I hadn't been so miserably careful to cover my own butt.

Thinking about Dave and Penny, I could feel my eyes begin to fill with tears. *This wouldn't do, not at all.* To ease my pain and confusion I concentrated on the task. My thin pile of notes became a stack of paper. I covered everything in enough detail to give the facts, and my notes included some of the feel of it all. I emphasized the brutal abuse of the Arabic children, and the helpless girls and women.

I looked up from my stack of notes. The wall clock said it was nearly two. I glanced over at our guard, sergeant Taylor, and saw him sleeping upright in his chair. Whoa. This guy provided my only line of defense and I didn't want him asleep. I slid my chair back on the tile floor. The screech woke Taylor with a jerk. He snorted and checked his watch.

"It's going to be a long night," he said, looking around the office. "Do you have some coffee around here? I could sure use a cup or two."

"Yeah, coffee. I'll go down the hall and make up a fresh pot. I could use some myself."

I got the pot from the first sergeant's office and headed down the hall toward the laundry room to set up the coffee. Nelson was nowhere around, so I checked the couches in the dayroom. He wasn't there either. Now, what?

On the way down the hall, I stopped by my room. I thought about our Taylor, our sleeping beauty, snoring in his chair. He didn't inspire a lot of confidence and maybe I needed to cover my own butt.

I opened my wall locker and pulled Dave's P38 from under the blankets. With a full clip seated, I released the slide to load a round in the chamber, toggled the hammer down, flipped the safety on and stuck it in my waistband, pulling my sweatshirt down over it. Maybe that was being over-cautious, but I felt better, safer with the heavy pistol pressing against my belly. After I made the coffee, I went back to the orderly room. The overhead lights had been switched off.

The AP still sat at the CQ desk, slumping forward in the chair. Shaking my head, I rattled the coffee pot on the hotplate and kicked the desk. He didn't respond. A cold, tight feeling grabbed my guts. I tapped him on the shoulder. Nothing. Now I was spooked. I flipped the light on. Turning his chair around to face me, shock slammed through my entire body. His throat had been cut, all the way across. The front of his uniform was a mass of blood. There was blood all over the desk. Blood on the walls. Everywhere.

I felt paralyzed. After a moment that seemed like forever, I started to reach for the phone to call for help, then stopped and pulled my P38 out of my pants and flipped the safety off. That simple action calmed me some, and my confidence returned, but my hands were shaking. There was a round in the chamber. All I had to do was snap the trigger through its double-action mode on the first round.

I grabbed the phone handset with my left hand, laid it on the desk and began to dial the Air Police with a shaky finger. There was a sound from the hall, faint, indecipherable. Swallowing hard, I called out, "Sergeant Nelson, is that you?"

When the Pres stepped in the doorway, I almost passed out from fear. "Ted? What's going on, man? There's nobody around. Where's the CQ?"

He came ambling in as calm as you please. I could have shot him—should have—then and there. But I hesitated. He reached behind his back. I knew he was going for his weapon, but instead of pulling the trigger, I swung the P38 at his head, trying to put him down without killing him. He ducked but my gun hit him a glancing blow across the top of the head. He fell, rolled over and came up with a forty-five in his hand. The double click as he cocked the hammer forced me to act. We both fired at once. He missed but I didn't. While I thought about that, he fired again and hit the phone Black plastic splattered all over the desk and over my arms.

In panic, I leapt through the doorway and ran toward the street-side stairway. A loud boom and I felt a sudden sharp pain in my left arm. He'd hit me. I kept running, dropped to the floor, and the forty-five boomed again. I rolled out of the hall, into the shelter of the anteroom of the stairwell to the roof. Rodrigo breathed hard and grunted. He worked his way down the hall toward me. Should I roll out for a snap shot? A close range shootout against his forty-five scared me. I heard the clatter as his magazine ejected and the smooth click of a new clip being seated.

I had to do something, something that would give me an advantage. And it hit me. I pounded up the stairs to the roof. The

P38 in my hand was much more accurate than his forty-five. On the roof—with more distance between us—better accuracy gave me the advantage. It was my only idea. I ran with it.

I scrambled through the open hatch and rolled out onto the roof, clearing the hatchway as Rodrigo fired a wild round in my direction. My arm started to hurt really bad as I scuttled toward the far end of the building. The streetlights glowed behind the hatch so he'd be in silhouette when he came onto the roof, over a hundred feet away. I lay on the flat roof and held my weapon with both hands, ready to fire. It was an easy distance shot with the P38. A more difficult one for his forty-five.

Rodrigo's head showed for an instant. A quick look around and he ducked. He popped up again in a different position. His grunt said he'd spotted me. I tried to back away, but felt the edge of the roof.

This is it. I'll fire from right here. My only way out was to jump off the roof, and I decided I wasn't that scared of the son of a bitch.

Rodrigo leaped through the hatch and rolled out on the roof. He kept low and slithered toward me. I steadied my shaking hands and squeezed off a round. He grunted, rose up and fired four or five quick rounds. Gravel kicked up in my face and I yelped, more out of fear than pain.

He stopped. My yelp must have sounded like he'd hit me. I played possum and waited. My skin crawled and my arm throbbed. I heard his strained breath and heavy grunt as he struggled and rose to his feet. He staggered and stumbled toward me. I waited. Finally he was within about seventy feet. I came alive, aimed for the center of his chest and squeezed off several rounds. He lurched to his left for several steps and fell to his knees. He collapsed, rolled off the edge of the roof and made a muffled thud as he struck the ground.

Then there was only the silence.

- 29 -

My left arm hurt like hell. I got to my feet and moved to the edge of the roof. In the glow of the streetlights, Rodrigo's body lay face-up beside the sidewalk. The blood on his chest glistened in the hard blue light of the mercury-vapor lamps. I felt cold all over and couldn't stop shaking.

Looking down at Rodrigo's body, I tried to take in what had happened, but my thoughts blurred in a slow-moving sluggish drift. Thoughts of horror or remorse might come, but right now, my body and mind felt numb. And tired. The screech of a vehicle skidding to a halt in front of the barracks shook me back to reality. I looked down and saw the AP white-hats on the men climbing out of the truck. They clattered up the sidewalk and around the building.

"Sir, I think this one's dead," a man called. They all looked up at the roof at once.

I stepped back from the edge, and called down. "Can you help me? I'm hurt. I've been shot." Someone asked if I was armed. I looked down and saw the Walther still in my hand. Blood dripped from my other hand, staining the gravel of the roof. I moved closer to the edge and looked down at the men below. "Yes, I'm armed."

"Listen up! Go back to the top floor and lay down your weapons where we can see them. Clear?"

"Okay." With my weakness and wooziness, a feeling of dread rose in me. Trying to make it down that steep stairway was going to be tough. I flipped the safety on, put the P38 into my waistband and stumbled back to the hatch. Then I eased myself over the frame and down onto the first step. I slipped, missed the next step and jerked my wounded arm. The pain was a shocking jolt, a hot poker jammed in my flesh. My trip to the bottom of the flight was made on my butt and my good side as I tried not to hurt myself again. I laid the P38 on the floor, kicked it away from me and waited on the bottom step.

A lieutenant led his squad into the small stairwell. He picked up the P38 and handed it gingerly to a big sergeant, then kneeled by me to get a better look. "All right, men, give us some room. Sergeant! Take two men and check the roof. We don't want any surprises."

As the men clambered past us he quickly inspected my injured arm. The lieutenant turned to the NCO in charge of the detail. "Get some medics up here so they can check this out."

"Yes, sir!"

The lieutenant turned back to me. "Airman, give me a quick summary of what's happened here."

I gave him the short rundown, and added, "Rodrigo, the guy outside, got your guard. Cut his throat. Our CQ is missing. He might have killed him too."

The lieutenant grunted. "OK. That's enough for now. We'll need a full statement later."

I sat there and tried to ignore the pounding pain in my arm. Medics crowded the stairwell with their gear and a stretcher. One of them looked me over and said, "Still bleeding some. That's kind of a mess."

They put me on the stretcher. "What was it?" he asked. "A forty-five?"

"Yeah. A forty-five," I said.

"Huh. You're lucky, Airman. It's a flesh wound. No bones, joints or arteries involved from the look of it. Right now, we have to clean that up and get a bandage on you."

They did first aid on my wound, gave me a shot, lifted the stretcher and started down the hall. We headed toward the base hospital for an official examination by a doctor. The shot—morphine?—finally began to ease the pain.

* * *

It seemed like hours before they got all of the paper work done. A doctor strode in with a nurse in his wake. He checked my chart, muttering. "The nurse says you've been walking in the ward and seem to be all right with that. How do you feel?"

"Pretty good sir. My arm's stiffening up, but the pain has eased off some."

"Just don't overdo it. It'll be good and sore for a while."

"Yes, sir. I'll try to take it easy."

He turned to the nurse who stood beside me. "Airman, take this dressing off so I can examine the wound."

She took the bandage off and he turned my arm over, looked at it, and grunted. Then he poked around.

I grunted when he prodded my arm. I wanted to scream at the doc but my military training kept me quiet—almost.

He picked up my chart, made some notations and handed it back to the nurse. "I'm going to release you now, Airman, but if you have any dizziness or the wound smells bad, you get yourself back over here, understand? Any heroics and I'll have you in the ward for a week. Clear?"

"Yes, sir. No heroics."

He prescribed some pills and turned to the nurse. "All right! Redress the wound and we'll get this man out of here."

Re-dressing the arm hurt more than the doc's inspection. When the nurse finished up with the bandage, they fitted me up with an Air Force blue sling for my bad arm and gave me some antibiotics and pain pills.

I headed for the door and realized an AP, a tech sergeant, was walking along behind me, armed, serious-looking and big. I stopped. "Uh. Are you going to follow me out of here or what?"

He squared up his shoulders and managed to look even more military. "That's my assignment, Miller. I'm your guard until they tell me otherwise. My name is Petit."

"Uh—I didn't know anything about having a guard."

"Airman Miller, Colonel Crawford assigned me to you, and where you go, I go. My team has a vehicle outside and one of my men is there now. The docs ordered bed rest, so I suggest we take you to your barracks."

We walked out of the hospital together. His man pulled the Jeep up to the curb as we reached the street and Sergeant Petit and I got in. "Sergeant Petit, can I ask a couple of questions?"

Sure," he said. "Ask away."

"What's the situation back at the barracks? Sergeant Nelson, our CQ, was missing. Is he okay?"

"Miller, he's dead. Our squad found him, strangled with a wire. And they found a wire garrote in Rodrigo's pocket."

If I hadn't been pretty sure Nelson was dead it would have been more of a shock. I still felt numb, detached.

The stairway up to the third floor was hard going, but I made it to the top with a rest on the second floor landing. Sergeant Petit installed himself outside my door with a folding chair from the dayroom while the other AP checked out the area. My eyes were heavy as I took my pills. I crawled in the sack already half asleep.

* * *

In the broiling heat of the brassy North African sunlight, I sweated. I squeezed my Walther P38 in both hands, ready to fire as I lay on the flat roof. The fine blowing sand turned the late afternoon sky to a dull red, choking me. On the gritty roof the sharp odor of scorched tar surrounded me. I eased back, as far away from the street as I could get and faced into the fading, shifting glow of the sun. To get me he'd have to come through the open hatch at the top of the stairway. He'd be in silhouette and I'd be ready.

His head popped up and he stared at me, grinning, taunting me. His soft, steady laughter mocked me over the moaning of the wind. I tried to back away but the edge of the roof stopped me. He had me trapped with no retreat. I had to face him here and now.

My heart pounded as he scrambled onto the roof and crawled toward me. I tried to fire, but the trigger wouldn't budge. My arms felt stiff and heavy and my hands started to shake. Sweat dripped down my face into my eyes. He crawled closer. His breathing and laughter got louder and my hands were frozen. I couldn't move, couldn't see, couldn't breathe. Then the cold, hard steel of his forty-five pressed against my forehead. I trembled. The sharp report and stunning impact on my skull overwhelmed me, crushed me.

My foot banged the locker, and the sound snapped me awake. I bolted upright in my bed and cried out, sweating and shaking, afraid of slipping back into the helpless horror of this nightmare. A sharp rapping on my door was followed by my guard asking, "Miller! Are you all right?"

Reassured that I was still safe in my room, I took a deep breath and called out, "Yeah. It's okay. I'm all right." I wiped my sweaty face on the sheet and tried to slow my breathing. I turned on the lamp and looked around. My head throbbed from slamming into the head-rail of my bunk and the intense emotions still gripped me. But my room and reality were coming back into focus.

It had been a dream. Only a dream. I lay there and tried to slow my breathing, hoping it wouldn't come back. Once was enough.

- 30 -

The next morning my mind was clear. The things that had happened to me made sense. I tried to figure out how I felt and what my next move ought to be—realities had to be faced and fences needed mending

Rotten feelings of guilt about my betrayal of Penny's trust made me squirm. There had to be a way to convince her that the last months had begun to create a difference in the way I felt about her, about people; that the stress of the last few days had begun a kind of moral remodeling. I needed to say all of this to her, somehow, to tell her how I'd changed and grown. And how important she had become to me. But it had a hollow sound to it, even in my own mind.

I dragged myself out of bed and moved with caution, favoring the bad arm. I cleaned up and put on my uniform and my new blue sling. Philosophical thoughts didn't make a very good substitute for breakfast. I opened my door and nearly ran straight into my AP guard, one of Petit's airmen. "Whoa. I forgot you were out there."

"We're here—"

"Until the colonel says to stop. Right. I'm ready for some breakfast."

He looked at his watch. "More like lunch I'd say. I can walk you over to the chow hall, if that's where you want to go."

I hesitated. "I need to make a phone call on the way out."

We stopped at the dayroom and I dialed Penny's number. The phone rang and rang. I hung up and tried again. Finally, I heard the receiver click, but the connection broke immediately. *What? They weren't taking calls? Damn!*

We were headed for the street side stairs, but as we passed the orderly room the CQ called out, "Miller. You have an appointment with Sergeant Wilson at the Provost's Office at 1400 hours."

"What's that all about?"

"Some kind of deposition or something. I don't know, just be there."

"Okay. I hear you, Sergeant. By the way, I remember working on some notes here last night. Before the shooting started. Have you seen them? I need them for the work I'm doing with—for some work I'm doing."

"Anything laying out—like papers, shell casings, the busted phone—all that stuff was boxed up and sent over to the Provost's office."

"Oh. Can I get my notes back, or get a copy made?"

"I don't know anything about that, Miller. Check with the First Sergeant or the Provost's office. That's out of my hands, for sure."

"Okay. I'll check it out when I see Sergeant Wilson. Thanks."

* * *

At 1400 hours, I stood in front of Sergeant Wilson's desk again, with my stolid Sergeant Petit waiting in the background. Finally, Wilson decided to notice me. He looked up from his paperwork and actually smiled.

"Good afternoon, Airman Miller. I heard about your adventure on the roof."

Not knowing how to respond, I could feel a wave of heat moving up my neck. He put me at ease. "Two officers will debrief you on the incident, one from our unit and one from the Judge Advocate General's office. They'll take a deposition about your fight with Rodrigo. You're in room 110, just down the hall."

I asked about my notes and Wilson promised to check on that for me.

We went down the hall and I knocked on the door. A first lieutenant opened it and looked me over. "You must be Airman Miller."

"Yes sir," I said.

"I'm Lieutenant Cooper." He jerked his head in the direction of a captain standing to one side. "And this is Captain Seigel from the Judge Advocate General's office." He turned to Sergeant Petit with a frown. "We won't need you for the next hour or so, Sergeant."

"Sir!" Petit barked. "I have standing orders from Colonel Crawford to keep Airman Miller under close guard at all times, until the colonel orders me to stand down. I have to be here. I'm sure you understand, Lieutenant."

The lieutenant stepped back and turned a bright shade of red.

The captain offered his hand and we shook. "Airman Miller, I've been appointed by my commander, at the request of Mr. Mackey, to act as your legal counsel during this questioning session."

"That's good news, sir. I was a little nervous about this deposition business."

"Nothing to worry about. We're trying to get the facts of your encounter with Rodrigo on the record."

"Yes, sir."

The captain sat down at the table. "My presence is a formality to some degree, but it's also good legal practice. As you'll recall, Article 31 of the Uniform Code of Military Justice requires that you be protected from compulsory self-incrimination."

Yeah. I could barely remember one day in basic training when we spent about eight solid hours listening stoically to a sergeant who gave us the high points of the UCMJ. We all signed a paper saying we'd been informed, etc., etc. About all I could clearly recall was struggling to stay awake as the sergeant droned on and on.

Captain Seigel consulted some notes. "Colonel Crawford told me to tell you—in exchange for your agreeing to assist in his investigation and act as a witness—no charges will be brought against you stemming from prior offenses or violations of military regulations during your time at Wheelus."

I thought about it. That was the crux of it for me, personally. Without a solid guarantee like that, somebody could blind-side me with a dishonorable or bad-conduct discharge before I even knew what was going on. "That's very encouraging, sir. But I'd like to hear him say that, himself."

"I don't think that'll be necessary, Miller. I have a copy of the colonel's memorandum here, signed and duly witnessed. He dug a paper out of his brief case and handed it to me.

I read through it, trying to translate the inflated legal jargon of the thing. It boiled down to a couple of paragraphs that seemed to say what the captain had told me. "Well," I said, "That looks pretty good. Looks like he's got me covered and out of harm's way on this." I hesitated. "Captain, can you get me a copy of that letter? One I can keep, just so I can be sure of what I've been promised."

Captain Seigel frowned. "That's not really necessary."

"With due respect, sir, it *is* necessary for me to have a copy. One with a signature and a witness. If it's not too much trouble, sir."

Instead of getting angry and pulling rank on me, he chuckled.

"Well said, Airman. You do have a right to your own copy and I'll see that you get one. Good enough?"

I breathed easier. Maybe this guy really was on my side, really was my counsel. Getting a letter from the colonel hadn't been a certainty, and now I felt relieved and more confident about getting fair treatment.

Captain Seigel gestured for me to take the chair next to him. "Miller, I'm staying with you through today's questioning, and I'll act as your advisor and legal counsel as long as necessary."

The lieutenant began the questioning from a long list written on his pad. He started with the evening Dave was killed in the parking lot. We proceeded through the events of that night, touching on the activities and performance of the AP assigned to the squadron.

I told him what I knew about that, and tried to move with caution, like you would in a minefield. "Lieutenant, it seemed to me that the AP knew what he was doing, but I'm not sure he appreciated the seriousness of our situation. He seemed sort of casual, like he felt tired or had something else on his mind."

I described the business about the radio and the AP's comments about our "shooting incident" with care and accuracy. "I tried to explain what was going on, but he told me to stow it. I think he was more interested in telling me about being on his OIC's shit-list than in why he was assigned as our guard."

"Airman Miller, you're making allegations against a man who can't defend himself—"

"Lieutenant Cooper, I'm trying to answer your question."

Captain Seigel cleared his throat and Lieutenant Cooper took a minute to write on his pad. He still didn't look too happy about what he was hearing.

We continued with the details of the discovery of the AP's body and the ensuing battle with Airman Rodrigo. We covered the basic ground and I interrupted him. "What about them sending a single AP to guard our whole floor? Why weren't we given a squad? Didn't they know we'd already had one man killed? Why—?"

Cooper pulled himself erect in his chair. "You've asked the wrong person about that, Airman Miller. Maybe you need to ask the provost himself. Or perhaps the wing commander. I'm going to continue with the official list of questions," the lieutenant said. "We need to get everything down."

Wing commander, my aching ass. "Well then, I guess I need a break. Where's the nearest restroom?"

I didn't need to go, but I sure did need a break from this twerp. Petit followed me down the hall and waited outside. I killed as much time as I could and we headed back to Room 110.

Walking down the hall, Petit slowed his pace and turned his face to me. "Miller— you need to cool it with the lieutenant. You're picking a fight you can't win."

"I hear you, Sergeant, and I *will* back off. But he's a jerk."

"Just try to cool it. You're nearly done, right?"

I sighed. "I know, I know. I'll try, Sarge."

He nodded. "Do. Do try, Miller." He shook his head and we re-entered the room.

The lieutenant seemed calmer and noticeably more courteous when we started in again. I wondered if he'd had a little talk with Captain Seigel while I was gone. He started back on his list.

Finally, we were done. The captain stood. "I think we can go ahead and wrap this up. We've covered the important ground and everything seems to be in order. Let's sign it. I'll need certified copies for my file, of course."

"Certainly, Captain Seigel."

"Lieutenant, I'd like to ask about a couple things now," I said. "Can you give me a minute or two?"

The lieutenant looked at his watch. "I suppose."

"Sir, about the other men in the squadron. Was anyone else hurt?"

"You know about Sergeant Nelson?" I nodded "Well, everyone else came through without a scratch." He snapped his briefcase shut, got up and left the room. So much for questions.

I stopped by Sergeant Wilson's desk to check with him about the meeting with the King's council. Another NCO manned his desk. "Look, Airman. I just got here and Wilson's in a meeting with the Colonel."

My meeting! And I was late already. He gave me the room number and Sergeant Petit and I took off running for the second floor conference room.

- 31 -

Petit and I slipped into the conference room, a big room, with good seating, heavy carpet and bright lights. We were a little out of breath from hurrying down the halls, and found the meeting well under way. A chart on the blackboard at the head of the table held a list of names in bold block letters, with a topic and time duration written beside each name. Right next to the bottom I read: A/2C MILLER— Employee Abuse at Club Tripoli—10 minutes

We sat on the back row and tried to look inconspicuous among the senior NCOs and officers seated around the room. A few faces were ones I recognized and I assumed that the others were the ones named on the board, the participants. Across the top of the blackboard was written tomorrow's date, with 0900 hours—The Palace.

After the current speaker wound up his talk, Colonel Crawford stood up. "We'll assemble here tomorrow morning at 0800 hours for a final briefing. Then we'll travel together to the palace," he said. "The Libyans will direct us to the meeting place and handle the formalities there. It's their meeting, but as I've said already, we want to take a firm stance with them. All of you on the list, here," he said, pointing to the blackboard, "will have today to polish your presentations. Now, let me introduce the remaining presenter, Ted Miller. Stand up, Airman Miller, so they can all see you. This is the bandsman who worked at the club, the man who's been helping with the investigation."

I stood up, feeling self-conscious. I was on display, but it didn't feel like being on a bandstand. I felt more like a specimen in a jar. I appreciated the colonel's keeping my discomfort brief.

"See me after the meeting, Miller. And that's it, gentlemen, unless someone has a question." He paused. "All right then, I'll see you here at 0800 hours."

I waited for Colonel Crawford to finish talking to a few of the officers, then followed him down the hall to his office. When we got to the door, he asked my guard to wait outside. We went in and the colonel closed his door and put me at ease.

"Sit down. I got the notes you'd worked on about your involvement with Club Tripoli. They were sent over from the band squadron, and I've looked them over. Here. You see these parts I've marked up? I want you to cover and emphasize those tomorrow."

I scanned through my notes. "Yes, sir. Do you need these back?"

"No, you keep them. Run through the material I marked there to make sure you can easily squeeze it into ten minutes. Try to take only about eight or nine minutes of your allocated time. That way, with a slight delay or stretch in your talk, you'll still get in under the wire."

"I understand, Colonel."

He looked around his desk at the neatly stacked piles of paper. "Good. Rehearse what you're to say. Work with Sergeant Andrews on this. He's an experienced, capable speaker." He looked at me and hesitated. "You've talked to Penny, I suppose?"

"Uh, no. No, sir, I haven't. Not since—since I told her about me and the club. The details."

"Well. She hasn't said much to me either, lately." He took a deep breath and looked around his desk again and I knew he had nothing more to say to me.

I gathered up my notes and stood to salute. He said, "Dismissed."

* * *

The next morning, we boarded the bus to go downtown and I felt ready to do my part. An escort of Libyan police and a junior member of the royal family met us at the main entrance on the square. They led us into an antechamber where a large fountain occupied the middle of the room. After a short wait, our host escorted us to the conference room.

Following a formal welcome by the prince, Colonel Crawford described the club in plain terms. "This hotel is an evil presence in your city, wearing a guise of light-hearted entertainment. True, there is music and dining and a floorshow, but be aware that their real business is in the realm of seduction, addiction and perversion—alcohol, narcotics, prostitution, gambling, usury and abominable practices."

An image of Rodrigo and the busboys flashed in my mind. I saw the faces of some of the council members harden as their interpreters caught up.

Colonel Crawford folded his arms across his chest. "Their prostitution activity is based on rigid control and helpless dependence of European and Arabic women."

I heard a harsh exclamation from someone at this point.

The colonel put his hands on the table and leaned toward the council. "The women provide the owners with enormous profits, but typically lose their physical and mental health, and eventually their lives. We will show you that the people of this club deal in murder, assault, and intimidation on a daily basis. Their debasement extends to the sexual abuse and degradation of young boys and girls, Libyan children employed at this 'nightclub.'"

He had their attention, and in the ensuing dead silence, the colonel introduced the first speaker. The council members began to interrupt the speakers occasionally and the exchange became lively. One councilman, an old man with a long beard and white hair, was particularly vehement.

Captain Myers expounded on the club's network for distribution of narcotics in the European community in Tripoli. "When we have to deal with the devious nature of a man like Scarlatti—"

"Explain yourself, Captain." The old councilman spoke with an angry glare. "The subtle machinations of this Italian seem to be too smooth and needlessly complex. It seems to a poor Bedouin trader like me these drug runners need to learn what swift desert justice is all about."

I thought, *If that old man is a poor Bedouin trader I'm a four star general.*

Captain Myers tried to continue. "With respect, Sheik, explanation is my goal. Be patient with me."

The sheik raised his hands, palms up. "But I am patient. To a fault."

He drew laughter from the other men on the council.

Finally, it was time for me to speak. The colonel introduced me and I moved to join him at the end of the table. "Airman Miller is the only person here who has worked in the club. Recently Miller attempted to leave, to quit his job with the Scarlatti family. That move nearly cost him his life. Fortunately he defended himself and overpowered the man assigned to kill him so he's here to talk with you today. Airman Miller."

As I talked the room became quiet. "I remember the faces of the women and the children working there, their hopelessness and their fear. I've heard the employees and the security guards brag about the routine violation of the Arabic girls on the cleaning staff, some as young as nine or ten years old. And the younger busboys. I've seen the expressions on their faces, leaving the hotel rooms of men like Rodrigo, limping away from their abusers."

To the hushed audience I concluded. "I still hear their frightened voices. No one could help them. They had no one to turn to."

The members of the council were silent for a long moment, and began talking quietly among themselves.

The old white-haired councilman spoke intently to his interpreter. He turned to me. "Why did you spend months and months working at this so-called nightclub when you were surely aware of the evil there? You have spoken of the cruelty and debauchery of the place." He tugged his beard. "And yet—you stayed and remained a part of it all. Why?"

Why indeed. The difference in perspective, the changes in me and my outlook were important factors. "To answer you, Sheik, I have to explain things I don't fully understand about myself. I began working there as a boy playing guitar with the band. It was fun and it gave me money for going to college when I get back to the United States. The wealth and glamour of the club seduced me. But gradually I came to understand what they expected of me, what I had to do. That's when I decided to quit. And they tried to kill me.

"Yes, I know. It took me months to travel that path and arrive at conclusions that now seem obvious to me, and apparently to you, too. Finally, the predicament of the children working there, trapped at that club and enslaved by their tormentors, became more than I could bear."

The councilman stared at me. "More complexity," he said. I wasn't sure how to interpret his response but he didn't pursue it further.

I looked at the colonel. He nodded and I sat down. I felt tired and drained but it was over. Gradually a wave of elation began to replace my fatigue.

The colonel then did a brief summation. Someone asked him why I had killed a member of my own squadron.

"The man that Airman Miller killed had given his entire

allegiance to the organization of Scarlatti," Colonel Crawford said. "He couldn't be considered an airman any more. Rodrigo had reverted to the status of a hardened criminal and—I think you'll agree—Airman Miller had no choice.

"In spite of the best efforts of the United States armed forces, we are never totally successful in keeping people who are clean and pure from being corrupted. And we cannot avoid, totally, the inclusion of evil men within our ranks. Such men, and those of the Scarlatti organization, are men without a code of ethics or morals. They *will* rape, assault and murder good people and we must always be on our guard against them."

He paused and looked around the room. You could almost feel the mood of the men present shift as the pause lengthened. The colonel raised both hands before him in an opened palm gesture. "We have come here today to ask your permission to take action against Scarlatti and his people. It is my hope that the United States Air Force and the government of the United Kingdom of Libya can combine our strengths to put these people out of business and out of Libya."

His words echoed my own feelings. The men of the King's Council of Ministers applauded politely, and the Prince thanked us for spending our valuable time in helping them understand the extent and severity of the problem with Scarlatti and Club Tripoli. Then he invited us to adjourn to the antechamber for refreshments while the council discussed the information we had provided them.

* * *

When we reached the chamber I sat down at the fountain to rest. Colonel Crawford came over and sat down next to me. "I want to thank you for an excellent contribution to the meeting. I watched those old men closely during your talk. Your description of the plight of those women and children moved them."

"Thank you, sir. I tried to keep it as simple and uncomplicated as I could."

"Well, it seemed to work. That detail may have had a larger impact than we'd hoped for. And I think they accepted your plea of innocence and immaturity as to why you stayed at the club as long as you did."

"Yes sir. I hope so."

"We'll see," he said. "The Prince said he wanted to give us their decision about Club Tripoli before we leave today."

I started to ask the colonel how he felt about my plea, personally, as Penny's father. I hesitated because I knew he was busy and concerned about the outcome of the meeting. Maybe it wasn't the right time but I couldn't see a better time coming.

"Colonel Crawford, what do you think? Do you understand how it happened? How I could drift over the line from doing my job as an airman? I didn't sign on to be any kind of thug with those guys, and taking a part time job seemed to me to be the only way I could hope to achieve what I saw, what I still see, as my potential. I didn't see how I could go to college back in the States if I got out of the Air Force as broke as when I joined. It wasn't like I had any kind of GI Bill to fall back on.

"Sir, a lot of guys I know—airmen, NCOs and some officers, too—a lot of men have part-time jobs off-base here and back in the States. If that's against any kind of regulations it's news to me. And to the other guys I know who work as musicians in the on-base and off-base clubs."

The colonel scowled and I figured I hadn't made my point. Or was he going to fall back on quoting the book to me, citing the old "conduct unbecoming" dodge?

He leaned toward me slightly. "Miller, you need to talk to your first sergeant or your CO about all this. It's more about time and place, about where and what you've been doing. In my view it was the wrong place and the wrong time."

He sounded like he was dodging my question. "Sir. How could I know that until it was too late? Too late to quit or come out clean. What does Penny say about it? Do you think I have a chance to—?"

"Boy, you're asking the wrong person. You'd have to ask her, straight up. She and I don't talk very much these days and I'm not very close to her thoughts. She's her own person and rather private. Like her sister, Cynthia."

"Cynthia . . . Penny's mentioned her only once or twice so I really don't know what she was like. She doesn't talk about her much. Says none of you do."

"Ah. Not much to say I guess." He sat up straighter on the bench, almost physically pulling himself together, checking his tie and cuffs. "One thing is clear. Your guilt is not an issue. We made a deal. You've kept your part and I'll keep mine. Total immunity for activities and transgressions while working at Club Tripoli, and working for me." He rose and I stood up too. "As for Penny, I'm afraid you're on your own. My rank and my influence don't extend to being highly persuasive with the female mind. Again, thanks for your help with the meeting."

I sat down on the bench again and watched the fountain for a while. Not much encouragement from the colonel but then I didn't really expect a lot. The dilemma was mine, mostly of my own making. I got up and strolled around the big chamber trying to make sense of the alien architecture and the lack of mass in what had to be a strong support system for the high ceilings. Where were the big sturdy columns and the thick buttresses around the edges? This sure didn't look like anybody's medieval castle.

It took a good long while but our guide from earlier in the day finally came back to the antechamber and asked the colonel to return to the conference room. The rest of us stayed at the fountain and tried to make small talk. Some of the NCOs and officers began to pace around the room and their behavior was kind of infectious. I discovered myself among the pacers with no recollection of getting up from my bench. There I was fidgeting like a little old lady.

At last the colonel returned. He stopped, looked at us all and didn't make a sound. We all tightened up as he hesitated. Then he put his thumb up high and said, "We did it, men."

He walked toward the front of the palace with the guide leading the way and the rest of us following close behind him. "I'll give you the details on the bus as we ride back to the base. We convinced them."

- 32 -

Our speakers for the meeting climbed aboard the bus, talking among themselves. After we were settled, the colonel stood at the front looking like a tour guide, and brought us up to date. "Basically the council has agreed to shut down the club and put Scarlatti and his crew out of action. I'll have to get the wing commander's approval of our specific level of involvement. Of course, the general may want to seek approval from his superiors as well, but I doubt it."

The colonel began to fold his arms, but grabbed the back of a seat as we rounded a corner. "We don't expect any problems to develop. I have a preliminary go-ahead from the general, subject to the details, to mount an armed raid on the club. The King's council has agreed and they have said they want to move quickly on this. Europeans and any U.S. civilians who have worked there will be encouraged to leave Libya voluntarily. Otherwise, they'll be charged and tried by the council. Apparently the Air Force will be asked to deal with its own people." Colonel Crawford looked in my direction. I started but managed not to duck my head.

He continued. "Scarlatti will be handled personally by the king. He'll have Scarlatti tried, and if he's found guilty it's a death sentence. He'll probably have him beheaded."

I had a quick, vivid vision of Scarlatti on his knees with his head down and forward, waiting for the sword. I shuddered, wondering where they drew the line between justice and barbarity.

The colonel paused. "I think the best news is that the council has asked the Air Force to provide special tactical squads to conduct this surprise raid. Our squads will take the place by force."

He turned to Captain Myers. "I'm appointing you as the field commander for this operation, Captain. You and your staff will provide the planning and work with the perimeter defense squads. There'll be additional training or refreshers on weapons and tactics. Of course the schedule and details will be available on a need to know basis only, to the participants in the raid."

I saw smiles on the faces of Myers and Wilson and some others on the bus. I knew they had favored taking their own troops into the club. Now they had sanction to do just that. Their voices formed a chorus of excited approval in the crowded bus. The colonel smiled broadly.

Back at the AP HQ, Sergeant Petit and his backup offered to take me to lunch. We went to the NCO Club for cheeseburgers and fries, the special for the day. I offered to buy their lunch but they wouldn't hear of it. Sergeant Petit shook his head. "No way. You're the lowest rank here and we invited you. The least we can do is to buy."

"Thanks, I appreciate that. But you know I'll be glad when we all get back to normal and people start to treat me like I expect. Chewing me out, pulling rank on me and stuff like that."

Petit grinned. "Be careful what you wish for, Miller. Wishes like that have a way of coming true."

Yeah.

The first sergeant had told me I could move around the base as long as I kept in touch with the CQ. My first thought hit me hard. I wanted to see Penny but I hesitated. *Was that a good idea?* She might need more time away from me to understand what I was trying to do. Yet I missed her and longed to hear her voice. So, in spite of my good intentions, I went to the phone booth off the entrance to the NCO club and dialed her number.

"Colonel Crawford's residence," her mother answered.

"Hello, Mrs. Crawford. This is Ted. Is Penny around?"

There was a short silence. "I don't believe she's available. I'll tell her you called."

Yeah. I'll bet you will. I'd try again later in the day. Maybe then Penny would answer instead of her mother.

I called the CQ to check for messages. He said there was only one. "You have a meeting scheduled with Captain Myers at 1600 hours. Expect to spend an hour or two in his office." With about three hours to go before the meeting, the APs took me back to my squadron. Of course they followed me upstairs as always. Sergeant Petit walked down the hall with me. "The usual drill, Miller. Lock your door and I'll post a man out here."

"Okay, Sergeant. I need some rest before my meeting with Captain Myers. It's at four, so don't let me sleep all day."

Taking off my uniform to avoid making wrinkles, I lay down on my bunk and fell asleep immediately. It seemed like no time had passed when the guard banged on my door. The noise jarred me awake and I glanced at my watch. It had been nearly two hours. "All right, I'm up," I called out.

I felt sluggish, but I got up and splashed water on my face and got my uniform back on. Feeling a lot better, I opened the door. "Let's go," I said.

We headed for the AP HQ building where I reported to Captain Myers in my best military manner. He put me at ease and told me to sit down.

"Okay, Miller, I'm in command of this operation and I've appointed you as my assistant, a sort of aide de camp, for the raid on Club Tripoli."

I felt my brow furrowing. "Aide de camp?"

He chuckled. "That's an old fancy term for military flunky, Miller. But it means you'll be at my side at the command post. And right behind me if I decide to enter the building."

"Will I be armed?"

"You'll have to be. I wouldn't take a man into a battle zone who can't even defend himself."

"Okay, Captain. Just asking."

He leaned back. "Of course that means you'll be getting additional training and practice with the weaponry, the forty-fives and the grease guns. I may need your knowledge, your familiarity with the club, when we go in. And I definitely need that knowledge and your experience with the habits of Scarlatti's people to help me plan this raid."

"That I can do, sir," I said. "I know the place and the people."

"Good. That's going to help with the timing and our moves. My orders are to keep casualties to a minimum. In particular, they want to avoid killing or wounding any of the hotel guests, the drinkers and gamblers. They also want us to take Scarlatti alive if we can. I—"

"Captain, I'm not so sure you can take him alive. Scarlatti is a little screwy. I've seen him act really strange sometimes. He's hard to predict."

"Well, that's a different slant on the man. Most people I've talked to seem to see him as levelheaded, a businessman. I'll have to warn the Libyans that it may not be possible. I won't risk the lives of any of my men just to take Scarlatti alive."

I interrupted Captain Myers to ask a question. "Sir, when do you plan to execute this raid? From what I've seen down there, if you choose a night on the weekend you're going to have lots of civilians underfoot."

He raised his eyebrows. "Yeah, I guess that makes sense. It is a casino and a nightclub. Does it slow down after, say, midnight?"

"Not much, Captain. Now, if you can stage this operation for a Monday night, or better yet, on a Tuesday, that's about as quiet as the place gets. Especially if you start sometime between 0400 and 0600."

He jotted down this information. I thought about the security guards. "Captain, the club's security guards aren't going to give you much resistance. They're more used to whipping up on the women and children, and an occasional drunk. They won't want to put up a real fight."

He looked irritated and turned to me. "Maybe, maybe not. But it's their lack of discipline that worries me. They might be out of control or unpredictable. We'll have to be prepared for anything."

Then he unrolled a set of drawings for the club. For the next hour, we pored over the hotel layout and living spaces. I tried to point out every little thing I was able to recollect about the club's halls, rooms, furnishings and stairways.

After more than an hour of answering questions about the layout and the security force, it seemed to me that we were covering the same ground again. I stood up and stretched. "Captain Myers, aren't we repeating ourselves? Seems to me we're covering the same things we talked about a couple of hours ago."

He narrowed his eyes. "Yes. We are. I've got to be dead sure about what's involved, here." He leaned back in his chair. "So far, almost everything you've told me has been consistent with what we've learned from our own agents who've visited the place and a couple of Libyans who've worked there. Your more detailed information has filled in some gaps."

"Glad to be of help, Captain Myers."

"You have helped, Miller. Why don't you take a break, while I get the team leaders together and bring them up to date? Be back here at, say, 1930 hours. Get some supper."

"Yes, sir."

* * *

We got back to the captain's office after dinner. He and I covered some more ground and it seemed to me that the plan was starting to gel. I couldn't think of anything else about the club or the layout of the building to tell him.

Then I remembered! "Captain. Scarlatti spends a lot of time in the evenings and at night, alone in his private rooms and office. They're in that tall tower at the northwest corner of the building. He uses several rooms there, including a small apartment."

I described the small tight stairway up the tower from the main building. The captain's brow furrowed. He flipped through his roll of drawings. The part describing the tower showed sketchy outline drawings with almost no labeling or dimensions. He grumbled and looked though the drawings again.

"Captain, I remember something Scarlatti told me. He had the whole tower redone and converted to his office suite only a few years back. These drawings must be older than that."

He looked surprised. "They are old. About twenty years, but they're the only ones the government office could find in their files. Here." He handed me a pad of lined yellow paper and pushed his can of pencils toward me. "Sketch these offices and the stairs. Estimate the steps in each run and show me how many turns and landings there are."

Sweat popped out on my brow as I struggled to recall the details. I told him everything I could dredge up from my limited exposure to Scarlatti's private suite. "Captain, please remember. I was only up there once, and I was in a hurry when I left. The details are fuzzy to me."

"Just do the best you can, Miller."

Captain Myers looked at my sketches. "Hmm. We won't have much to go on there." He tossed his heavily chewed pencil aside and got a fresh one from the can on his desk.

He was silent for a while as he puttered with his notes. "I'll brief my command in the morning. As of now, the mission is scheduled for tomorrow night. We'll leave here on Tuesday at 0400 hours, and commence at the club at 0500. Get a good night's sleep tonight. I'd guess you won't get much tomorrow night."

It had been a long evening. I got up, feeling tight and stiff. "Good night, Captain Myers. And sir, thanks for including me as your aide." He waved me away and returned to his notes.

I left his office and headed back to the barracks with my APs.

33 -

The next day crawled by. I checked in at the nurses' station in the morning. Everything looked good with the wound. They gave me some more pills and a few more words of advice. The doctor didn't certify me for full duty, but I felt pretty good. Back at the barracks, I pulled my guitar out of its case, and hit a couple of chords. As soon as my left hand rotated to line up with the neck of the guitar, the bruises and stiffness in my upper arm grabbed my attention. It was tight and still hurt. I ran a few scales and strummed for a minute or two and it didn't get any better, so I put the guitar back in its case. A few minutes playing at a time, stretching out to longer practice sessions, would help the arm. I figured it would come back soon enough if I didn't push too hard. I think my growing tension about the coming raid was part of the problem and I didn't expect that to improve.

Sergeant Petit took me over to the library to pick up something to read and I spent most of the rest of the day reading and sleeping in my room and occasionally playing guitar gently. Not doing much of anything, just waiting for the early morning kickoff for the mission downtown and trying not to fret and worry. The day crept along and gradually moved to a close.

* * *

At 0300 hours, Petit's backup AP banged on the door. "You said three, Miller, and it's three."

I got up and put on my sage green fatigues. My sling stayed in my locker. It made me look like an invalid. They might even leave me behind if I showed up wearing it. I finished tying the laces of my clunky black brogans and grabbed my steel helmet. We headed for the Jeep and the AP HQ building.

I was nervous as a cat on moving day. Captain Myers handed me a forty-five in a holster, with two clips of ammunition on a web belt. He wore a forty-five himself. "Miller, you can use this for a last-ditch self-defense, or on my orders. Clear?"

"Yes, sir. On your orders."

Myers' troops were already waiting in a big Air Force truck. A Jeep pulled up to the curb and we climbed in for the ride downtown. When we arrived at the Castle Square, Captain Myers assembled the two squads of APs. Each man carried a forty-five, a grease gun, and an array of stun and concussion grenades and extra clips hanging from their belts. Captain Myers saw me checking them out.

"These men are the best, our crack troops. Most of them had combat experience in Korea—base defense against the Chinese and North Koreans. I've been working with them and they're well trained and disciplined."

A small Libyan police squad joined us. They looked eager too, but I wondered about their training and experience.

Our men divided into their two squads and we took our positions with as much stealth as we could muster. The primary invasion team deployed to the front entrance, while the command post and reserve troops grouped at the rear of the club. My squad crouched behind the courtyard wall in the employee parking lot with the captain and me, waiting for the signal from Captain Myers to open the back gate. Sergeant Petit was the ranking enlisted man for the group, the NCOIC. I'd worked with him in some weapons training sessions, but I didn't know he was second in command of my group. The reserve team looked alert but relaxed. I breathed way too fast and my hands shook.

As we waited, the door in the gate opened with a loud creak. One of the kitchen workers stepped through it, looking furtive and carrying a big box. He saw us and froze. The poor son of a bitch fainted and one of the APs caught him and eased him to the ground.

On Myers' signal, we immediately moved forward and deployed to cover the rear door. The clattering load-and-lock noise of the squad's weapons made a sudden startling outburst, immediately followed by the detonation of concussion grenades at the front door. The silence of the night was completely shattered. The chatter of automatic weapons fire and the loud crumping sound of the stun grenades replaced the predawn quiet and electrified the peaceful city square at five o'clock in the morning. The Libyan troops in our group began making a warbling, high-pitched savage wail, the ululation they used in the desert.

Myers turned to me, a huge grin spread across his face. "Listen to that, boy! Does that raise the hair on your head or what?"

We heard people screaming inside. The sounds of chaos intensified as the reserve team had their first customers. Several club security guards burst through the back door, waving their weapons around. They saw our reserve team. One guard fired his pistol in our direction. Our team cut them down with a devastating volley.

Things settled down pretty quickly. It seemed like I'd been right about the club's security guards. But the noise and commotion increased again. Muzzle flashes blazed through the second story windows. Glass showered down into the courtyard. It sounded like the front door team had made it past the first floor resistance. The operation progressed quickly and smoothly. A group of partially dressed men and women, hotel guests, chattering nervously in several European languages ran up to the back door and stumbled over the guard's bodies. They fell and screamed, trying to get clear.

Captain Myers snapped, "Sergeant Petit, have a couple of your men clear the stairs. Get those bodies out in the parking lot."

They dragged the bodies out of the way and helped the guests. The Libyan squad led them out to the parking lot and tried to calm them down.

Two women rushed up to the door leading a group of cleaning girls and busboys out of the club. Maria di Gioia seemed to be in charge and kept them relatively quiet, but some of the younger children were hysterical. I was glad to see that Maria had come through the raid okay and I called out to her. She gave me a sharp angry glance and returned her attention to the children. I shook my head and tried to concentrate on the progress of our mission.

Judging from the sounds, the raid was winding down. Grenades blew out a couple of windows on the third floor, but the chatter of the automatic weapons had turned sporadic.

One of our troops came running down the hall and stopped at the command post. "Sir!" he said. "My commander says to inform you that we have secured the first three floors of the club and are conducting a room by room search for remaining hold-outs. Civilians and hotel guests are confined to the main dining room."

The captain asked, "Casualties?"

"Sir, we're not completely certain about who's who, but there are about a dozen Club Tripoli people dead or wounded. It started as a clean smooth sweep but some of their guards went nuts. Firing at everybody, completely out of control. We think we have three hotel guests injured and at least one dead."

"What about our men?"

"Just two or three walking wounded, sir. The team leader wants to send these men out to the command post and receive replacements to help keep the prisoners organized."

Myers gave the order. The runner left with the replacements in tow.

We'd begun to relax a little when the sound of the firing intensified. Captain Myers' frown deepened. "Petit! Get a man in there to find out what's happening."

"Sir!" The sergeant sent an NCO inside to get a report on the apparent change. The automatic weapons hammered in spaced bursts as intermittent muzzle flashes were visible through the windows of the tower. The team was taking the stairway leading up to Scarlatti's office suite. The flashes progressed upward and rounded a corner of the tower. We couldn't see them anymore, but we could still hear them. A new sound began high in the tower, the high-pitched chattering of a weapon with an unusually rapid rate of fire. The heavy, pounding of the grease guns fell silent.

The captain slammed his fist into his other hand. He grabbed a sergeant by the arm. "Thompson, get your men in there with the flamethrowers and report to the team leader. He'll take it from there." The tactical squad went tearing into the club. We heard them slamming up the stairs to the tower entrance.

Captain Myers tensed up even tighter than before. He turned to me. "That thing had the sound of a German machine pistol, a Mauser? Is it Scarlatti trying to make a stand? If the son of a bitch wants a fight, he'll sure get one."

Flames and smoke poured from the tower windows in dense black columns. Another column rose from the parapet at the top of the tower. I no longer heard the explosions of the grenades and the small arms and automatic weapons fire diminished. Now the smoke thinned and began to clear. I wondered what was happening. In that instant I remembered the elevator I'd seen in Scarlatti's office. The one I'd forgotten to tell Myers about. *Oh, no!* I jerked his sleeve. "Captain! There's an elevator in that office suite that runs up from the wine cellar. He may try to use it to get away."

"What? What elevator? Can you find it in this wine cellar?"

"Yes, sir."

He turned to Sergeant Petit. "Pick two men and go with Airman Miller to this basement elevator. This bastard's not going to get away. Miller! Get a grease gun from one of these men—Clemons—and head for that elevator. Double time, move it!"

Clemons thrust a grease gun and an extra clip into my hands and we were off.

We ran down the hall and took the stairs as fast as we could, down through the storerooms and on to the western-most corner. There was the wire cage and the retracting door to the elevator shaft. At that moment, the little elevator arrived.

As the door began to open, Sergeant Petit ordered, "Get down!" We dropped to the floor. Out came Scarlatti, eyes wild, holding a machine pistol with both hands, screaming in Italian. He ripped off a blast of fire. Petit and I squeezed off tight bursts from our grease guns as another started its ripping pop just behind me. It only took the one fusillade. We'd hit him with a dozen rounds of forty-five caliber lead in the upper chest and throat. His eyes locked on mine as the machine pistol slid out of his hands. He crumpled and fell to the floor of the wine cellar. Petit lowered his grease gun as I cleared my own weapon.

* * *

We reported back to the captain. Sergeant Petit stood at attention. "Captain Myers. We found the elevator and Mr. Scarlatti. He didn't get away, sir. Miller got him with one tight group in the upper chest."

I started to protest to Petit who just grinned at me. Myers looked shocked. "Well, Miller. I guess we won't take him alive, then, will we?" He looked at me and shook his head. "You accompany me back inside and show me this escape route. I need to see the body, too."

Captain Myers and I went in through the back door with me leading the way. I took him down to the wine cellar. When we reached the body, the guard who'd been posted there snapped to attention. Scarlatti lay in the pool of blood where we'd left him.

Myers looked him over. "Sergeant," he said to Petit. "Get this guy photographed and turn the body over to the Libyan squad. They said they wanted him and they can have him."

We went back upstairs. The sights I saw in the main floors of

Club Tripoli were as shocking as the sounds of the initial entry into the club. Now in dead silence, the carpets smoldered, adding to the stink of gunpowder, cordite and dust. The richly polished paneled walls bore scars and tears from bullets ripping across rooms and down halls. Shattered glass littered the floors in the bars and the dining room. Mirrors, chandeliers and wall lighting hung in disarray, covered with broken plaster and dust. Working our way toward the rear stairways, we saw rooms whose delicate French doors had been blown out into the halls by stun or concussion grenades.

The command post for the invading team was near the hotel kitchen, placed in the sheltered alcove off the main dining room. The swinging doors leading to the kitchen had been ripped off their hinges and thrown aside. Captain Myers stopped to talk to the officer in charge of the primary invasion team.

The first lieutenant looked tired, but he snapped to sharp attention when Myers addressed him. "Well done, Lieutenant. I'll write this up in my report to the wing commander. I think you'll be hearing from him as well."

"Yes sir, Captain. My men deserve the credit for putting these guys down and taking charge. I'd like to provide a list of the men I feel were instrumental in the success of the raid."

"Do that Lieutenant. Your team took the brunt of the action and that's the way we'll write it up." The lieutenant snapped off another sharp salute and turned to his NCOIC and the problems at hand.

About twenty or thirty people were still being held in the kitchen. His men moved them out in small groups under guard to the rear parking lot. They would soon have the captives secured.

As I examined the debris and damage to these once-elegant rooms and halls, I felt amazement for the low level of civilian casualties. But, like Myers had said, we had to be prepared for anything. Even the club guards going nuts. I found myself wishing that Scarlatti and his inner circle could be paraded by and forced to view the shattered remains. Then I remembered the pair of young men who had reveled in the sumptuous surroundings of the club, Dave and I, pretending to belong to the group of wealthy young Europeans who patronized the place. A sense of loss and loneliness settled in my belly. I longed for the comfort and warmth of Penny and Dave. What happiness we'd known seemed to belong to some different place in a distant past.

* * *

Our driver brought the Air Force Jeep around to the parking lot and we followed the big Air Force truck back to Wheelus with the morning sun in our faces. Captain Myers reported to the colonel and held a debriefing. They came out and the captain looked tired. "Miller, you'll have to keep quiet about tonight's events until we tell you otherwise," Myers said. "You can talk to your CO and first sergeant. I informed them about your participation in the raid. Otherwise keep the lid on."

"Yes sir. I'll wait for permission."

"Good. Turn in your weapon and clips to the quartermaster." Captain Myers started to go, and then turned back to me. "And thanks for all your help with the mission."

"Sir, I was afraid I'd messed up by forgetting about Scarlatti's elevator."

His smile didn't reach his eyes. "You remembered in time, Miller, but you sure did give me a jolt."

I started back toward the barracks and was nearly to the snack bar when it struck me—my guards weren't with me. Yet I felt safer than I had in a long time.

I reported to the CQ and went in to see Sergeant Andrews. The Old Man came in. He looked me over and sat down. "I see you're still with us."

"Yes, sir." I gave them a compact summary of the results of the raid.

Then they let me go. I went to my room, sat on my bunk, and tried not to think about the raid. I longed for a return to the way things were, to have my life back, but there was no way to seek forgiveness or to be allowed to go back to the before. My stubbornness and stupidity haunted me. It was over, yet it was all still there, still real. Starting over seemed altogether too painful a process. I finally fell into a restless, troubled sleep, tossing and turning through my recurring nightmare.

* * *

Around four in the afternoon I needed some coffee and a change of scene. I walked across the street to the Oasis. Sitting near the windows drinking coffee, I saw Captain Myers come in for his late afternoon break.

He got his glazed doughnuts and black coffee and sat down at my table. "So, how are you?" he asked. "Recovered from all the excitement?"

"Yes sir," I said. "Life's settling down. Nice and quiet."

"I hear you. I'm glad I didn't miss the show, but a little peace and quiet is going to suit me just fine in my last few days at Wheelus."

"Are you rotating back already?" I asked.

"Yeah, next week if the big Constellation doesn't break down. Like they say, the world's best three-engine transport. Anyway, I'm ready to go."

With a pang of envy I realized I'd let his departure date slip my mind while I worried about my own problems. I was starting to feel normal again and not favoring my arm so much.

He noticed. "Is the arm getting better already?"

I moved my arm around to show off my state of health. "Yeah, it is getting better. And 'already' depends on where you're sitting. To me, it seems a lot more like 'finally.' The nurse gave me some stretching exercises to do, but it's not that big a deal. It'll probably clear up on its own, but I'll do the exercises she showed me."

I did some gentle twisting motions and got away with it. "It's not sore enough to get me out of much work, though. Playing guitar is getting easier too, but now my stamina needs to be rebuilt. That's the first thing that goes."

We drank some coffee and I wondered how the investigation was coming along. I could see the possibility of things just drifting back to the way they were before. New people, maybe, but the same old crap. "Have they wrapped up the loose ends with Scarlatti's family and the organization yet? What about the people in Morocco and those guys out at Homs?"

"It seems kind of quiet right now, but some of the people at Marrakesh are sure to try to move in and fill the void. There's just way too much money to be made in those rackets to expect people to lie low for long. Homs is a different story altogether. The Royal Tank Corps ran a raid parallel with ours and cleaned out the Inn. The word is they'll keep the inn and turn it into an EM club, but it won't be getting back in business any time soon."

"Well, those guys need a place like that," I said. "Do you think there's any way to keep the gangsters out of Wheelus? They didn't seem to have a lot of trouble recruiting and building before." *God!*

Did I say that? I could feel a hot flush of embarrassment climbing my neck.

The captain looked down and stirred his coffee. "We can try, I guess," he said without looking at me. "But it won't be easy. We're not the highest paid organization in the world."

I thought he was going to say something else, maybe something about Dave and me and the easy money, but he shifted his focus instead. "You know, Ted, I think you're different, now. You learned some hard lessons at that miserable club, but don't let your guard down. Don't be tempted to get involved in anything like that again. It's not worth it. People like that—the ghouls—they'll devour your soul."

I shivered. I suddenly recalled the images of Dave and the others. "Captain Myers, I still remember the faces of all the men who died in this mess. I can see them in front of me as clear as I see you right now."

His eyes took on a distant look. "I know. If you talk to a combat veteran, you'll hear almost the same words from him."

"Like Sergeant Wallace and his buddies from the war? How he still sees them and talks to them?" I shivered again. "I can't explain it very well, Captain. I have trouble coming up with the right words."

He sat there watching me. He didn't say anything. He must have understood some of it anyway. He drank a little more coffee, then pushed his cup away. "Son, that's part of what I meant about learning and growing. You're only a little older than you were when you got here, but you're not the boy that got off that airplane a few months ago."

We remained silent for a while. I'd miss him when he left for the States. But the memory of his patience and help over the last few months would stay with me.

Captain Myers stood up. "Miller, I've got a desk covered up in paperwork so I'd better go. Our raid was easier to carry out than write up in a report." He shook my hand and left.

* * *

I went back to the barracks, to my room to try to think. So much had happened, so much had been lost. It seemed like everything had changed. Dave was gone and Sergeant Nelson. Scarlatti had died an awful death, violent and ugly. And Rodrigo. Of those still here, only

Charlie and Pat seemed unscarred and undamaged. I was a wreck, I thought, a sad, mournful shell of the person I used to be. And Penny seemed as hard as stone, like she had tossed us all aside and moved on to the future she'd planned before any of this had happened.

I lay there worrying, tossing on my bunk, looking for some kind of common thread or an underlying pattern that would tie it all together. For Dave, Scarlatti, the Pres and me—maybe it was as simple as old-fashioned greed. We all saw a way to make a lot of quick easy money without the effort and dedication it would take to match the available gains in honest, hard work. Some of the others, like Nelson and some of the people from the club, had been caught in the middle, more the victims of our greed than through any fault of their own. In spite of my attachment to Richard and the rest of the squadron—and even Charlie, Pat and Penny—they had all been like observers, like disinterested spectators on the sidelines of a brutal, repugnant game. Captain Myers had seemed the closest to caring or being involved, but he was leaving soon. I couldn't keep depending on him.

I longed for a return to the way things had been, to be able to take some pleasure in the simple things, like the people around me and the music we'd made and enjoyed making. I longed to have my life back. I guess I just wanted to be forgiven and allowed to go back to the before. I didn't want to pay for my mistakes or admit my errors, my total unthinking behavior. Go and sin no more? I was too far down to believe it was going to be that easy. And starting over seemed way too painful a process. I finally fell into a restless, troubled sleep, tossing and turning through my nightmares.

Somehow, despite my intentions, that afternoon was the last time I saw Captain Myers. His office was just down the street from my barracks and I meant to go over there and get his new address back in the States, but he got busy preparing to go home and I was stewing about how to get back together with Penny, worrying about my own miserable affairs. He shipped out before we ever got together again.

- 34 -

I knew Penny would be leaving soon and her last few days at Wheelus melted away. One afternoon I saw her car in the parking lot at the BX. I went inside and found her talking to Patricia. I walked up to the counter where they stood. "Hello, Penny. Hi, Pat. Hope I'm not interrupting anything important, but you were both here and I couldn't just walk right past you. So how've you been, Penny?"

She ducked her head, an almost imperceptible movement. Her eyes flicked right and left, then narrowed as she asked, "How are you, Ted?"

The situation was awkward, but I had to keep going. "I'm doing pretty good. Tried to call you a time or two, but I can't seem to catch you at home."

"Oh. I've been really busy, getting ready to go to Atlanta. So much to do."

Patricia looked down at the counter top in silence. No help there. "Penny," I said, "let me buy you a Coke at the snack bar. For old times' sake." She didn't respond. "Come on, I won't bite. I just want to talk."

Two women entered and Patricia turned to go, saying "I have to get back to work."

She wouldn't meet my eyes and I let her off the hook. "We'll see you later, okay."

I turned to Penny. "Ready?" She looked annoyed, but I didn't expect her to be submissive about it. Not her.

She flipped her ponytail, started toward the door and stopped. She cocked her head toward me and frowned. "Well? Are you coming?"

We walked over to the snack bar and claimed a table. I got us Cokes, carried them back to the table, and sat down. "Penny—"

"Ted." Penny sat with her hands folded in front of her. Her eyes were narrowed and she held her mouth closed with her lips compressed. She took a deep breath and asked, "What's this all about? I feel like you're forcing me to sit down and talk when there's nothing left to say."

"Then don't talk. Listen. This is about you and me. We haven't talked for weeks and you owe me an explanation."

She looked up, shaking her head. "I owe you? No, I don't think so. Things have happened. Everything's changed."

"I haven't changed. Don't try—"

"You have changed, Ted! I thought I knew you, but you've turned into a stranger."

This was my one chance at any kind of reconciliation and my calm restraint was slipping away. "Penny. Things haven't really changed. I still love you as much as ever."

She looked up, shaking her head. "No. You've gone from a happy, talented, charmer to an introspective, moody, grasping worrier. You've turned into a thief, a criminal—"

"I am not a thief—"

"You're a criminal. A loser."

My hands squeezed the edge of the table. "Believe me, Penny. When I finally figured out what they expected me to do for them, I woke up. We had it out and I quit the place. Your father put me to work on his criminal investigation."

"You had to work for him. Or go to jail."

"Stop it! If you'll just listen to me, and let me tell what happened between Club Tripoli and me, between your father and me. Give me a chance to explain."

She slammed her hands down on the table. "No! You listen. I trusted you with everything. I gave you my heart and my love. Everything. And you betrayed me, sinking down into the mire of that filthy club, doing degrading jobs and disgusting little crimes."

The truth hurt, yet I had to try. "Oh, Penny. What's happened to us? To your love for me?"

Her lips quivered and tears filled her eyes. "That's the worst part, Ted." Her voice had risen to a strained, high-pitched whisper. "My love is still there, still strong. That hasn't changed. I do love you. Oh God!"

Penny leapt up from the table, knocking over her chair. Without another word, she hurried to the door, threw it open and ran from the shop. She crossed the parking lot to her car. By the time I got to the front door she had jumped in, started the engine and was backing out. My worst fears had come true. Standing there at the door, trying to ignore the rude idiots who stared at me, my strength evaporated. With my world shattered around me, I left the snack bar and remembered the last thing she'd said. She still loved me. Remembering the pain of her expression and her tears, she clearly meant it. She did love me. Did that mean I could hope for some kind of future with her?

I dragged myself to the bus stop to wait for a ride back to the barracks, not knowing whether to hope for the future or forget the whole thing.

- 35 -

The day arrived. While I'd tried to maintain hope, the shadow of her coming departure cast a pall over everything. The dread of her leaving made the time go by even faster. Dawn had brought a replay of my old nightmare about the gunfight on the roof of the barracks. Lying there, shivering from the cold sweat of that recurring dream, I felt certain the day would not improve.

* * *

Penny's family stood with her at the passenger terminal on the Wheelus flightline. I'd wheedled the flight number and departure time out of Patricia. Showing up alone I stood around, awkward and out of place, I didn't join her family but stayed out of the way near the chain-link fence, trying to blend in with a group of airmen going home to the States. The colonel stood with his family around him and looked preoccupied, while Penny's mother fidgeted and Sandy seemed a little lost. Penny and Patricia chattered together and Charlie stood there, watching the F-100s and checking his watch. He noticed me standing apart near the fence and walked over. "What's up, Ted? Aren't you going to say goodbye?"

My attempt at a smile failed. "No, I don't think so. I shouldn't even be here. I tried to stay away—but I couldn't force myself to do it."

Charlie looked down at the concrete. "Yeah. Well, I'll keep you company for a minute." As we stood there waiting, Sandy broke away from her family group and joined us.

"Ted . . . I saw you over here with Charlie, and you looked so sad. I haven't seen you since that day at the beach. How've you been?"

"Okay I guess. It's not the good old days, but I'm getting by. What about you? Going to miss your sister?"

She grimaced. Sisters never change, I thought. I felt a little better here with her and Charlie, more like a real person instead of a wraith haunting Penny's sendoff. Sandy took my hand and her eyes teared up. "I've tried to talk to Penny about you, but she just shies away. It's like Mom has her brainwashed. It's all about the future and Agnes Scott, I guess. But I miss you. And so does she, behind her big tough act."

I looked up into the cloudless afternoon sky. "Sandy, I know you mean well, and I appreciate what you're saying. But I don't have much hope right now. I don't think I have a future with Penny."

She looked down and sniffed. "Sometimes I think Penny's smart—and sometimes I think she's just dumb. Oh, Ted."

"Hey, come on now, Sandy. People don't always get what they want. And you can't always tell whether it's for the best or not. Knowing takes time. You need to wait and see, to get some distance away from all this. And I do too."

We'd both run out of things to say and I felt miserable, dreading the moment when Penny would get on that plane. Sandy took my hand. I felt something there, a piece of paper. *What?*

Sandy couldn't avoid her mother's steely stare any longer. She said, "Take this. Look at it later. I have to go." With a quick hug, she turned and trotted back over to her family. Charlie rejoined Patricia and I took a deep breath as I tried to be calm and simply accept what was happening. My muscles ached from their tightness—like guitar strings about to break.

The last call for Penny's flight departure crackled over the loudspeakers and she walked out to the big Constellation. She turned and waved, then climbed the roll-around stairs and boarded. I watched the plane taxi out and take off into the brilliant sunshine, beginning the long gentle turn to the west that would take her over the city and the big harbor where we'd met.

Her airplane dwindled to a bright speck in the western sky. And as that final image faded, my dreams faded with it. Would I ever see her again? I opened my hand, and there on the small piece of paper Sandy had given to me was Penny's new mailing address—and a single word. Write.

The End

Printed in Great Britain
by Amazon.co.uk, Ltd.,
Marston Gate.